a

trick

of the

mind

Penny Hancock grew up in south-east London and then travelled extensively as a language teacher. She now lives near Cambridge with her husband. She has three children. Her first novel, *Tideline*, was published to rave reviews and was a Richard and Judy Book Club pick in 2012.

Also by the same author:

Tideline
The Darkening Hour

a
trick
of the
mind

PENNY HANCOCK

**SIMON &
SCHUSTER**

London · New York · Sydney · Toronto · New Delhi

A CBS COMPANY

First published in Great Britain by Simon & Schuster UK Ltd, 2014
A CBS COMPANY

1 3 5 7 9 10 8 6 4 2

Simon & Schuster UK Ltd
1st Floor
222 Gray's Inn Road
London WC1X 8HB

www.simonandschuster.co.uk

Simon & Schuster Australia, Sydney
Simon & Schuster India, New Delhi

A CIP catalogue record for this book is available from the British Library

Hardback ISBN: 978-1-47111-506-6
Trade paperback ISBN: 978-1-47111-507-3
eBook ISBN: 978-1-47111-509-7

Typeset by Hewer Text Uk Ltd
Printed and bound in Great Britain by CPI Group (UK) Ltd, Croydon, CR0 4YY

For Andy

CHAPTER ONE

April

What was I thinking about, as I drove down that winding country lane with its blue shadows dappling the road ahead? Of how hard it was to leave someone, I remember. Even when you knew it was right. Loving a person, while needing to get away from them, was a paradox I couldn't explain.

I felt an unexpected kind of sorrow, almost grief; anyway a hollow in my chest that ached, to be driving towards the sea without Finn. The image that kept coming to mind was of a limb, deliberately cleaved from my body.

I was into deep Suffolk, with its ancient trees and lush foliage. Towering hedgerows were silhouetted against the twilit sky, topped with a haze of may blossom. Fresh green smells drifted in. The road had been empty, apart from a solitary jogger I'd avoided on the verge when I'd first turned off the A road, cursing him for not wearing something Hi-vis. They thought you could see them, these runners, even when the light was low. As it was now. It was what Finn called the magic hour, poised between day and night. A photographer's favourite time.

I was grateful for Pepper, my neighbour's Norfolk terrier. He filled the Finn-shaped space next to me. I had promised the old man I'd look after the dog while he had his heart op, that I'd guard him with my life. When we'd set off I'd assumed the little dog would stay on the back seat with his chew – instead he had jumped into the front and had his paws up on the dashboard to see where we were going. Was it even legal to have a dog in the front? I ruffled Pepper's fur. His nose shot up, his eyes reflecting the soft light, full of love.

I'd turned the music up. Beyoncé yelled that she didn't want to be a broken-hearted girl. I could hear Finn saying, 'How can you?' – leaning over, tuning the radio into something folky or traditional. *Proper* music. This weekend, for the first time since college I didn't have to worry what he thought. I was taking control of my life at last. I was free of a relationship that had been holding me back for years! My mood swung upwards again – I felt the way my class of five-year-olds must do when I opened the door of the stuffy pre-fab at three thirty and they spilt out like crabs heading for the sea. Grateful for space and time to play, to stretch their limbs. To do what the hell they liked.

'Ssshh, Pepper!' He'd begun to bark when there was a clunk and a jolt and the car veered sideways.

'Whoa!' I said. 'What was that?'

I slowed, my pulse racing, turned down my music and looked in the mirror. I could see nothing, only a bare branch, sliced off by the storms of last week, swinging over the tarmac. A few broken twigs and thicker tree parts were strewn across the dark road. The impact had knocked Pepper onto the seat. He'd stopped yapping and now he wriggled onto his front. 'You OK, Pepper?' He wagged his tail.

I glanced again in the mirror as I drove on, slowly, my heart thumping hard.

There were only shadows on the road behind me. Nothing, just the branch, a remnant of last week's storms. It must have caught the left-hand wing mirror and slammed it so it was flat against the door now. Yet my heartbeat quickened and the thoughts started up: 'Turn the car round, go back, check you didn't hit anyone.'

I *had* checked. It was just a branch.

'You hit a person standing on the side of the road back there. Go back.'

Before, I'd have turned the car round. I'd have found a turning place, and I'd have driven back, my palms sweating, to the point where I believed I might have knocked someone over, and there would be nothing there, no injured person, no crushed body. Reassured, I'd turn again and drive on. I had done it, to Finn's amusement, even when there hadn't been a jolt – once when the wind had buffeted the car so it had rocked, another time when the lights changed to amber as I crossed a junction. The thought would enter my head that I'd hurt someone, and I had to go back to check. But not any more, not now I was casting off old ways.

I continued, slowly. I leant forward, and scanned the road ahead for bends that were easy to miss in the near-darkness. Nothing was left of the sunset in my mirror but a smear of pink, low on the horizon. Ahead, the bright rhombus thrown by my headlights picked out trees flaunting young leaves and reassigned them to darkness. I was used to London, where it was never dark, where traffic lights and shops and streetlamps and the constant peal of police sirens kept you company. Here, there were so many bends in the road you couldn't see round. Deep blue coppices you couldn't see into. Tricks of the light and shadows that looked like something else. But I would not let the little jolt take hold in my mind.

We were going through a village now, its houses lit up, the last one before we got to Southwold. I preferred being among houses. My heart rate slowed and I returned to my reverie.

'You can't plan your life the way you plan a lesson,' Finn had said.

'This is just a feeling, there is no plan, Finn.'

'I love you, Ellie. What's the point in destroying what we have?'

'I need to move on. We were just kids when we got together. Things have changed . . .'

'Is it this exhibition?'

'Not just that.'

'What? I need to know.'

I couldn't say it. That his love, his tolerance, had begun to rein me back. I had to free myself if I was ever to change, become the person I was capable of being. We were almost through our twenties, it would be too late, other people had established themselves in their careers, won prizes, got there. I'd been coasting – accepting a status quo I knew didn't make me happy – for too long.

Now things were happening for me at last.

A gallery in May's town was holding a show of artists in aid of the charity Mind and the paintings I had submitted had been accepted. It was an up-market gallery that only accepted high-calibre artists. I felt a frisson of excitement again at what all this meant for me. And so I'd invited friends, we were going to spend the weekend in my Aunty May's house by the sea, walking, eating, going to the Private View on Saturday night.

The air coming in the window had changed texture now to something sharper as we entered the town and drove past the familiar shop fronts – the fish and chip shop, George's antiques, Adnams wine cellar – and I was turning off down a lane where flint-walled cottages lined the pavements, and the faint waft of wood smoke mixed with the tang of the sea.

I turned right and the buildings fell away and I drove over the golf course, the wind buffeting the car.

'Nearly there, Peps.'

Past the water tower, a solitary circular building black against the sky, and at last over the humpback bridge. Left on the unmade track past the Harbour Inn and the black ramshackle fishing huts and jetties along the estuary, bumping over things on the track: rope, or nets, and stones. I looked past the tilted black masts of boats. Nothing beyond but the North Sea and the vast sky that symbolised my future – open, limitless.

Left at the end, and then I turned sharply right onto the shingle track, rattling over rough ground, finally pulling up outside my Aunty May's cottage, so familiar, the sight of it sent me plummeting back into my childhood.

It was like coming home.

The house was in darkness, of course. It stood, its back to the road, its broad low form staring across the dunes and further out, to the sea. I sat, wanting to relish the moment. The first time I'd come here alone since my aunt died. Without Finn, I was able to sense everything.

The past within the present.

Appreciation that Aunty May had left *me* her house.

The strong bond my aunt and I had always shared.

It all gathered around me, filling me with warmth, and a sense of completeness. This was where I belonged. I knew at last what it meant that my aunt had left me her house, it was the passing of the baton – she wanted me to take the house forward, to bring life back into it, to fill it.

I clipped on Pepper's lead and we got out. Silver breakers were just visible smashing on the sand a couple of hundred metres down the beach. The wind slammed into me as I came round the car. I stumbled against the bonnet, bruising my hip.

'Shit!'

Pepper was tugging at the lead, begging me to let him run about. His fur blew upright so he yelped in surprise. I picked him up and kissed his ears. 'Sorry, Peps, I can't let you off the lead. Do a wee and we'll go indoors.'

I adjusted the wing mirror, congratulating myself again for resisting the urge to turn back after the tree caught the car. And I was buoyed by the same sense of joyful anticipation I'd felt when I arrived here as a child.

CHAPTER TWO

I tapped the gatepost three times without thinking, a life-time's habit. A second's apprehension as I slotted the huge key into the lock and pushed open the door onto the darkness inside. The house smelt, as usual, of mildew, and my feet slipped on the sand that always coated the floors with a fine gritty layer. It got in somehow, even when the house was locked, through minute cracks, or under the door. I flicked on the lights. I went through to the kitchen, dumped my bags, Pepper at my heels. I turned on the immersion heater, switched on the fridge. I would warm up the place, turn it back into a home.

Upstairs the mattresses were cold under my palm. I ran back down and filled the kettle. The hot-water bottles gave off a familiar old smell of warm rubber, winter nights, childhood. I tucked one under a scratchy blanket on each mattress. I'd asked my friends to bring their own bed linen. May's was a bit random, a few thin duvet covers, some crumpled sheets.

I put on May's old Roberts radio for company and 'Dancing in the Moonlight' tinkled in the background.

Pepper followed me, as if he couldn't bear to be a foot from me, and I chatted to him, glad of his company. 'We'll light the fire, put out flowers, candles, chill the fizz. The place is going to be warm and beautiful by the time they arrive.'

I could do this on my own! Play the hostess, run a house.

I filled one of May's old pans with water ready for the pasta. Chiara, my flatmate in London and best friend, had said she'd bring a pudding. I'd asked Louise, who we'd flat-shared with at art college, to make a salad. I'd brought the pasta, two sauces and a block of fresh, crumbly Parmesan. Bread and Parma ham, melon and artichoke hearts. We were going to eat – those of us who ate at all, Chiara barely did – at May's beautiful, circular kitchen table. A proper dinner table. You couldn't play the hostess in our cramped London flat. It was a novelty to do it here.

I grated the Parmesan, unwrapped the antipasti and put them on plates. I went up to the room I was going to sleep in – May's old bedroom at the front – and unfolded the dress I'd bought for the Private View party. I'd fallen in love with it, in a vintage store in Bethnal Green. It had a silk under-dress and the rest was green lace, and when I put it on I felt ridiculously pleased with myself, as if I was stepping into a new skin. I hadn't worn feminine clothes with Finn, he pre-ferred me in my painting overalls.

This room wasn't musty like the others; it still smelt how it smelt when May was here, of clean air, windswept washing, and wide horizons. Yes, I thought, the sense of possibility, of being different.

The others should be here soon. It was almost ten. Chiara, I knew, had had a meeting after work and Louise was picking up her new boyfriend from the airport, so I didn't expect them much earlier. The voice of the newsreader on the radio chattered in the background as I busied myself, placing the dress on a hanger so I could gaze at it from the bed, and organising my underwear into May's empty drawers, arranging my spare jeans and jumpers in colours on a chair. I was filling the spaces May's death had left, rekindling the life in the house. I refused to feel sad any more. She wouldn't have wanted that.

As I moved from the front bedroom, which overlooked the dark dunes, to the back one, overlooking the road and the marshes, the thoughts were emerging slowly like an old film developing in my unconscious. I felt slightly light-headed; I put it down to impatience for my friends to roll up. My palms were damp – I assumed it was due to excitement about seeing Louise after all this time, sharing our news, talking about our art, wondering whether she'd changed.

My heart raced as I heard the crunch of tyre on shingle, and a beam of light swung across the room through the window. Someone was arriving. Pepper bounded down the stairs, yapping.

Chiara and her boyfriend Liam came in, dumping their bags, kissing me on the cheek, carrying bottles into the kitchen.

'Sorry we've been so long. There was a diversion on the

road back there. This is amazing, Ellie, you didn't say it was actually *on* the beach. Wow! What a perfect spot!'

'I know!' I was brimming with pride as I hugged them. 'I'll show you around.'

They followed me upstairs, making appreciative noises at the three bedrooms, the low-ceilinged bathroom with its claw-footed bath, then down again – exclaiming at the long sitting room with its wood-burning stove. I still couldn't believe all this was mine. They wandered to the picture window at the front, peered through though there was nothing to see now but tiny lights far away on an expanse of darkness.

Chiara put her arm round me.

'It's just beautiful.'

'I feel so privileged.'

'Doesn't it feel sad though?'

'It did, at first.' I didn't want to burden my friends with the grief I had experienced when I'd heard the news. All that was six months ago now. 'But you know Aunty May would have loved the thought of us here this weekend,' I said.

'Ellie's aunt was a painter too,' Chiara told Liam. 'And she fostered kids, didn't she? Talking of which . . . look at this!'

She pulled a photo from her purse and waved it under my nose.

'Oh, Chiara!'

Shadowy limbs and etched sinews not unlike the clouds smudged against the sky in my rear-view mirror on the way here. A tiny head with a turned-up nose. It hit me in an unexpected way, the reality of the new life within my friend. I crushed a second's panic; I was going to be left behind, my friends were settling down, starting families – the feeling again that there was so little time to get it right.

Liam put his arm about Chiara and they gazed at the scan picture of their baby together – a vision of perfect happiness.

'I tell you what though,' Chiara said, slipping the photo away again. 'It must have been nerve-wracking for your aunt, watching kids so close to the sea. There's no fence between the house and the beach, is there?'

'Get you! Already thinking like a mum!' I said. 'People didn't worry so much about health and safety in those days. Kids looked out for each other.'

'Well anyway, I love it,' said Chiara. 'It suits you, Ellie. All these beautiful paintings!' There was one of May's landscapes on every wall, a cluster of them on the stairs. 'Now, can I take our stuff up? Before we relax?'

I helped Chiara put her sheets onto the warmed mattress, pulling them tight, tucking them under.

We sat for a minute on the bed.

'It's going to be odd seeing Louise after all this time,' she said. 'Can you believe she's been in Oz for two years?'

'I know. It's weird.'

'I wonder if she'll look different. I suppose we've all changed. Two years older and me with my bump.'

'It barely shows yet. You look gorgeous. Blooming.' I kissed her cheek.

Chiara smiled, stood up and wandered to the window. 'I bet there's a great view.'

'Yes. Wait till the morning!' I said, then wished I hadn't. Something about that sentence filled me with unease. But why? I was here, in my aunt's old home, that I'd always loved, with my best friends and Frank's little dog. Nothing to worry about. I would be the new woman painter – replacing my aunt – with a dog and a house by the sea. An image I'd always dreamt of for myself. I looked over my shoulder three times, though, just in case.

'How long did your aunt live here?' Chiara asked when we were back downstairs. She was moving about the kitchen, picking things up and looking at them, curiosities from another era – a quilted tea cosy, the aluminium pans people no longer used. A glass egg timer filled with sand. Everything had May's mark on it; she had painted her glasses, made candle holders out of pottery and decorated them in her distinctive style, pretty muted colours, reflecting the sand and sea grass, the sky outside. Ochres, lilacs and blues.

'As long as I remember. My very earliest memories are of holidays down here with May. But listen, it's late,' I said. 'You must be starving. Let's have the antipasti and we can eat properly as soon as Louise gets here.'

'I'll make Bellinis for those who aren't up the duff!' Chiara said. 'Ooh look, you got artichoke hearts. And Parma ham. I've taught you something. I brought the pudding, like you asked, a tiramisu.'

Luckily, since I wasn't much good in the kitchen, Chiara was the greatest cook I knew. Yet she hardly ever ate a thing. Her baby bump barely showed though she was over eighteen weeks gone. The not eating was something I knew not to mention. She covered it up by feeding everyone else.

'Babes, you've spilt something on your dress,' Chiara said. 'Oil, I think.'

I looked down and was startled to see that there was a dark stain across my hip. I must have spilt something on it as I got the food ready. My stomach turned over, my pulse began to race again. Anxiety, with no obvious focus. Just that uneasy feeling that threatened to spoil my weekend.

'Bugger!' I said. ' I'll stick it in the wash.' My mouth was dry. 'Could you just light these candles, while I change?'

Upstairs I pulled the dress over my head. It was mad to feel anxious – my friends were here, everything was good. Yes, I'd left Finn, but that was something I'd been planning for months. I'd forgotten to switch off the radio and the presenter burbled on in the background. Something made me tune in to the next item on the news.

'Police are appealing for witnesses after a hit-and-run incident on the A1095. Anyone on the road at approximately eight thirty this evening and who might have seen the pedestrian, who is in hospital in a critical condition, is asked to come forward.'

I stood, rooted to the spot. The anxiety I'd barely registered, my damp palms. It was all slotting into place. The car had jolted. Veered sideways. There had been oddly shaped shadows on the road behind me.

But I'd ignored the voice that urged me to turn round and check.

I hadn't gone back. I hadn't gone back.

CHAPTER THREE

Aunty May died too soon. Not age-wise, although I'm learning that however long a life, it is never as long as it *could* have been.

May was my mother's much older sister and I loved her. It was six months since she'd died. She'd been in my life for as long as I could remember so I'd thought she would be here forever. I'd been planning to visit her the weekend I got the news.

'We didn't know, none of us knew she'd go and die,' my brother Ben reassured me, but it made no difference. I wanted to wind the clock back. I had put off visiting May, the last weekend of her life, to spend a day shopping with Chiara! I'd thought I could go the following weekend and was now fighting the belief that if I'd gone I would have been able to prevent her dying – ever.

At May's house I always had to touch the gatepost the right number of times, check outside the picture window before sitting down anywhere, look over my shoulder three times whenever a bad thought came into my head. Talismans I'd thought up as a child and still relied on to keep people – my aunt in particular – safe.

I knew these things made me look odd – tapping, counting, moving things into the right position. Finn thought they were funny, light things. He laughed at me. He didn't know how I depended on them – especially when it came to anything to do with May.

'You're taking steps down bonkers alley here, Ellie. Tapping a gatepost, avoiding cracks in the pavement, sacrificing lambs – none of these things affect what was going to happen anyway. You should have been an ancient Greek. Or a character from the Old Testament.'

I knew this. I wished I could be more rational.

They found Aunty May on her bed, two empty pill bottles beside her, a hastily scrawled note saying she had simply had enough, that she had reached her journey's end.

When I heard she had left me her house it felt like a strange, mixed blessing. I was grateful, of course I was – no one gets to own a house at my age unless they have extremely wealthy parents who can fork out for them. But it was all tangled up with the feeling I'd got something badly wrong. The owning of it was tinged with guilt. Why did I deserve the house? And why hadn't she left it to my brother as well?

It was clear my mother wasn't too happy about it either.

'You must sort it out immediately and put it on the market,' she said. She was so agitated, so restless when it came to anything to do with Aunty May. 'Before it gets damp over the winter.' She was quite adamant about it.

'Sell it, repay your student loans early. Get the debts from round your neck. You might want to start a family one day, but if you don't clear them you'll be forty before you know it. And still in the red. You think you've got forever. You haven't.'

'It'll need a lot of maintenance, Ellie,' my father said. 'For once I agree with your mother! You'd be better off putting it on the market the minute we get probate and letting someone else sort it out.'

'I'm worried Aunty May would be upset if we sell,' I said. 'Surely she left it to me for a reason?'

It didn't occur to me then that my parents were reeling, as we all were, from May's suicide, that getting shot of her house was their way of obliterating the pain of this, the shock.

My brother seemed unfazed by my inheriting it, however, and offered to help me sort it, get rid of May's clothes and other personal things – bottles of shampoo, packets of paracetamol – that had been left as if in suspended animation, in her kitchen and bathroom.

'We'll clear it up, it'll be a way of putting Aunty May to rest,' Ben said.

Perhaps May had left me the house because she and I were both artists, something that had always bonded us. And because she knew I *would* hang on to it, value its quirkiness, its idiosyncrasies, however impractical, while if she left it to my mother – or Ben even – it would have been a photo in an estate agents' window before the earth had settled on her grave.

*   *   *

The house still contained her in those first few weeks after she died, back in October.

I thought the house was watchful, or perhaps it was Aunty May who was watchful. I stood in the front room on the day after her funeral, and looked out over the sea grass to the shingle dunes.

I saw my child self holding Aunty May's hand, with my little brother Ben, moving west into the wind with our heads bent and our buckets and crabbing lines clasped to our chests, our voices snatched up and carried out to sea. Sea-gulls swooping and crying overhead. I remembered perfect evenings that went on forever, when it never grew dark, the light simply fading as the stars appeared one by one, and May allowed us to stay up, our bare feet curling into the cooling sand. I could feel the warmth from the fires we built with driftwood. May baked potatoes wrapped in foil on them. I remember burning my fingers trying to pull them out, the sweaty white flesh searing my tongue. I could remember the white ashes that spiralled up when finally we had to admit that the dark and the cold had beaten us and it was time to dowse the flames.

As I stood, cherishing those memories, the house stirred, creaked. I don't believe in ghosts, but that day, I felt Aunty May's presence. Her breath and her footfall. She had not left yet, or perhaps the house had not released her spirit. The wind chime placed on the back porch (it would have been rattled to death by the easterly winds on the front) tinkled as if she'd just passed, even when not a breeze stirred the air. And in the fine veil of sand that coated the worn boards and lino-leum inside I could make out the fresh imprint of her slippers.

As I moved into the kitchen, something fell onto the counter – rocked there for a moment, making that faint, regular sound a coin makes as it spins to a halt. I went across to peer at what had dropped but couldn't find a thing.

There was the corner of something jutting from one of the floorboards. An edge of fabric. I pulled at it and wriggled it and tugged at it and at last it slithered out. It was a child's bib, made of cotton with a hand-painted picture on the front – in May's distinctive style, a fabric painting of a small lopsided figure with a crooked leg outside an old house with the words 'Crooked House' above it, and the words from the rhyme inscribed beneath it. Where had I last heard that song? Even in the Key Stage One classes at school we didn't sing nursery rhymes any more – it was all calypso or African call and response chants or Indonesian folk songs. But I could hear a voice sing quite distinctly: *'There was a crooked man and he walked a crooked mile and he found a crooked sixpence upon a crooked stile.'*

The bib. It might have been mine, or Ben's. Perhaps it had lain hidden under the floorboards since I was a child and first came down to stay with her?

I tucked it into a drawer in the duck-egg blue, Fifties sideboard that had been there forever. Ben and I would sort these drawers later. They were stuffed full of tea towels and linen and trinkets that didn't fit on the shelves – napkin rings and half-used birthday cake candles and biscuit tins rusting at the edges with faded pictures on the top. I picked up one of these tins, with a Victorian reproduction of a little girl on the lid, and prised it open. Inside was a piece of paper inscribed with the words 'A piece of you'. I lifted it up. Underneath, a lock of fair hair. I gagged, put the paper back and the lid back on the box, stuffed it into the drawer and closed it.

Beside me, the curtains moved almost imperceptibly.

I took a step back. Let some quiet seconds go by. Someone, I was convinced, stood in the doorway through to her back room. I thought I saw a shadow. I had the sense of a presence. But when I turned, there was no one there.

I knew without question that May hadn't fully left yet.

So to clear out her paintings and canvases and to sell her house to a stranger seemed brutal to me. Like a violation of everything that made May who she used to be, who she still was.

That night I'd shown Ben the bib and, gingerly, the hair, and he laughed and reminded me that May had always been a bit eccentric, although we knew her so well, it hadn't seemed so to us.

'Always collecting odd bits from the shore. Bird skulls and dried starfish and bones for her art. And remember when she took us right out in that tiny rowing boat, onto the sea, and you were crying and saying you wanted to turn back and she seemed not to hear you? And in the end I shouted at her and she did finally turn the boat around?'

The memory began to surface, fleetingly bright and hard, before it shimmered and slipped away again.

'I thought we were going over the sea to France,' Ben said. 'I wasn't afraid that she was taking a risk, I was afraid because I thought there were dragons across the sea!' He laughed. Now Ben mentioned them, other things began to come back to me.

Moments when May seemed to not be there. Times when she kept us up so late at night it began to feel wrong, as if she had simply forgotten that children need to go to bed. Once she had fallen asleep herself and Ben and I were still playing around her and I had taken it upon myself to take Ben up to bed. I must have been six or seven then, and Ben only three or four.

A sort of darkness, underlying the things that we did that were more exciting than anything I'd known before.

The house had lain empty over the winter. It had needed time. I had needed time.

After Christmas I had come down with Finn a couple of times. I didn't know much about houses, how quickly they deteriorated when no one inhabited them. As if they languished from grief themselves. Finn didn't know much either, I was soon to discover. I told my mother not to worry, though, that we'd do our best to maintain it. We aired it – throwing open windows – and went around sweeping away cobwebs and mouse droppings and the dead insects that collected far more quickly than I would have imagined.

I painted the back porch.

Finn managed to fix a lock on the back door. He put up a banister on the rickety stairway, using, ingeniously, an old broomstick. He was resourceful like that, any old bit of driftwood and he could turn it into a shelf, or a stool, a table. May had met Finn, and she had liked this about him. His inventiveness. Now he hung curtains on pieces of rope he found down by the fishing huts. I used to love this about Finn too when I'd first moved into the Mile End flat. His makeshift constructions – everything he touched he could turn into something useful, or into a piece of art.

But it was dawning on me that I didn't want this here. If this was going to be my house I wanted to do it my way, bring something different to it, bring new life into it. I wanted to renovate it with my own, more minimalist ideas. It was the first time I'd ever owned something that was completely mine. And I wanted to make the decisions.

'We don't need money, we don't need to consume,' Finn argued, bending a piece of wire into a loo-roll holder for the downstairs bathroom. 'Most things can be constructed out of recycled found-objects.'

I began to find his presence irritating, stifling. He never gave me any space.

'Show your mum you can look after it and she'll stop badgering you to sell up,' Finn said, sitting outside on the dune, smoking a roll-up. That was when he'd put his arm round me and said the words in my ear. The words that tipped everything over the edge so I knew it had to end. 'We can bring our kids up here,' he said.

And now I'd decided to come, invite friends, bring some life back into the house, to do it my way.

I wanted to let the last feather-like ashes of May's memory fall back, to settle out there on the salt flats.

Then I could start afresh.

CHAPTER FOUR

My mobile sounded in my bag, startling me out of my catatonic state after hearing the radio news. I stared at it, as if it might explode in my face.

It was Louise.

'It's taken us forever. The road was closed. There was some accident, and we went on a mad diversion through the depths of the countryside. It really is the sticks out here! But we're nearly there now. We're in the high street by a pub. What's it called, Guy? Oh. The King's Head.'

I gave her directions and went downstairs to tell Chiara.

'Great.' She filled our glasses. Liam held his up and tiny bubbles shot out of its top in a fountain. I saw him through the golden liquid, smiling, his face distorted by the glass.

'Congratulations, Ellie,' he said. 'Happy house-warming, and bloody ace job getting those paintings into the exhibition.'

Had I hit something on the road back there? The impact had slammed my wing mirror back against the door. Who was to say it wasn't me who had hit the man, injured him, maybe fatally, and hadn't stopped?

The car had jerked, tilted to the left. I'd been distracted by Pepper. I hadn't gone back.

'Ellie?'

'Yes?'

'I said shall I put the pasta on now?'

'Sorry. Yes, of course, let's get the dinner on the go.'

No. I was being a fool. Letting irrational thoughts control me, when I'd resolved not to, any more.

A beam lit up the table in the sitting room as a car swung onto the shingle and there was the crunch of tyres and the slam of car doors, and the door burst open and Louise stood there, bleached and blonde and tall and gorgeous and we hugged each other. I realised I'd been feeling a little anxious about seeing her after all this time. Louise, like me, had continued to work as an artist, when we'd all left art college, and had emailed to say she'd sent some of her work to the same gallery, when she heard they were looking for contributors. There were only six artists exhibiting, however, and Louise hadn't been chosen. In her shoes, I might have found this tricky, but perhaps this new man she'd met in Australia, who, by all accounts, she was madly in love with, had helped cushion the blow.

'Louise!' I said, and we kissed on the cheeks and hugged each other the way we'd always done.

'I bought you these,' Louise said. She thrust a huge bouquet into my arms. 'Lilies for your new house!' Her curly hair had grown long and her teeth looked very white, like the lilies.

'You look fantastic, Louise,' I said. 'Even more beautiful than you already were.'

I filled a large vase with water and arranged the flowers so they fanned out, their stiff waxy petals white and bloodless, leaving a dusting of pollen on my sleeve. A vision of roadside shrines of flowers like these burst into my head. I'd had the music on loud, and I still heard a thump. Does a branch make a thump? I'd been looking at Pepper, not at the road. I hadn't listened to the thoughts in my head that told me to turn the car around, go back, check.

And now someone was in hospital and I had no idea how bad it might be.

'We've got three things to celebrate,' Louise said, taking a glass from Chiara.

'Ellie's exhibition, Chiara and Liam's new addition, and . . .' She stopped and smiled up at Guy, the tall blond Aussie she had brought with her, and he took her hand and held it out.

'We're engaged,' she said, 'and just look at the ring.'

'It's gorgeous, Louise. Congratulations.'

I don't think anyone noticed that I hardly ate. I moved the pasta about my plate, and smiled, but all the time the thoughts kept coming at me. The impact on the car, the way it had swerved as I looked at Pepper. I rifled through the images in my memory – could I have been mistaken? Were those broken branches I saw in the mirror, lying on the road? Or were they bits of a body, broken and scattered?

But the impact would have been bigger if I had hit a man, wouldn't it?

What if the man was dead? Might I be his *killer*?

When we'd cleared the dishes, I ran upstairs. It was eleven o'clock. There would be local news. I turned on the radio and listened. The item told me that the young man in the hit-and-run incident on the A1095 was in a worse condition. No one had come forward. The incident had happened at approximately eight forty-five.

Well that sorted it.

It had been eight fifteen when I'd gone along that stretch of road. I remembered glancing at the clock. It couldn't have been me.

No way.

'Police are appealing . . .' I switched it off. Went downstairs. In the kitchen I smoothed my hair in the glass, composed myself. The others had rolled a joint and the pungent smell of weed permeated the sitting room. Liam lolled back, a hole in the knee of his baggy jeans, with Chiara dressed in her assortment of mismatched vintage clothes leaning back against him. I loved my friends. I wanted to join them in their happy haze, but the thought wouldn't leave me.

It was a quiet road, and there were all those shadows. If the man, boy – the radio hadn't specified his age – had been lying there, unable to get up, it could well have taken half an hour before another driver spotted him, which would mean he could have been hit at eight fifteen, as I drove round that bend.

If the driver had knocked the man over and only realised later, what would they do? If they only realised after hearing the news item that it was them?

Would they go to the police?

Or would they keep quiet?

If they went to the police, how crazy that would sound.

'I only just realised.' As if they wouldn't have noticed before.

The police would think they were crazy, or a liar, and they *would* be crazy or a liar, because no one could hit a person at that speed on a road and not know it straight away.

Everyone was dazed with fatigue by now, discussing the cultural differences between London and Sydney.

'I'll just take Pepper out for a wee,' I told them, and clipping on his lead I went outside. The wind had dropped a bit but the rain was coming down in a fine mist. The sea swished and crashed against the beach, over the dune. There was a smell of rotting things. Was it the same smell I had breathed in with such relish earlier? Now it smelt rancid, fishy, unpleasant. The wind must be blowing up from the fishing huts huddled over to the west of here, where lobster pots and abandoned boats and discarded fish carcasses had been left in the brine and were beginning to fester.

I opened the passenger door of my car and switched on the ignition and the lights. I walked around it.

Nothing I could discern, no dent, no scratch. Pepper was snuffling away at something on the car, licking at it. I looked more closely. Or was there something there, close to the wing mirror, where it had folded in with the impact? A dark patch. My heart rate sped up again. I pushed the wing mirror back into place and saw that the glass had shattered. No! I imagined a person stepping out from the shadows, taking the impact from the wing of the car without my seeing, then being thrust back against the tarmac into the depths of those tall hedges. My hand strayed to the dark patch on the car that Pepper had been licking. It came away with a dark sticky brown stain. The same as the stuff on my dress?

It was blood.

I knew what I had to do.

I would drive back the way I came. I would remember, if I went the same way and looked into my rear-view mirror, re-creating my journey, whether I had hit a man or whether I hadn't.

If the worst came to the worst and I realised there had been someone there, who had stepped out maybe at the last minute, who I must have rammed with my mirror or even with the whole nearside of my car, I would go to the police, confess, tell them that I had no idea until I heard the news.

Either that or I'd know once and for all that I hadn't done it.

But I must go now. It could not wait until the morning. By then the scene would have changed. It would be light, things would have been cleared up or washed away by the rain.

I went indoors. Everyone was sprawled on the sofas now except Louise, who was leaning back against Guy's knees while he played with her hair, pulling at a curl, straightening it out and letting it spring back. They were talking about some trek they had gone on into the outback, the amazing russet-red colour of the sand and the mountains.

I could only see the blood on my dress. Was it human blood?

'Aboriginal art,' Louise was saying. 'I had no idea, I'm going to use it in my work.'

I went over to Chiara and spoke into her ear. 'I've got to get some dog food. I think there's an all-night supermarket in the town,' I said.

'You're not driving?'

'I've only had one glass,' I said.

Chiara frowned.

'You OK?'

'I'm fine.' I wanted to go now. I couldn't bear to wait any longer.

'Do you want me to come?'

'No, it's OK. Thanks though. I'll leave Pepper here if you don't mind. Won't be long.'

'Can't it wait till the morning?'

I shook my head.

I couldn't speak any more. My mouth was dry. Because my real reason for going out at midnight in the car in the rain seemed completely absurd, but I would never rest until I had gone back and done what I should have done to start with.

Checked.

It was darker than I'd thought it would be and the rain drummed against the windscreen, obscuring the view further. I tried to remember where it was I'd felt the impact. I screwed up my eyes, looking out for the broken branch. Anxious about my driving, I went slowly, peering in my rear-view mirror, checking all around. The road twisted. It was difficult to see anything but the beam of the headlights reflecting off the wet road.

I had been driving for maybe fifteen minutes when I thought I saw it. The branch, bent in the middle like a long arm dangling its fingers onto the narrow road – it would be hard to miss. I couldn't stop here, it was close to a bend, so I drove on and then, just a couple of hundred metres further on, there was a police cordon, the cones, the place they taped off where the man was hit. A notice asking for witnesses. And more tree parts, snapped off, scattered on the road. Now doubt played through my mind. Which branch had I hit?

I had to drive for another five minutes in order to reach a junction where I was able to turn and come back, reliving the journey I made earlier this evening when I had been so convinced I was taking my life in a new direction.

I was ignorant about impact, and thrust, and momentum, all those things we were supposed to learn about in physics that seemed pointless – of no relevance to my life as it was at that time. If I'd listened, I might have had some idea of what it might have felt like. Whether I might have knocked into a grown man and only heard the slam of the wing mirror, experienced a tilting of the car to the right. Whether the impact could have thrown him far.

What speed had I been travelling at when I came down this road? How fast would you have to be going to do that? I wasn't a fast driver – something my more reckless friends laughed about. But I hadn't been thinking clearly this evening. I'd had the music on loud and Pepper had distracted me with his barking. I might have been going at forty, possibly fifty. Don't they say if you hit someone at thirty you can kill them, but at twenty they survive?

I certainly hadn't been going slowly enough, in that case, to hit a man and *not* kill him.

The radio had said he was alive though. Injured but alive.

For a few moments this skewed logic reassured me – I had been going too fast to have hit and not killed a man! Hoorah! I couldn't have hit him – if I *had* he would be dead.

Then the truth flashed back. He might be brain-damaged or his back might be broken. He might be crippled for life even if he wasn't dead. It might be worse than if he'd died.

I passed the spot again, the tape and the cones and the police cordon. I looked into my rear-view mirror.

I could see nothing but the bough of the tree. Nothing else on the road, nor in my memory. But if you did something so ghastly might you wipe it from your mind? Might you shut down, unable to relive that awful vision, the intolerable knowledge that you'd just destroyed a life, while you were so full of your own rosy future that you didn't even bother to look where you were going? I had been distracted by Pepper. I was talking to him, telling him we'd be OK without Finn, and so I could have hit the man, and passed it off as nothing but a broken branch on the road.

The other branch was round the next corner. There was a lay-by just in front of it so I pulled up.

There was a strong wind blowing now, buffeting the car

so it rocked as I opened the door and got out. The wind almost blew me back into my seat as I stepped onto the tarmac. It was pitch dark. No traffic, nobody, nothing. I stood for a moment, my senses straining. The wind must be blowing in from the sea, there was the faint smell of salt on it, mixed with vegetation. I was thirsty. My mouth dry.

The wind whistled through the hedges, shifting a plastic bag that had caught there, blowing it up so it billowed white in the night. The rain had stopped but I wished I'd put on a fleece instead of just this cardigan over my T-shirt and jeans. I pulled the cardy closer around me and headed back up towards the place where the cones were, the signs saying 'Accident', the calls for witnesses.

There wasn't much to see. The cones had been moved back and the yellow tape flapped now on the verge. A car was coming, its lights appearing and vanishing as it approached along the bendy road. I drew back into the hawthorn, out of sight. As it passed something glinted in the hedge, lit up momentarily by the car lights. I moved across. A shard of glass, it looked like, caught in the hedge. The police must have missed it. I looked about. It was difficult to see any-thing else in the cordoned-off area once the car had passed. I don't know what I'd expected. A shoe? Blood? A body part? I shuddered.

But I had something.

I had the bit of glass. I could check whether it matched the glass from my mirror where it had broken and if it didn't I could leave this whole thing alone and get on with my weekend.

I turned and started to walk back to my car. Round the

bend, along past the tall hedges, and then the tree branch loomed into focus, just beyond where I'd parked, hanging over the road, ragged at the ends, sticks strewn about the road; several cars must have driven into it. Then I could see, a little further on, the mangled body of something, squished up against the verge.

I bent down. A bird. Feathers flattened against the tarmac. Not much left of its head. Quite a large bird, black and white. A magpie? Stupid to let the old wives' tale affect me, but nevertheless, I regarded magpies as unlucky. If I'd hit this one, if it had flown into the side of my car, knocked my wing mirror, then fallen concussed, if it had lain there as other cars passed, flattening its head into the road, I didn't want to think too much about it.

But this was my explanation. I *had* hit something. I *had* seen something on the road in my rear-view mirror, but it was just this poor bird.

I shivered. I must get back. As I set off, towards my car, I noticed a track I hadn't seen earlier, on the same side of the road as my car. It was a narrow single track, difficult to spot, as it ran just below the level of the main road. A battered van was waiting there, in the entrance, near an open gate, parked, its lights off.

Who had parked here, at night, in an entrance to a farm track? Was that someone sitting there in the driver's seat? A head silhouetted against the sky, which had brightened a little as the clouds parted in the wind, revealing a watery moon.

My heart did a little skip as I saw it.

Why hadn't I spotted it before? I began to hurry.

As I drew closer to my car I wondered why I hadn't left my

headlights on. They would have lit up the road so I could see what I was doing.

I was certain then, that I heard the gentle thunk of a door closing.

The van door.

The wind dropped, I could hear the tread of footfall on rough ground. Someone was coming down the track.

I walked faster, fighting the urge to run, my ears straining – how close were they? I was aware of the solitary figure I made on a remote part of this deserted road at night. I'd told no one where I was going. If anything happened to me . . . I might disappear and they would have no idea where to begin to look. I'd let my preoccupation lead me into the jaws of real danger.

The footsteps were accelerating now, they'd grown heavier, were getting close.

I reached my car. Fumbled for the keys I'd dropped deep into the small pocket of my cardy. I tried to control the trembling of my fingers. Why had I locked the car door? Had I imagined there might be a car thief out here at this time of night? I should have left the headlights on, the door unlocked for a quick getaway. I'd been operating on automatic as if I'd parked in the street outside our Mile End flat where people were paranoid about car theft, instead of in this country lane.

Why hadn't I brought Pepper?

I longed to be with the others now. Not here, driven by the kind of irrational thoughts I'd believed I'd stopped having.

The figure from the van was closing up now, his stride long. I glanced up. His face – what I could see of it, the bottom half shrouded in a scarf, the top shaded by his hoodie – was pale in the night.

I pressed the button on my key fob twice.

My fingers were weak. Nothing happened. I was frozen, my fingers disconnected from my brain, my will. I forced them to do as I wanted.

He was maybe ten metres away, his feet scrunching on the road, closing in on me.

At last the locks clacked open. I pulled open the driver's door. Fell in, slammed it shut.

Pressed the lock again. My fingers felt like rubber.

I put the key in the ignition. He was there, a face hovering a few inches from the windscreen.

I started the engine. Put my foot on the clutch.

A thump on the window. Then the face disappeared from view. He was coming round to the door as the car jerked into motion.

I had my foot on the accelerator. I pulled away too quickly, stalled. He was at my door now, his eyes leering above the scarf that shrouded his mouth and chin, a broad nose, eyes set far apart. I tried again to get the car started. It hiccupped, lurched, stalled again. He had hold of the door handle. I didn't want to look at the face, and I pulled away, but I did look, caught another glimpse, this time he was mouthing something. I left him on the verge, shouting inaudibly as I headed back to the sea.

'Where have you been, Ellie?' Chiara stood in the kitchen doorway. 'You were ages! I was going to come and look for you!'

'The shop was shut. I tried somewhere else, but . . . you know.'

'We tried your mobile,' Louise said, joining us, 'but you'd left it in the sitting room. We were worried.'

'I'm fine,' I said.

'Scatty as ever,' said Chiara, putting her arm round me. 'She went for dog food! At this time!'

Louise yawned. 'I could've sent Guy to get some in the morning. He'll want a run.'

'You are nutty sometimes, babes,' Chiara said. 'Pepper isn't going to starve if he doesn't get breakfast at the crack of dawn. You're over-compensating for Frank.'

'Who's Frank?' Louise asked.

'The old man across the corridor from us in London,' Chiara said. 'Ellie's taking care of Pepper for him while he has heart surgery. He told her he was afraid Pepper would die before he did.' She was chuckling. 'And Ellie told him she was sure he wouldn't.'

'That was tactful!'

'I felt dreadful. It sounded like I was hoping Frank would die first,' I said. My voice came out weak, wobbly.

'She was being nice,' Chiara said. 'Weren't you, Ellie?'

'I didn't want him to worry, he was going through such a lot.'

'So you offered to look after his dog?'

I shrugged.

Chiara hugged me.

'Ellie's always kept an eye on Frank. She's got the kindest heart. My philosophy is if you always try to do the right thing – in the end you're bound to do the opposite!' She squeezed my shoulder. 'I keep a bit of a distance myself.'

'Anyone would've looked after the dog in those circumstances,' I said.

'I wouldn't,' said Chiara. 'Dogs should live outside as far as I'm concerned.'

'How long's it going to be though?' Louise asked. 'You might have adopted him permanently, if the old man dies. What sort is he?'

'A Norfolk terrier.'

'Cute!' Louise ruffled Pepper's fur, and Pepper, out of character, growled.

I didn't sleep that night, I lay and listened to the hiss and suck of the waves on the shore. I'd hit something, and a man had been injured.

His life might be ruined. I imagined he might be a young man, a teenager perhaps? His parents would be beside themselves. Or his girlfriend. Where had he been going? Was he alone? When would they have heard that their son had been hit on the road and the driver had gone off without stopping?

I could go to the police, but what would I tell them? That I had been on that road last night, that no, I hadn't seen a man on the road. No, I hadn't hit anyone, as far as I knew. But something had caught my wing mirror and I'd found blood on the door? That I was haunted by the fear I should have turned back? That I regularly had the compulsion to go back and check on things, so it was difficult to untangle what was rational, what irrational. What would they do? Keep me in for questioning? It might take all weekend. I had important buyers coming this evening. And anyway it sounded bonkers. It *was* bonkers.

Then how come there was a hit-and-run on the same stretch of road where something had flung my wing mirror back against the door? And the doubts started up all over again, smashing into my brain, then receding, like the waves.

CHAPTER FIVE

The first thing I did the next morning was put on the radio.

The item was not first on the local news, it came on after two or three other things about the wettest April on record, and a fishing crisis.

'The man knocked down by a hit-and-run incident last night has been named as Patrick McIntyre. He remains in critical condition in hospital. Police continue to appeal to drivers to come forward.' I switched it off.

I got up and dressed, and downstairs pulled my long boots on over my jeans. Louise's lilies seemed to glow on the hall table

I didn't want to see them. Flowers were for roadside accidents. Lilies were for death. I went outside, Pepper at my heels. Tapped the gatepost three times. The air was fresh and a wind blew in off the sea.

I knew I shouldn't, but I couldn't resist bending down to

check the bonnet of my car where the blood had been. It had washed off in the rain. All evidence gone. As I turned to go back indoors, a voice disturbed my thoughts.

'May's house! You burgling May's house.'

I looked up. The man on the bike down on the road was about fifty but was staring at me wide-mouthed – a child's expression. I remembered him – his name was Larry, a local who'd been here forever. He lived in one of the fishing cottages along the harbour. He stood and stared at me, his lower lip trembling.

'You burglar!'

'I'm not a burglar, I'm May's niece. Ellie.'

'May gone. Girl gone. Gone. Dead. Don't come back.'

He'd got the out-loud logic of a young child spelling out to himself something he'd been told but didn't quite understand.

'Yes, Larry, May's gone. I'm sorry.'

'Not coming back.'

'No she's not, I'm sorry, Larry.'

'You killed the lady.'

I stared at him. I didn't need this.

'No, Larry. No. May died. I didn't kill her.'

'Bye-bye, lady,' he said.

'Bye, Larry.'

I wondered if Larry's 'she's not coming back' was his way of differentiating this from the time she had gone into hospital, leaving the house empty for several years.

I was eighteen and at art college when I heard that Aunty May was back in the blue house. I knew by then she had been sectioned, had been in and out of hospital but had been discharged at last.

I had been shocked by the change in her. She had aged terribly in the years since I'd seen her. Her hair, once lustrous and chestnut, up in a bun, was white, her eyes, once intense and full of sparkle, were haunted. She had lost weight, her skin, I thought, was the colour of the white cuttlefish we sometimes found on the shore.

It took months for her to regain her old sparkle, to start painting again. That was when we'd started meeting up, for painting weekends, quiet, creative times that we spent together and that bonded us once more.

Chiara was in the kitchen in her dressing gown, filling the kitchen with an aroma only she could produce from a packet of coffee. She'd brought Italian pastries and was warming them for everyone else in the oven of May's old Baby Belling cooker. 'I'm going to get Liam up now. *Il mattino ha l'oro in bocca*,' she said.

'Which means?'

'The morning has gold in its mouth,' she said. 'We mustn't waste it. How much do you need to do for tonight?'

'I need to check all the paintings are hung properly and the price list.'

'It's so exciting! Aren't you excited?'

'I am.' And I was.

The clouds had shifted in the night winds and the April sun was shining through the kitchen windows and outside there were tiny blue flowers in the tough sea grass. The air was translucent here, the sand looked white, the grasses a soft fringe against the pale blue of the sky.

Chiara put her pastries on the table, a burnished heap surrounded in flakes of gold leaf. They gave off a warm buttery smell. Chiara was right, the morning had gold in its mouth.

I fed Pepper with the dog food that I'd had all the time.

Louise and Guy came in.

'We thought we'd walk up to the town along the front,' Louise said.

'OK, but first we need breakfast,' Chiara said. 'Liam doesn't function before he's got food in his stomach.' Liam had come in, his fair hair standing up in spikes, his face puffy with sleep. He leant his head over and put it on Chiara's belly.

'He needs feeding too,' he said.

'Or *she*,' Chiara said.

'Are you going to find out?' I asked. 'I think I'd want to know.'

'No.' Chiara said. 'I want a surprise!'

'Suppose you're tied up with the show this evening?' Louise said, peeling herself from Guy, sitting down, pulling pieces off a pastry to pop into her mouth.

'There's quite a bit to do,' I said again, though the paintings were all hung, with the special magnets I used, something that had impressed Valerie who owned the gallery.

She had said they'd sort out the refreshments. All I had to do was turn up, talk, schmooze with potential buyers, Valerie had reassured me. 'You'll charm them. You're talented and you look the part, just smile a lot and answer their questions.'

'What does she mean by my "looking the part"?' I'd asked Chiara.

'You've got the distracted arty look! And the pallor of someone who is too full of ideas to feed herself properly. A kind of young Tracey Emin. Or maybe it's the clothes. The vintage stuff. Anyway, you'll look great.'

'I'll have to pop in there this morning,' I said now.

A thought was stirring within me, a way of putting my anxiety about the hit-and-run to rest once and for all so that I could concentrate on the weekend.

I looked at my friends, Louise with her tan and Chiara with her barely perceptible pregnancy bump, and thought how much I loved them and needed them. How although we'd all got older we hadn't changed fundamentally, none of us dressed that differently from how we'd done as students, or changed our basic values. We had all been struggling – to raise a mortgage in Chiara and Liam's case, to get work in the art world in mine and Louise's, making do and dreaming that one day we could leave our part-time day jobs and become professional artists. Was it all beginning to happen at last? I couldn't let the worry spoil it.

Louise walked to the window. Looked out past my car to the dunes. 'It's really atmospheric here. Inspiring for you.'

'I knew you'd get it.'

'I think it's the thresholds you get here, the border between land and sea, sea and sky, life and death. The kind of themes you use in your work. A liminal landscape.'

'Exactly! And what I want to do too, is somehow show the layers beneath what we see?'

She turned and grinned. 'I've hardly done any work over the last few months. You're way ahead of me,' she said.

'Oh, I don't know about that,' I said.

'Right! I want to get out there,' Liam said. 'Are you girls coming? Shall we take Pepper, if you're busy at the gallery? A walk in this sea breeze will shift the hangover, won't it, hey, Pepper?' Pepper jumped up and snaffled at Liam's hand, his tail going madly.

'The forecast's good,' said Guy, looking at his phone. 'It's going to warm up by lunchtime. Though what warm means here is anyone's guess.' He looked up at us all and grinned and Louise moved away from the window and leant over him, wrapping her arms round his chest and kissing his hair. I might be moving up in the art world but she had found love. Why was it so difficult to get all three right? – the relationship, the work, the house?

I told my friends I was popping to Ipswich to get some extra magnets to hang paintings.

'Try not to be too long,' Chiara said. 'I know you're nervous about tonight, I can see it. But everything's going to be fine. I'll sort everything else so that you can focus on your viewers.'

'Thanks, Chiara.'

'*Prego!*' she said. 'You know me, nothing I like better than an event to sort.'

I looked into her big brown concerned eyes.

I could talk to Chiara about the hit-and-run now. I could ask her, so do you think it's possible it might have been me, and Chiara would say, 'No, honey, don't be daft.' Or she would say, 'Look, if you go to the police you'll be wasting their time. You know this is crazy, don't you? You would know if you'd hit someone.'

'But there was a jolt,' I'd say. 'I remember a jolt on the road that I ignored! The music was on loud. I was talking to Pepper. Then there was blood on the bonnet!'

'A body would make more than a jolt,' she would insist. 'You would have seen it.'

'In the dark? While I was looking the other way?'

Instead I said I'd see them later and watched them walk away.

I knew what I was going to do. The thought had come to me, loud and clear.

I should have gone back and checked. But it isn't too late. I can go to him and find out how bad it really is.

If he is going to die, if he's critically injured, though God forbid, I have to tell the police I might have hit him.

It is the right thing to do.

But if he's OK, I can forget all about it, come back, get ready for tonight, put on the new dress, go to the Private View, take the first steps into my new life as a proper working artist. Without Finn.

I didn't give it any more thought. I locked the door, got into my car.

As I drove away from town I was overcome by envy for my friends and their freedom. I had a horrible presentiment that what I was doing was going to intefere with my plans. That it would take me away, not just from my tired old ways – the things I wanted to move on from – but from everything that was precious to me too, and that I'd never get back. My friends were walking along the shore with my dog, on their way for a lunchtime drink. The perfect spring weekend that I had planned and envisaged.

While I was about to find out whether I'd killed someone.

CHAPTER SIX

I wasn't sure if the hospital would let me in. I didn't know what the rules were these days, about visiting times, about who they did and didn't allow in. And all I had was a name. Nothing to prove that I might actually know or be related to him.

I hated hospitals. The facelessness of them. The long corridors. The blue signs. I was glad this was a small one – the ones I disliked most were those vast teaching hospitals more like underground cities, with long tunnels of blank walks, and double doors and signs to departments where people must be suffering, or gasping their last breaths, with hurried harassed overworked medical staff and grieving relatives and anxiety. I even hated the car parks, the endless rows of vehicles that have carried the wretched and the bereaved to this building no one really wants to be in.

But I forced myself. If I could just do this, reassure myself the victim was alive, recovering, I'd be able to relax.

*   *   *

It didn't take too long to find, on the outside of the town, and the visitors' car park was full, it being Saturday. I prowled around the bays for a while and finally squeezed into a space at the far corner near a spinney of trees. A gaggle of people were smoking beside the entrance, under the sign saying 'Secondary smoking – think of the people who are breathing it.' That was something Finn and I would have laughed at once.

'Ah. Yes. Patrick McIntyre. Came in last night,' the receptionist, a woman with platinum-blonde hair and geek-chic glasses told me, checking her screen. She glanced up at me. 'He's on the trauma ward – third floor.'

I got into a lift and pushed through the double doors. My heart was thumping. I didn't know if I'd be allowed into the ward. And I hadn't worked out what I was going to tell the nurses about why I was here. Let alone what I'd tell the man himself, or any relatives that might be hanging around. I had a half-baked idea I could say I was a journalist, covering the incident, but I hadn't thought it through.

All I knew was I had to prove to myself for once and for all that even if there was the tiniest chance I had knocked this man down that at least he was OK. He would live.

The ward doors were locked. I pressed the button on the intercom and a man's voice asked who I was. I said I was here to see Patrick McIntyre and the door clicked open.

There were two nurses at the station, a man and a woman. The man barely looked up when I approached and muttered Patrick's name.

'He's in recovery still,' said the woman, who was about my mother's age. Her blue eyes ran up and down, assessing me.

'And you are . . .?'

'I . . . I'm a friend.'

She smiled.

'Tom'll show you.'

The male nurse got up, his legs so long and spindly they barely looked as though they'd hold him, and told me to follow him. Wasn't he going to ask my name? Any other questions?

'How is he?' I asked Tom's back, as he strode ahead of me. 'How's he doing?'

'He's doing well,' he said. He turned his head without stopping, glanced at me. I wondered if he was older than me, or younger or about my age. He still had acne and he wore lots of silver in his ear. Younger, definitely.

'The consultant's doing an assessment on his scans, will have the results later, but he's comfortable. The op went well. He's heavily sedated. You might not get much sense out of him yet.'

'How long will it take for . . .?'

'Hard to tell, if he continues like this he could be out in a week. But you never know, there can be complications with head injuries.' *Head injuries!* 'On top of the blood loss.'

I swallowed.

'You're his girlfriend then?'

I nodded. I couldn't speak. He didn't look round, didn't seem to care one way or another.

He pushed open another door. 'Don't be shocked by all the equipment. It's not as bad as it looks. He's lucky, his back's OK.'

We went into the room.

I looked over my shoulder three times, to make him be OK.

'Please be OK. Let me not have caused you any serious harm,' I whispered. 'If it was me. Please though, please let it not have been me, let me get away from here. Back to my new life.'

He was on a bed under the window.

Beyond, the trees were tipped with green, just coming into leaf. The sky was blue, it was a beautiful day. I could see my car, the culprit, down below. I wanted to be in it, to get away as fast as I could.

I looked back at Patrick. There was a drip set up. His legs were hidden under the tent of hospital sheeting.

I shut my eyes, then opened them. Forced myself to look at his face.

I was shocked. Patrick McIntyre was about my age. Late twenties, I guessed. What had I imagined? In spite of the nurse's assumption I was his girlfriend, I had been thinking of perhaps a teenager, a youth, someone a bit wayward. Not a fully grown man. Short dark hair protruded from the dressing on his head. A bronzed face, and his forearms, that were folded across his chest, strong and golden and smooth with that ridge of muscle; the thought came to me unbidden that this was a man who should never have ended up like this. *What a waste*, was the thought that slid in. I forced it out again. It would be a waste, of course, whoever it was. But somehow, seeing all this health and vitality cut down like this seemed unfair, unbelievable. I thought of Guy, out there on the beach with my friends. Of my brother Ben, with his glossy golden girlfriend. Bright successful good-looking types.

Patrick looked like one of them.

'He might be able to hear, it's worth talking to him. He'll be pleased to know you're here. And it'll help bring him round.'

I glanced up at the nurse, checking to see if he was testing me out. I could be anyone, couldn't I? I wanted to ask again, is he going to be ok? But the words stuck in my throat. My hands felt light, as if they didn't belong to me.

'Got anything with you that might jog his memory when he comes round? Photos. Anything like that?'

Why? Why would he need his memory jogging?

'Just in case there's a little bit of amnesia,' the nurse went on. 'He had a blow to the head, the way he landed. Though it'll be impossible to know until he's fully conscious. He's still under the anaesthetic. But familiarity as soon as possible is always helpful.'

I forced myself to behave as I imagined his girlfriend might in this situation. Efficient. Sensible.

'I've got my phone.'

What was I doing, playing along like this? I rummaged through my bag, my hands were slippery, sweaty with nerves. I pulled things out – trying to control my movements as I did so. My diary, an appointment card for a haircut, my purse, dumping them on the bedside table until I found my phone that had slipped to the bottom.

I clicked it on. Smiled up at the nurse.

He wasn't even looking. He was studying a chart at the end of Patrick's bed, filling it in. After a while he left, closing the door gently behind him.

*   *   *

51

There was not much in the room apart from the beeping monitor and the drip. A trolley, out of reach of the bed, with a plastic jug of water on it. A couple of laminated signs Blu-tacked to the walls advertising patient liaison services. No flowers, no cards. It was probably too soon. Or maybe this man was far from home, and family and friends.

I ran my eye up and down Patrick's body.

'Please don't die,' I whispered. 'Please don't let me have killed you.'

His chest rose and fell, his breath just audible, his closed lids a delicate pale lilac.

I wondered what colour his eyes might be when they were open. Brown, I guessed, dark, intriguing brown.

His full lips were pale and dry. On his chin a neatly clipped, black beard. This part of him, at least, had been spared, I thought. His face was intact.

I tried to visualise the moment of impact on my car. I recalled the journey for the millionth time. The light fading behind me, darkness up in front. My music up loud and Pepper distracting me for a second – or was it longer?

A shock ran down my body into my legs. The jolt was quite hard. The car had wobbled, swerved, I'd righted it and driven on, fighting my need to check.

I *could* have hit Patrick as I looked at Pepper, caught him, if, say, he'd stepped out from the verge, perhaps waving me down, perhaps hitching a lift. I remembered the jogger then, how I'd barely seen him until I'd almost passed. It was completely possible I had seen no one on the road, because I was looking down when it happened, and hadn't heard the full impact because Beyoncé had been singing about not wanting to play the broken-hearted girl.

I visualised it all as I stood there beside him, the impact as he stepped out, losing his foothold, knowing he could do nothing to help himself as he ricocheted into the air, the flipping over, the legs buckling, the head-first crunch onto the tarmac.

I stood up. I needed to get out. I couldn't stay here, knowing something no one else in the world knew. Or I could tell someone. Who? I could tell the tall nurse with his skinny legs. What would he care?

I could go to the police.

Then other thoughts tumbled in. My friends, all waiting for me to return and entertain them for the weekend. The show this evening at which I was to raise money for Mind. There were important buyers coming.

And anyway it was insane, wasn't it?

There had been nothing but part of a tree on the road, and the bird. That was what had caused the blood on the bonnet.

I stared at his well-toned body. He was well groomed; neatly clipped sideburns, as well as the beard, and, I noted, über-clean nails. He had tanned skin with a sheen of health on it.

His lips turned up a little at the corners as if he was dreaming of things that amused him.

Would he still have that look when he came round and found he'd been knocked over by a stranger?

I looked about the room.

I mustn't be long. Anyone might turn up at any time, ask

what the hell I was doing here, a stranger at his bedside. But maybe if I found out who he was, where he was going last night, I would perhaps be able to fit things together, prove it wasn't me.

There wasn't much here. A locker. I opened it. A wallet, packed with credit cards.

An iPhone. I flicked it on. He didn't have a pass code, the icons came straight up on the screen. There was his Facebook, impossible to resist a quick peek. I clicked on it.

This must be him, squinting into the sun. He was in a suit, his arm round a woman. She was Asian-looking, Chinese, Korean maybe.

He was grinning, creases radiating from the corners of his eyes.

The woman was smiling adoringly up at him. I examined her. Slim, beautiful, in flimsy black evening clothes and high heels. Behind them, just visible, was a line of deep blue sea.

His 'Friends' list was there, his life in mates in front of my eyes.

I scrolled down the list. There were a few men standing beside yachts, several were in wetsuits. A couple of tanned, smiling women.

I had to leave. I put the phone away. I'd take a quick look in his locker then go.

An expensive-looking watch.

A receipt in his wallet printed out from the internet, a flight booking receipt. He'd flown back from Corfu in March.

I closed the wallet.

'I'm sorry,' I said, taking up his hand, feeling its weight, the black hairs that curled over his knuckles, a chunky ring, not on his wedding finger. The nurse had told me to speak to him, but what to say?

'Please, whatever you do, don't die,' I said. 'It was an accident. I was on my way to Southwold. To my aunt's house. You might know it, the blue clapboard house on the beach. If you don't die you could come one day. When you're better. You and your girlfriend. Do please get better.' A last plea, it came out with a sob.

'I want you to know I never meant to hit you.'

The door opened and I swung round.

A nurse. Small, neat, Filipino.

I steeled myself, opened my mouth to say I was leaving, but she smiled as she checked Patrick's monitors and made notes on his charts and ticked things off.

'It was bad luck,' she said, pulling his sheets straight. Picking up his file from the end of his bed. 'He's handsome. But silly boy. Lucky his injuries aren't worse.'

'Is he . . . is he going to recover?'

'We hope,' she said. Then she winked. 'Don't you worry. You must tell him no more walking in the dark. Impossible for drivers to see you on those dark country roads.'

'Do they know what happened?' I asked, my voice weak, tremulous.

I should have gone, but I liked this nurse, there was something comforting about her small neat briskness. She would never get into the kind of mess I'd got into. I imagined her home, a minimalist retreat, with tiny cups and a china teapot of green tea. Clothes hanging on a rack of uniform hangers, ironed, no clutter. I imagined her children, I had children like this in my class. Pretty, clever children – children who played violin and got top marks in maths and were fluent in both their mother tongue and English and often other languages too, who wrote beautifully and were sweet with it. It was a stereotype I was creating, I knew, but for now it soothed me.

'Who found him? Who reported it?'

'Another driver phoned the ambulance. The police are still making enquiries. They have two suspects.'

She paused. Looked straight at me.

'You must be verr-ry worried. You his girlfriend?'

I nodded, stupefied.

'He often get in fights?'

I shrugged. 'Not usually, no.'

'Not what police think. It was hit-and-run, you know? The car hit and drove on. Shameful! They think it was after a fight. He had alcohol in his system. Witnesses saw him in pub earlier. They think the driver went after him deliberately. But you're not to worry. Police will sort it all out, they will come back to talk to him when he comes round. They will be in touch.'

I stared at her, my tongue sticking to the roof of my mouth, wanting to ask more.

But she nodded and went out as briskly as she'd come in.

So. There had been a feud, in a pub. Someone had deliberately gone after Patrick, in a drunken rage! It had nothing to do with me.

It was still awful to imagine this poor man being mown down by some drunken louts, but it meant I could disentangle myself.

The sun came in, and the room was warm; it was quiet apart from the beeps from the monitors. I wanted to run after the nurse and hug her, thank her for reassuring me. My fear seemed to evaporate. All my limbs went floppy, relaxed, as the crazy thoughts that had been taunting me loosened their hold.

I didn't need to go to the police, there was no need to confess to anything.

The man in the bed was OK anyway, he wasn't going to die. I would walk out, put this whole crazy incident behind me. No one need know that for twelve hours I'd been obsessed with the insane idea that I might have killed someone.

But I had to leave. Before someone turned up. Accused me. A stranger by the bedside.

Probably almost as much a crime in itself as a hit-and-run.

'I've got to go,' I whispered. 'I'll make sure you're OK. I'll check the local news. I'm so glad you're not going to die. It's all going to be alright.'

I picked up my bag.

I turned round at the door to have one last look at him. My heart jumped a beat.

His eyes were open.

I blinked. Took a step away. But no, it must have been a trick of the light, for they were as they had been when I'd come in, his eyelids shut, smooth, the black eyelashes curling gently against his cheek.

I turned my back on him and pushed open the doors.

'Hey,' came a voice from behind me. 'Let me see you.'

CHAPTER SEVEN

I bolted. Down the corridor past the nurses' station, ignoring the demands to disinfect my hands, not stopping to speak to the nurse, Tom, who was rifling through files, and whose eyes I imagined burning into me as the door to the ward banged behind me and I leapt down the three flights of stairs.

I don't know how I got to my car. But within minutes I was accelerating out of the hospital car park, and driving fast back out of the town. The sky was huge and yellow and relentless, I felt raw beneath it, exposed. I wanted to get among tall buildings, among cramped streets. I wanted to be in London, people of every nationality hurrying past the windows, each in their own world, not looking at anyone else. Where everyone was anonymous.

When the man in the bed had spoken those words to me I'd panicked, left without turning to face him. If he shouted out that he'd never seen me before, what would I do? What if he asked the nurses who I was, what I'd been doing there? I mustn't think any more about it.

I clutched the steering wheel, leaning forward to make sure there was no chance I might hit anything else by accident. How was I going to get through the exhibition tonight, entertaining my friends, Louise and her boyfriend and the public? I'd have to be the sparkling hostess when I had this new knot of anxiety deep in my stomach, that I might be accused – if not of running the man over – then of being some sort of imposter. But I had no choice. I'd been gone for over an hour. I couldn't stay away any longer.

Southwold was busy. It was Saturday and day-trippers had driven in, their cars filling the parking spaces along the streets. Groups ambled along the pavements, stopping to look in shop windows, to gasp at the price of property in the estate agents or to buy overpriced cheese from the delis, or designer sailing wear from the clothes chains. I parked near the church and walked down to the promenade.

I stood leaning on the white railings. I could see my friends and Pepper down on the beach. I could see myself at six years old, sitting on one of the posts along the groyne. Picking at stones that had got wedged into holes in the wooden pillars by the tides, in a hopeless quest to get them all out. Far away to my left, beyond the lower promenade with its pastel-coloured beach huts, was the pier.

I looked at my friends caught eternally in the sunshine of a spring Saturday, not knowing that this moment was passing even as they threw the ball to and fro. They thought everything was perfect. They had no idea how quickly what we cherish and look forward to can switch to something dark and frightening and out of our control. But I was their host. I was responsible for making this weekend good for them. And the man was alive. He was unlikely to ask who I was. He'd only seen my back, so everything *was* alright.

I went down the steps, between the steep banks of brambles and dog rose and nettles to the promenade with its pretty beach huts, then took my boots and socks off and ran down the rest of the concrete stairs to the beach.

Feeling the cool sand beneath my feet, I walked over to my friends. Pepper ran towards me and jumped up and I picked him up and kissed his warm fur.

I would try from now on to forget about the hospital. It was unlikely anything would come of my visit. You had to live in the present, as my yoga teacher was always reiterating. Be mindful of now. I would devote myself to being a good hostess for my friends. To the Private View tonight. Tomorrow I'd help Chiara make breakfast for everyone. Kippers, as Liam had suggested, with lemon, and poached eggs and slices of that lovely three-grain bread you could buy at the deli.

Later we could take the walk over the footbridge to the other side of the estuary, to Walberswick, and have coffee in the café there. I would begin again. I would have the weekend I intended to have when I first invited everyone down here.

I stood welcoming people in the doorway of the gallery. The glass of Prosecco that Valerie thrust into my hands as soon as I arrived gave me a warm glow. The incident with Patrick had gone distant, ethereal. The hospital visit, too, had faded, seemed unreal. I would leave it like that, a tiny aberration, and move on.

'Your pictures are looking fantastic, come and see.'

I followed Valerie through the whitewashed ex-chapel, arched windows at either end letting in bright, white, seaside light.

The paintings were set off by the space. I could hardly believe they were mine.

'I love your idea, using these magnets to hang them. Very cool,' she said.

'It's what everyone's doing in Oz,' said Louise, standing beside me.

Valerie said, 'They look great, don't they? I like things on board, unframed. And they're certainly in good company.'

One or two of the other artists sold through up-market galleries in London. I knew for a fact that one had a painting in the Tate. I'd been chosen to show my work among long-established artists. I felt a twinge of pride. If only the other people I loved and cared about were here. Aunty May, of course. But Dad too, trapped by his agoraphobia to the confines of his little studio flat in Greenwich. My brother Ben, off on some business trip. My mum, tied down by work.

It was busy but quiet. People moved about with catalogues, murmuring. They looked wealthy and middle-aged, well dressed in that casual, we-have-natural-good-taste way. Understated, but very expensive fabrics. I smiled. Shook people's hands. Answered their questions about my inspiration (rivers, mostly the Thames, though I'd started working on the Blyth recently), where I worked (no one could believe

I didn't have a studio but worked on the sitting-room floor in our Mile End flat), my themes (the boundaries between land and sea, water and sky, light and dark, life and death, layers beneath the surface) and who my influences were. I mentioned one or two people who had also, in different ways, taken inspiration from rivers – Alexander Pemberton, Frank Creber – and used layering and texture as part of their works – Andrew Taylor, Paul Klee, Rothko.

My most revered artists? Turner, and Whistler. My all-time favourite painting of the moment I told them was Whistler's *Battersea Reach*.

As I stood and chatted, Larry came past on his bike. He stopped outside the window and pressed up against the glass. He spotted me, pointed, and said something. Watching the big unformed movements of his mouth I guessed he was talking about May being gone again, but it was impossible to hear through the window, his breath steaming up the glass. He moved to the entrance, stood in the doorway, and repeated, 'Lady gone. Not coming back.'

A middle-aged couple edged past him and he repeated whatever he was saying, pointing at me. They shrugged, smiled, and moved on through the door.

I turned my back on the window and when I next looked, Larry had gone.

Most people were examining the labels before they looked at the pictures. It's often the name that captures the buyers first. They read it, then look at the painting, trying to work out in what way it warrants the title.

Left to me I wouldn't have bothered with them. The work,

I believed, and Finn would certainly argue, should speak for itself. None of my works were exactly figurative, though they were based on scenes, and there were allusions to shapes, forms. I allowed these to develop until I reached a point of resolution. But the galleries liked titles because they sold. People wanted to feel they'd bought something that they understood or recognised. They also loved to buy a painting that suggested somewhere they had been or something they had experienced. Anything with local place names sold.

Valerie came over to me about half an hour in.

She leant her head towards mine and spoke in an undertone, nodding towards a man in a suit with a petite silver-haired woman.

'They asked me to introduce you. Come on.'

They were looking at my picture that was based on the creek over near May's house, where it was broad and flat, where the sky was massive and the horizon melded into the edge of the water. I'd begun it in the winter during one of my visits after May died, trying to express this blurring of boundaries, the water reflecting the sky, the sky reaching right down to the water's surface, the sense of an underlying menace beneath the beauty. I had used the same blues and silvers Whistler employed, and it was a painting I was quietly proud of.

'Can I get you a drink?' Valerie asked.

'Sure,' the man said. 'And perhaps you could help, we were wondering about the starting price of this.'

'This is Ellie, the artist. I'll leave you to chat while I fetch the list,' Valerie said.

'How are you?' He was grey-haired, but his skin was

smooth. He seemed to shimmer as if everything he wore was made of the best-quality silk in that indeterminate shade of grey that speaks of exquisite taste. 'So *you're* the artist. Wow! We were admiring this piece.'

The woman, who had a pleasantly lined face, pink lipstick, and twinkling turquoise eyes, took my hand. 'You're a very talented young woman,' she said. 'We've picked you out. My husband runs a gallery in his restaurant in New York. We'd like to have a chat with you sometime, could we have your card?'

'Ellie?'

Valerie had come back with the price list, gave me an almost imperceptible nod, and moved away to greet another gaggle of well-dressed people who had just arrived.

'We'll put in a bid for this. But we wondered whether you took commissions.'

The man flipped a card out of a calf leather wallet and put it into my hand. 'Here are my contact details.'

I groped in my bag for my diary, where I kept cards like his. It wasn't there. I slipped it into my purse instead.

'We're looking for something for a restaurant in the Meatpacking District, a fish place. Something similar to this, but it must be six feet by four. Are you interested? We need it by August.'

'Of course.' Trying to suppress the rising excitement I really felt.

'I'll call you to discuss details. Give me your cell number.'

'What did he say?' It was Chiara, when the man and his wife had moved away.

'He's buying the big oil,' I said. 'And they commission work.'

She beamed at me and I allowed myself to beam back.

'Bloody hell! Exciting! I knew you'd do it! At last the world is recognising your true talent.'

'What's all this?' said Louise.

'Blimey!' she said, when Chiara had filled her in. She held up her glass. 'Guy! Liam, over here. Listen to this. That's so fantastic for you, honey. I'm thrilled.'

I smiled at her, and she looked pleased for me. She really did.

CHAPTER EIGHT

Liam had to leave after our kipper breakfast on Sunday morning, as he was doing the sound check for a gig in our local pub that night, and I was relieved that it meant Chiara would be coming back in the car with me. She would be my other pair of eyes, like a second pilot, ensuring I wasn't distracted. A chaperone to make sure I didn't get obsessed with some daft idea that I'd hit someone on the road!

Last night my friends had stayed up late.

Liam had got the fresh fish he'd talked about the night before from one of the fishing huts – sea bass – and wanted to do it in a salt crust as he'd seen all the TV chefs doing, and Guy offered to help, so we women sat by the woodburner with bottles of wine and talked. It was like old times – in our first year when we'd shared a student flat at art college. One of those memorable evenings when everything seemed to slot into place. Louise told us the whole tale of how she'd met Guy trekking in the outback, and then we all admired Chiara's tiny bump and talked about names for her baby. And my friends wanted to know all about Aunty May, about my special relationship with her and why she'd left me her house.

'We sort of bonded over painting,' I told them. 'My mother was working, or on research trips, or writing retreats, drumming up plots for her romantic fiction. Before she and my dad split up, he would be working at the museum, and so they would send us down to Aunty May's in the holidays.'

As I sat and related those holidays to my friends I could actually feel my little brother Ben's hot little hand in mine as my mother deposited us on the train that took us from Liverpool Street to Darsham where Aunty May would pick us up and drive us back to her house.

'Aunty May let us have more freedom than we ever had at home. We had whole days out on the beach, or in her beach hut, swimming, crabbing, building sand castles.'

'Sounds idyllic.'

'It was.' I was thinking about what Ben had said, when we'd cleared her things out of the house back in the winter.

'Looking back, though,' I said, 'I realise she could be a bit vague, distracted . . .'

'Ah-ha. Like you!' Chiara said.

'Really?'

'Der!'

They laughed.

'Anyway,' I said. 'My happiest memories are of being with her. Nights on the beach in midsummer when it barely grew dark. Visits to see the insects trapped in amber in Dunwich museum. She told us some moments in life are perfect, like the amber. Precious and glowing with an almost unearthly light. Those holidays were like that for me.'

I paused, remembering. 'Then she would say, only you have to beware. Sometimes insects get trapped in the amber when it's soft and then it hardens and they are trapped there forever. Even the most perfect things can be treacherous.'

'I guess she must have decided later that there were no more amber moments for her, because why else would she have committed suicide?' Louise said.

'What an odd thing to say, Louise,' Chiara said, looking at her.

I *had* loved those holidays, but I was only young. I'd loved going painting with my aunt, out on the shore. But even back then I'd always had to do my three taps on the gatepost to make sure May wouldn't die while I was here. Why, I wondered now, had I been so frightened, even at such a young age, that Aunty May might die? Was it to do with being left in charge of my little brother in this house that was so far from the world I knew, from streetlamps and shops and traffic lights and buses and the things that made the world feel safe to me?

If May died while we were there we would be left all alone with nothing but the sea, and miles of unchartered countryside between us and civilisation and I would never be able to let Ben out of my sight in case he ran away and drowned.

And so although I was happy to be with my aunt by the sea, I tapped the gatepost, to keep Ben and May safe.

*   *   *

Now as we drove back towards London, Chiara holding Pepper on her lap on the front seat, I was aware of that lift in my heart again, that felt like happiness. The weekend *had* been a success in the end. It had been so lovely spending time with my friends. They *had* helped bring life back into May's house. And, although I didn't say this out loud, the knowledge my art was going to appear in New York gave me a delicious warm excited feeling in the depths of my belly. I was moving on at last! May would have been thrilled for me.

I might have been tempted to do a detour through Cambridge to see my mother, tell her my news. But she hadn't made it to my Private View and I didn't want to guilt-trip her. She was busy. This was a full-on time of year for her, she was finishing a novel and would feel she ought to stop and pay me some attention, but would be distracted, her head in a storyline. I'd just have to save it for another occasion.

'*Madonna!*' Chiara said, as we sat in a traffic jam coming into London. 'Does everyone have a second house on the coast? I could do with a wee – it's the baby, pressing on my bladder.'

'Are you OK?'

'Yes. I can just about hold on. Distract me, tell me a bit more about these Americans. How soon do they want the commission?'

'I've got till August,' I said, leaning forward, afraid of taking my eyes off the cars in front.

'It's fantastic, Els, just what you needed.'

'I know!' I looked at her quickly, unable to suppress a grin. 'I feel blessed, actually. Things seem to be slotting into place.'

I pushed the thought of the man in the hospital out of my mind; the incident was done with, he was alive. He would be OK. He would probably forget he'd ever seen me. It was over.

'Ellie! Oi, Ellie! Wakey-wakey. I think you are.'

'I am what?'

'Missing him. Finn. I was going to say something on Friday night. You seemed distracted.'

'I was nervous. About the exhibition.'

'Are you sure you're doing the right thing? You can still move on in your career and stay with him too!'

'I just have to try this,' I said. 'I just have to see.'

'OK.'

' Look, Chiara, it wasn't Finn I was thinking about on Friday. I've sorted it now, and it probably sounds bonkers. It was just that – you remember on the way down Louise was delayed, and you and Liam had to go on a diversion? There was an accident on the B road into Southwold?'

'Yes. A hit-and-run. It was on the news.'

'I thought it was me.'

'What?'

'When I heard the news, I became convinced I might have been the hit-and-runner . . . it haunted me all that night. I had to make sure it wasn't me. I know now it wasn't.'

Chiara laughed.

'You *thought* it was you?! You are bonkers, Ellie. You would have *known* if you'd run a man over – it was a man, wasn't it? Fully grown?'

'But I bashed into something on the road. It smashed my

wing mirror, look, see?' I gestured over to my left, where the mirror was smashed, one piece of the glass missing.

'Oh, I see. Yeah. But still, I've hit a baby deer, in Scotland, much smaller than a man, and believe me you damn well know if you've hit something that size,' Chiara said, 'the impact's terrifying. I had whiplash after that and it was just a little thing. You're a nutcase, that's all there is to it. It's just like the time you made me go all the way back to the flat with you because you were convinced you'd left the gas on and might be poisoning poor old Frank and all the other neighbours!'

She chuckled.

I didn't want to mention that I'd actually gone so far as checking by visiting the hospital. It would sound completely mad. Over-the-top – obsessive.

We'd turned off down the Mile End Road now and were crawling past the fried chicken shops and the Asian food stalls and the mosques. The air coming in was warm and fuggy with smells of the city, exhaust and oil and a fainter sweeter smell of good spicy food. Police cars sped past us. The man who arranged all his fruit in plastic ice-cream tubs on the pavement, exposing them to a constant smothering of exhaust, sat outside his shop on a fold-out chair. We passed women in wildly patterned headscarves pushing buggies, caught glimpses of men in djellabas and leather jackets inside cafés, chatting in groups. Another world to the middle-class enclave that was Southwold.

'Look,' Chiara said, and I glanced at her. Her tone had changed. 'While we're on the subject of moving on and all that, I have to tell you . . . I've been putting it off, but . . . oh dear, this is hard.'

'Go on.'

'Well, it's just that Liam's found somewhere in London Fields. It's a flat, but there's a garden. He's put a deposit down.'

'Oh.' Was her suggestion I go back to Finn a way of softening this blow?

'I know. I'm sorry.'

'So, you'll be moving out?'

'But you're going to be OK, Ellie. If you carry on like this you'll be leaving your teaching job, you'll probably move down to Southwold, won't you? Become a full-time artist.'

'I don't know about that.' I tried to keep the panic out of my voice. I knew Chiara and Liam were looking to buy a house, it was to be expected now they were having a baby, but I'd imagined it might take months. I'd imagined I would have moved on long before they had. The thought of being left alone in our little flat without Finn, without my best friend, unnerved me.

'Ellie? Things had to change some time didn't they?'

'Of course.'

'And you'll be OK. We'll both be OK.'

'Sure.'

'See you at the gig later,' Chiara called over her shoulder as I dropped her at Liam's house in Tredegar Square, and I went on to our road, a cul-de-sac just past Stepney Green Tube. Amazingly I found a space just next to our building.

Chiara was right. I'd be OK. I would focus on the commission for New York. I'd been so preoccupied, I was forgetting the money I'd just made at the gallery. Nearly two thousand pounds. If I sold any more paintings I could put a deposit down and rent a nicer flat. I'd move to a quieter area, perhaps drop another day's teaching, spend more time sending out proposals for commissions. I'd socialise in new circles and might even meet a new man. It was what I'd wanted!

I dragged my bag from the boot, took Pepper up in one arm. We climbed the steps to the front door. I was met by the fusty smell of a building lived in by many people, and stumbled over the heaps of junk mail no one bothered to pick up from the slimy floor. Yes, I would definitely move, once Chiara had gone. I wouldn't be able to afford to live here alone anyway. Chiara had, as usual, left her domestic mark on our little kitchen with its window overlooking the B&Q car park. Fresh tomatoes and lollo rosso and some interesting-looking cheese in the fridge. Oranges in a bowl. The flat was just bearable with her homely touches, but I couldn't imagine living here alone, or sharing it with anyone else.

This conversion didn't work. The building had been chopped up into flats so the landlord could make maximum money out of the limited space. The circulation of air was poor, cooking smells infiltrating the bathroom and the cut-in-half bedrooms, and the sounds from other flats came through badly engineered partition walls.

I dumped my bag on the shoddy grey carpet and went to listen to the messages on our landline answerphone. There was one from Mum asking me to let her know how the house had seemed this weekend, whether I'd had further thoughts on selling it. Another message from the suppliers I'd contacted about some canvas and stretchers.

Then there was one that sent a chill from my toes up through my body to my head. I had to hold on to the bookshelf to steady myself.

'Ellie? This is Patrick. The nurses said you came to visit me. They've told me I have amnesia and to get in touch with you as soon as possible. You're not supposed to use mobiles but these hospital phones are hell to use, you have to get a card and fiddle about so it's easier for you to call me. I'm pissed off. They're saying I'm going to need major rehabilitation. Call me, will you? It might help, they say, if we can just talk. Here's my number. Oh and . . . You looked so pretty when I saw you leaving.'

I slammed the phone down.

How did he get my number?

How did he know my name?

CHAPTER NINE

I stood for several minutes beside the phone in the kitchen, trying to ignore the drip from the ceiling our landlord had failed to fix. A pigeon was preening itself on the windowsill. One of its feet was deformed, a pink stump where the claws should have been. I looked away. Played the message again.

Was this a punishment for not going back and checking whether I might have hit someone on the road? A man – a stranger – was stalking me. Stalking? The man in the bed had seemed so strong, so wealthy, and good-looking, I couldn't imagine he called people he didn't know out of need. That glamorous woman on his iPhone showed he was hardly desperate. And anyway, it was *me* who had gone to see *him*. Stalking was the wrong word. He had phoned me because he believed I was someone he knew.

I would call Chiara, confess I'd gone as far as visiting the man in hospital, that now he'd rung me thinking I was someone he knew, and we would sit in the pub and have a good laugh about it. She would tell me to forget it.

I picked up my phone, relieved to have a signal now I was back in civilisation, and pressed Chiara's number. It went straight to voicemail.

Flustered now, I played Patrick's message again. His tone was relaxed, friendly. The anaesthetic – and he must only just have been coming out of it when he woke and saw me leaving – must have confused him. That was when I remembered my diary, missing when I'd gone to get it out at the exhibition. I got my bag and put it on the kitchen table. I rummaged through. My make-up bag was there. My purse. No diary.

I'd emptied my bag in the hospital, looking for my mobile, when the nurse had suggested showing him photos. Had I missed putting the diary back, in my anxious state?

If he rang again I would tell him that we'd never met. That it was a mistake. If he asked how my diary had got there I would say I had no idea. There were any number of explanations – someone might have found it elsewhere and brought it in while visiting someone else. Who knows?

Everything would be cleared up and I would never see him again.

With this thought I went through to my room to unpack my bag, shaking everything out onto the bed, then pushing it into the washing machine. The clothes I wore at the hospital seemed contaminated, I wanted the weekend washed off them.

I put on my yoga trousers and a vest top and spread a rug out on the floor. I lay down and lifted my thighs into the Bridge. Lowered myself. I moved into a Fish, arching my back, folding my legs into a fishtail shape, lifting my shoulders from the mat and resting the tip of my head on the floor. I lay on my back and did a Happy Baby pose – holding my toes – usually guaranteed to evoke a sense of being in the moment. I lay back, tried again to empty my mind.

The phone went almost as soon as I'd relaxed. I heard it click on in the kitchen, the recording asking the caller to leave a message.

'Ellie! I'm a bit drugged up. You didn't call back! I need your help to get me through this. Someone ran me over. But they can't find who did this to me. It's all getting to me now. Please phone, no one else has.'

Was he crying? Was that a sob I could hear?

Should I pick up the phone? Explain? Or pretend I wasn't here?

I could perhaps ask to speak to one of the nurses, tell them that their patient was ringing me in the mistaken belief that he knew me. I hesitated, then made for the phone, grabbing it just as the line clicked shut. That settled it. I would leave it.

The poor man must realise, as his memory came back, that he'd never met me, that it was a mistake. The diary would be thrown away and my visit forgotten.

I sidled into our cramped bathroom, put the plug in, ran a deep, hot bath and got in. Reflections of bathwater danced on the ceiling, white on white. Police cars whooped along Mile End Road outside. Cars, their windows down, went past, music turned up loud, the bass reverberating. The bathroom door was ajar. I hadn't bothered to lock it since there was nobody here but me. I thought for a second that I heard someone opening the main door into the flat. Pepper began to yap. No one but me and Chiara had a key. But Chiara was at the pub with Liam. I froze. Someone was moving about out there. I could hear the creak of a floorboard, the sitting-room door's squeak.

There was a smallish window in here, frosted glass, big enough if I pushed it up to crawl out of onto a garage roof. If I'd locked the bathroom door, I'd have had time. I sat up, pushed my hands down on the edges of the bath, stood, dripping, reached for a towel.

I stopped, listened again. I'd left my yoga clothes strewn all over the sitting-room floor. Nothing could have given an intruder a better indication of my vulnerability, in the bath, on my own.

My options: one, lean across, slam the door to buy myself time, jump out and slide the lock across. Two, confront whoever had come in. It couldn't be Patrick from the hospital. He couldn't have recovered already. But his voice on the phone had unsettled me. So, option three, climb straight out of the window onto the garage roof off the road.

I stood in the water, wasting time deliberating when I should shut the door, lock it, get through the window. Then I was certain, footsteps were coming towards me across the sitting room. I was out of the bath, grabbing a towel. I stood, the toilet brush in my hand raised, the only implement I could find with which to defend myself, a towel wrapped round me.

A shadow fell across the gap in the bathroom door.

CHAPTER TEN

'Put the toilet brush down! I surrender.'

'Finn!'

'Oh my God, you thought I was an intruder?'

'Of course I bloody well thought you were an intruder! What're you doing walking in like this?'

I pressed the towel closer around me.

'I came to see how it went.'

'Christ! You could've given me some warning. Now if you'll excuse me I need to put some clothes on.'

'I'll open a beer then.'

My eyes prickled with tears of relief, and something else. I'd gone all weak, as if someone had been holding me up, like a marionette, and had let go of the strings. My nerves were highly sensitised, twitchy, because of the man called Patrick, those phone calls. I'd thought Finn was him! How ridiculous when Patrick was stuck over sixty miles away in hospital.

Finn and I had spent hours in the past naked together but I couldn't let him see me like this now we weren't together any more, so when I'd thrown on some clothes I joined him in the sitting room where he was on the sofa, head bowed.

He looked awful close up, as if he hadn't slept for days. But that was nothing new. Finn led the kind of life where he could forget to go to bed for weeks on end. Pepper had trotted straight over to him and jumped up onto his lap. Finn fondled his silky ears with his finger and thumb.

'You brought your own beer?'

He shrugged.

Finn was on a permanent tight budget – his bringing beer was uncharacteristic.

'Finn! I've got wine in the fridge, you know. You needn't have worried.'

'I can pay my way.'

I wished what I felt for him was a wash of love. Instead what I felt was pity.

'I'm not suggesting . . . oh, never mind. Anyway, it gave me a shock, your walking in like that. Where did you get the key?'

'I saw Chiara in the pub. With Liam. She said she was worried about you, so I said I'd come round, and she gave me her keys.'

'You should have knocked! It's not on to just walk in like that.'

'I won't do it again.'

'Please don't, Finn.'

There was a silence. I'd never spoken to Finn in this bossy way before. I softened.

'What was Chiara worried about?'

'She just thought you might avoid joining us. So I came to find you.'

'I was going to come,' I said. 'I needed to unwind first.'

He looked up at me through his floppy fringe. 'Sorry to snap,' I said. 'It was kind of you to come.'

'Not really. Selfish motives. I've been missing you.'

I poured myself a glass of wine.

'But next time – I do have a doorbell.'

'It feels unnatural to ring the bell. I've never had to ring your bell before!'

He flicked his fringe aside and looked up at me with his earnest brown eyes. His elbows rested on his knees, he looked forlorn. I had to resist the urge to feel too much sympathy for him or I'd be tempted to crawl back to him.

'Finn, things are different now. You can't just walk into my flat any more, please accept that. It isn't . . . easy for me, for either of us, after all this time, but we have to give it a go, for a bit longer.'

'Do we? Chiara said she thought you were forcing your-self to do something counter-intuitive, she feels it's a forced decision, not an instinctive one, to end it with me, and I think perhaps she's right.'

'Well she's not. But anyway, how are you? How're things? How was your weekend?'

'Oh, you know,' he said.

'I don't know. Not if you don't tell me.'

'It was a weekend.'

'Finn, I'm sorry.'

He gave me a sceptical look. He knew I'd invited friends down to the cottage and excluded him.

'It's painful for me too, but I've got to try this. It's the only way I'll ever find out.'

'Find out *what*?'

'I've already told you.'

I had said that Finn belonged to a younger me. I was changing, but he didn't seem to be.

'So. How was the second home by the sea?' he said.

'As you know. It's an old windswept clapboard house with mice.'

'Hmph. Any roof in Southwold is worth millions. Even those beach huts are hundreds of thousands. You know you've landed yourself a pile. But anyway, what about the Private View. How did it go?'

'It went well, Finn.'

'I don't suppose you only got the freeloaders I get, draining the wine you've had to take out a bank loan to provide, eating the crisps, leaving you to clear up the mess, and wondering what you're going to do with all the bloody crap you've made and have nowhere to store.'

'It was in a good cause. People buy when a percentage goes to charity, so I sold a few. It doesn't make me a Turner contender.'

'Chiara said there was someone interested in giving you a commission, in New York?'

Finn and I had shared a studio at art college, we'd collaborated on several big projects. We had even developed our own secret 'language' when we were first in love, sending each other hidden messages in our paintings, words embedded in the collages we made, that we knew (though no one else would) to piece together to make sentences. He had told me he loved me for the first time like this. And I had told him the oddities about him I found irresistible. 'Your fringe,' I had stuck onto one painting. 'The way you pull your ear.' He saw the fact I was developing my own style as another kind of rejection of him. My moving away from the conceptual pieces he loved was something he found difficult, interpreting it as another sort of insult to everything that made him himself, Finn.

He sat hunched up, his baggy jumper swamping his emaciated body. His black hair hanging over his pale, earnest face.

'You're making this hard for me. For both of us.'

'I don't mean to. Sorry, Els.'

I looked at him as he stared into his beer. The trouble is, when you've been with someone for as long as we'd been together – could it possibly be five years? – you're so used to touching each other, *not* to feels like a strain. Unnatural. I longed to put my hand out as I would once have done, to squeeze his thigh. But I mustn't mislead him.

Then he glanced up.

'Look, when you're ready,' he said, 'if you like, I'll come and do some more work down there for you. No one will know we're . . . connected. I'll be the odd jobs man. I've collected some oilcans I found down on the river, on the tideline, I could customise them. You need some garden furniture, don't you?'

'Finn, if we're going to do this, it's best we just don't see each other at all – for a bit at least.'

'Will the Southwold gentry disapprove?'

'Stop it!'

'That's what it is though, isn't it? You don't want a penni-
less acolyte following you about!'

'Finn, please.'

'You're going up in the world, Ellie. A long way up. Out of
my reach.'

'No. That's not true.'

'A fucking New York commission!'

I didn't want to hurt him, yet it was unavoidable and the
more I tried to skirt round the truth, that I couldn't spend
my life with someone I wasn't one hundred per cent sure
about, someone who wanted to hold me back, preserve me
as the anxious, obsessive compulsive student I'd been when
I first met him – the more I avoided telling him these things,
the deeper I was digging myself into a different hole, making
it look as though I'd become blinkered by commercial success.

We were silent for a bit. My exhibition seemed to hang
between us, obliterating the chance of any proper communi-
cation.

'It wasn't such a great weekend after all,' I said. 'You didn't
miss much. I spent a lot of it fixing things at the house.'

'Ah! That's the reality, you see,' Finn said. 'The reality of
ownership. The more you have, the more you have to work
to maintain it. You should follow my example and never
own anything of any worth whatsoever. That way you are
free of all ties. The only thing I'm responsible for is Tommy.'

Tommy was the stray cat that had taken residence on
Finn's windowsill, in his room in a shared ex-local authority
flat in Bow.

'How is Tommy?'

'He's bored. He's fed up with being homeless and wants to move in with Princess, the feline up the road in the big house. He's got tired of the vagrant life. It's lost its appeal. He wants to settle down.'

'Aah. Like *The Aristocats*.'

'I love that film. I used to watch it when I was little, when I was off school.'

'Me too.'

'You coming to the pub?'

'No. I think it's best not to.'

I would have an early night after all. It was a teaching day tomorrow. He looked at me. His dark eyes full of warmth, full of that twinkle I was so drawn to at first. For a few seconds I wondered if I was, after all, making a mistake. I was afraid I might weaken. I had always loved his determination to reject the consumer world. I'd always loved him because he was so *true*.

'Come back to mine tonight. I want to wine and dine you,' he whispered into my ear. 'I've got baked beans. And a bottle of Blue Nun.'

And, of course, because he made me laugh.

'Ellie,' he said at last. 'I don't want to ask it but it won't leave me alone until I do. Is there somebody else?'

Now he was making me impatient.

'Of course not! Please go.'

And he left.

CHAPTER ELEVEN

When Finn had gone I tried to focus on making a salad, the way Chiara did, with olive oil and salt to bring the juices out of the tomatoes. I'd have to get used to cooking for myself once she'd moved. So I'd better practise. I was sprinkling on the salt when the phone rang. I picked it up, spilling half of the salt on the counter.

'I wondered if you'd like to come down this weekend, Ellie.'

It was my mother.

'Miriam's away and I could do with some company.'

'Aren't you working?'

'I've just finished a novel so I've got a bit of time to play with. Thought I could take you to the ADC on Friday night. There's a production of *Othello* we could see.'

'That would be lovely!' I rarely got to see my mother alone these days, since she'd moved in with her lover, Miriam. And she had probably picked up on the fact that although we could get by together, Miriam and I regarded each other warily. Miriam knew I couldn't help blaming her for my parents not getting back together, though my mother hadn't met her until several years after my parents split. It was unfair of me, but I still regarded her as an imposter in our family. We hadn't quite worked out who had the most rights to my mother's attention. I couldn't relax when Miriam was there, and usually cut my visits short.

I agreed to stay with Mum on Friday night, and continue on down to May's on Saturday to pick up my unsold paintings from the gallery and do a bit more sorting of her things.

I nibbled at my salad, which tasted nothing like what Chiara would have made – the tomatoes were hard and tasteless – then gave up and threw the spilt salt over my shoulder into the eye of the devil. I was a fool, believing in these things. I didn't really believe in them. But I didn't want to risk it. This was the problem with relying on talismans to feel safe in the world. When you ignored them, the free-floating feeling it left you with meant other superstitions popped up in their place. I was covering the bases. Taking precautions. The way I supposed some non-religious people prayed, just in case.

The phone went again as I swept up the scattered salt. My mother made a habit of changing her plans and not being able to see me and I prepared myself to feel let down.

'Ellie, it's me.'

'Who?'

'Patrick.'

For a few seconds I considered slamming the phone down. He spoke into my silence.

'Why didn't you ring back?'

'I—'

'I'm still me! Or that's what they're telling me. Still the old Patrick.'

What was I supposed to say?

He spoke though, before I could decide.

'When are you coming back to see me?'

I opened my mouth but nothing came out.

'I may be in here for days. But you're the only one who bothered to come – do you realise that?'

I tried to formulate an explanation in my head.

Instead I asked, 'Was I really your only visitor?'

'Absolutely.'

I felt a wave of responsibility, mixed with compassion for him.

'And they haven't found the bastard who did this to me. They thought they knew, but their suspects had a watertight alibi.'

'But I thought . . .'

'It wasn't who they suspected. They're looking for someone else, maybe someone unconnected. They think from forensic evidence it was a car, not a van.'

An uncomfortable surge in my belly. Doubt raising its head again. If it wasn't the people they thought, it still might have been me!

'There's a massive investigation going on, but it isn't going to give me my walking back, is it? It isn't going to undo what's done.'

'What? What do you mean, give you your walking back?'

'Didn't they say. . . didn't they tell you I may never walk again?'

I couldn't speak. His words reverberated round my head. *Never walk again. Never walk again.*

I clutched the kitchen doorjamb, feeling the grey carpet sway beneath me, the room recede and then swing back into focus. I wished I'd gone to the pub with the others after all. Where I could have hidden my head in the sand – or deep in a glass of wine.

'They just keep telling me to take it one day at a time. My leg was completely fucked as you must know. They say it could take weeks to learn to walk again. Fuck 'em. I'm gonna prove them wrong. At least I'm recovering from the bop on the head.'

I waited a few seconds, or maybe minutes. The silence on the other end of the line blossomed around me, filled up my room, the growl of traffic outside faded beneath the beating of my heart. I must put a stop to this. I should put the phone down, walk away.

Chiara had said it couldn't have had anything to do with me. But I hadn't checked! And now, when I shut my eyes, limb-like forms lying in the shadows came back to me. Bits I'd tried to convince myself were just storm-blasted sticks and debris from the trees but that now took on human shapes, scattered belongings in my mind.

I had ignored the compulsion to go back – now this.

'I need to see you, Ellie.'

This man believed he knew me! I owed him something, some explanation, some support.

'I'm not sure if I *can* come. It's difficult . . .'

'I'm going crazy! It's bad enough being stuck in bed unable to run or sail. There's nothing to do! No one to talk to. I thought you, of all people, would be here for me.'

I could see his body in the bed. The strength in him, crushed under car wheels. I couldn't just ignore his plea. I had become inextricably involved, by visiting him, whether I'd hit him in my car or not. I realised this now. If no one else had visited him then I had to. He shouldn't be allowed to suffer alone in this way. I tried to visualise this man called Patrick. Dark hair against the pillow. Muscular arms on the white sheets. A leg propped up. The beep of his monitors. The damage I was no longer sure I hadn't caused.

'Please, Ellie. Please.'

I took a deep breath. I owed him this.

'OK,' I said. 'It's OK. I'll come.'

'When? I need you soon.' His voice was soft now. Vulnerable.

'I'll come tomorrow evening,' I said.

'That seems a long time to wait, time goes so slowly in here.'

'I can't come before, I've got work . . .'

'Promise me then.'

'I promise.'

I put the phone down.

And I shivered all over.

The kids' bright little faces trooping into class were a welcome distraction the next morning,

I had the Year Ones, five- and six-year-olds, an age group I enjoyed. Young enough to still be innocent but old enough – most of them – to tie their own laces and wipe their own noses.

Billy nudged me, waving a photo cut out from the Sunday paper under my nose.

'What's this, Billy?'

'Charles and Camilla,' he said. 'On a Royal Tour.'

I smiled up at Joyce, my TA. Billy had a passion for the royal couple. He brought in photos he'd cut out of the tabloids almost every day. He had even named his guinea pigs after them.

I got through the day, too busy to give my encroaching visit to Patrick any more conscious thought, though a persistent knot in my stomach accompanied me. In the afternoon I got out some air-drying clay and let the kids make as much mess as they wanted – I'd get them to finish early and spend half an hour clearing up so the cleaner wouldn't have a fit when she came in after school. Then I'd read them a story to keep them quiet for the last fifteen minutes before I could let them go.

I opened the classroom door at three thirty and the children streamed out. Apart from Timothy. He always hung around when the others had bolted for the door, eyes fixed on the computer screen.

'C'n I do the pooters?'

'OK, Timothy. How's your weekend been? Did you do nice things?'

He shrugged.

It wasn't strictly within Health and Safety guidelines, allowing kids to turn the computers off. But Timothy loved switches, putting things on, turning them off, plugging them in. He loved watching screens fizzle on, and snap off. And I knew, better than anyone, how when objects held this kind of power over you, it made you miserable if you were prevented from carrying out your compulsion. It was Timothy's way of feeling he had some control over something, when he had so little in his life at home.

After a while I said, 'Isn't your mum waiting for you?'

'It's me chil' minder today.'

'We'd better see if she's outside.'

'Don't wanna go much.'

'What d'you mean? It's going to be a lovely evening, you can play outside, with your mates, can't you?'

My stomach had begun to churn. I wanted to get on the road. Get this visit over and done with.

It was almost impossible to understand the next sentence Tim uttered. Other people – staff as well as children – were impatient with him because it was so hard to decipher what he said. His language disorder meant words must feel to him like moths flitting around a darkened room, refusing to be caught even though he knew they were there. I had to give him time.

'What did you say, Timothy?'

'Me dad'll be there. Me stepdad. Hate 'im.'

'Why though? Why do you hate him?'

Another shrug.

I didn't want to ask him closed questions, put words into his mouth. I waited to see if he could explain something he might well not understand himself. At last he said, ''Im shouts at me. When I ain't done nuffin'.'

I would have liked to have put an arm around him, give him some kind of affection. We weren't supposed to touch the children in our care of course, but sometimes it was what they needed. He looked so starved of it, his body held rigid in a rejecting – or rejected – hunch.

His objection to his stepfather stirred something within me. Something that had been reignited last weekend, when I heard the radio report for the first time and the thought that I might have caused the accident crashed into my head. Getting the blame, trying to right it. The road to May's house. A choice ... making a decision that got me into trouble.

I thought again of that lock of hair in the box in May's kitchen drawer that had made me gag. It had had a physical effect on me, as if my body remembered something my mind refused to. Shame, embarrassment, the need to turn away. Something I'd turned away from ever since. Needing to tell, not being able to. How Timothy must be feeling.

'Timothy, you know you can always tell me or Miss Hatfield if you're upset about something that happened to you. D'you want to tell me more now?'

We'd wondered whether shouting was the least of his problems. Whether Timothy only reported the things he dared to report. The Child Protection team had been alerted. I wished I could take him home with me, or even better, to Aunty May's cottage, to spend the weekend on the beach, take him to buy ice-cream from the hut on the promenade or those shiny coloured windmills that flipped about in the wind. Give him a proper, carefree childhood.

I remembered a chat I'd had with Chiara quite soon after I'd started teaching.

'Babes,' she'd said, 'you make such assumptions. Not all kids had your upbringing. It doesn't mean they're unhappy. In fact in some cases quite the opposite.'

'No,' I'd said. 'It's not to do with the money, the

background. They're really needy, some of those kids, emotionally I mean. I want to make things better for them.' I
might have added that my upbringing hadn't come without
its undermining legacies.

But then she said, 'It's not your job. You have to keep a
distance. Don't get so involved.'

It was pointless being told not to get involved.

You had to have a heart of stone not to.

Now I glanced at the clock. It was almost four. I was desperate to leave. But I didn't want to leave Timothy alone in
the office to wait for his child minder, who was often late. I
let him potter about, helping me tidy things, suggesting he
sharpen the pencils, another job he loved.

'You *are* a help, Timothy. I usually don't get time to
sharpen all those colours. What a superstar you are!' He
gave me a rare and therefore all the more engaging smile
and we high-fived one another. As he opened his mouth to
say something a shadow fell through the open door.

'There you are!' His child minder had come to the classroom, a sticky-looking pink baby sucking a dummy in her
arms and a toddler wrapped round her ample thigh.

I had to stop off to buy Pepper some dog treats from the
minimarket on my way home, and take him for a quick run
around Victoria Park.

Then at last I could set off. I was on my way to unravel the
web I'd got entangled in when I'd felt the car jolt and swerve
to the side.

CHAPTER TWELVE

It was already six o'clock by the time Pepper and I were heading away from the sprawl of the London outskirts, the industrial estates and random billboards set up in barren-looking fields advertising bathroom refits and office space. I'd let myself into Frank's flat and found he had a carrier cage for Pepper, and I'd put him on the back seat – a precaution against further mishaps.

At last, we got into more rural scenery.

At this time of year the verges frothed with towering cow parsley, and the fresh green hedgerows were laden with the white gauze of hawthorn, the vast dome of the sky a smooth blameless blue, like a hospital gown, I thought, startled by my own simile. Once I would have seen this landscape as something exquisite, now it seemed to throb with hidden meaning, menace perhaps, thrill. I might weave this scene, these colours, into a painting one day.

Where could the man in the hospital have been going that

night? There was only the village of Reydon, a small smattering of houses before you got to Southwold at the end of that road. If he was heading for Southwold he was probably a local – I couldn't imagine a London weekender would be walking down that road at night. I wondered about his family, his friends, the woman on his Facebook page. What had Patrick imagined when he found my diary? He must believe I was someone else. The woman he thought he'd begged to come down wasn't me.

So who was she?

I left Pepper in the car in the hospital car park.

Patrick McIntyre, I was told at reception, had been moved into a general ward. I took the lift, buzzed at the door again and when it opened went to the nurses' station where they sat filling forms behind their desks. Patrick was at the end of the ward by the window. The beds were mostly occupied by older men, white-haired and half asleep. So when I spotted Patrick, he seemed to glow, a golden vision, his alert face in sharp contrast to the age and pallor of the rest. He was sitting up, no more tubes, a successful recovery by the looks of it.

He looked up expectantly as I crossed the room to his bedside and I remembered he'd said no one else had visited. I couldn't believe he didn't have loads of friends who would want to see him. It was what his phone suggested. He frowned at me, as if the effort of trying to remember almost hurt.

Pale blue eyes. Not brown after all. Framed by long, child-like lashes. A physical jolt passed through me. They were dangerous eyes, I thought. Eyes that could get away with anything and probably always had. His expression changed as I approached, from one of perplexity to one of recognition.

'Hi!' he said, his face breaking into a puzzled smile. He had very white teeth.

His mouth formed two little creases like brackets. The neat black beard across his jawline that had been shaped expertly was beginning to grow.

'I'm Ellie,' I said.

'I'm sorry if I looked confused, Ellie,' he said. 'The nurses had to help me recall stuff.' A nice voice. Deep, smooth. 'I lost my memory. But I don't know how I could have forgotten you. Ell-ie,' he said, as if he was trying out my name on his tongue, 'Ell-ie', as if it was something he could taste.

I didn't know what to say, what would make things worse for him, what better.

'Is it OK?' I gestured to the end of his bed, as there was no chair, and sat.

I wondered what he knew about me, what he didn't know, what he thought he knew, but didn't. And what I was prepared to tell him.

'Someone ran me over,' he said, blinking at me with his little boy's long lashes. He had an impish smile, a twinkle. Like Robbie Williams – who I'd had a bit of a thing for in my teens when he was young. I liked it.

'Someone ran me over and drove off. A hit-and-run. They thought they'd found who did it – they assumed it was the lads from Blackshore, but of course it wasn't.'

'Who are they?'

103

'Just some guys I got into a silly brawl with. They wouldn't go that far. So now the police have drawn a blank, and I've told them not to pursue it. What's the point? I'm sorry I ruined our weekend.'

I could say something now or . . .

'Ellie,' he said, and he reached for my hand. 'Thank goodness you've come. I was worried you'd given up on me after you saw my wrecked body that first day after it happened.'

'No. Really, it's not like that, I . . .'

'You didn't get in touch. I don't blame you. I'm not much of a catch like this—' he waved his hand over his body. 'And I suppose you're busy with work – do you know, I've forgotten what work you do. It's so weird. It's like there's a great dark room in my brain that I know is full of stuff. I grope about trying to find things that I know are there, but can't put my hands on them. But now you're here, I forgive you for not coming sooner. It's good to see your beautiful face.'

He frowned, looking intently at me, as if he was trying to convince himself he should know who I was.

I don't know why, but an impression of his mother came into my mind. What a doting woman she must be, how he would have enchanted her all his life, how he would have enchanted every female young or old who crossed his path. I should be careful!

He squinted up at me.

'I can't stop thinking about that bastard. How could he have done a thing like that, and not stop? They must have known. Don't you think? You couldn't bash into someone even on a dark road and not realise you'd caused a life-bloody-changing injury to someone?'

He spread his arms, to frame the legs that were stretched out stiff beneath the covers.

Then, with a flourish, keeping his eyes fixed on mine, he threw the sheet off.

'Look at this.'

I don't know what I'd been expecting.

A cast, perhaps. Some kind of dressing certainly.

Not this.

I tried to take a breath. No air went in.

My hands went up to my face. I couldn't breathe. Didn't want to look. Didn't want him to show me this. The room spun. I'd gone hot. Everything fizzed. I was going to faint.

'No,' I heard myself say. 'No!'

Both of his legs were bandaged. But one of them was dressed only as far as the knee.

The rest of the leg, from the knee down, was missing.

'Come on. It's OK. I'm alright.' His words seemed to come to me from far away.

I squinted through my fingers. He was gazing at me, questioningly. 'It won't make you fancy me any less, will it, Ellie?'

I needed to get away. I rushed back across the ward and asked for the hospital toilets. I reached them just in time to throw up. In the mirror my face was the same colour as the pale walls. I threw cold water at it. Then I stood, clutching the cool porcelain of the basin for I don't know how long. I was trembling uncontrollably. I wanted to run away as far as I could. Turn back the clock, never drive alone to Suffolk, never listen to the radio, start to think that I might have hit someone, visit them in the hospital. I didn't do it, I couldn't have done. It was a bird. But they hadn't caught the person

who had done it and I was on the road at the right time, and
. . . now this!

It was as bad as if I'd killed him.

Worse?

I had to go to the police, as I should have done straight
away, and say I was afraid I was responsible for this man's
atrocious injuries.

My whole life, the one I'd been anticipating as I set off for
Southwold that April night, free of Finn, painting for galleries, going for weekends in the country with Pepper, that
whole vision wobbled like a mirage before it vanishes.

I stood for a little longer.

Then I began to breathe a little more steadily, to force
myself to take some action. I had to confront this. It put me
in a position of responsibility, being given this information.
I had to be brave, I had to be adult. Patrick had to deal with
it, after all.

And now I was here to help him.

Back by his bed he took my hand again and drew me to him.

'You didn't answer. Does it stop you being attracted to
me?' he asked. 'Look at it, take it in, tell me.'

I made myself look at his poor poor stump again.

The thigh had been heavily dressed.

'My thigh was only superficially damaged,' Patrick said.
'But they had to dress it to stem the bleeding. Amazing, isn't
it? That part of it could be so completely wrecked while the
rest remained intact. They even found the bag I was carrying
– I had bottles of beer in it. Completely unscathed. Yet my
lower leg was well and truly fucked.'

I forced myself not to flinch as I looked at it.

'They say I'll need quite a lot of practice to get back on my feet . . . foot, I mean.'

He smiled ruefully and I wondered if he was on some sort of sedative or painkiller that prevented him from feeling the full force of this trauma – its implications for the rest of his life. The little curves that held his mouth in parenthesis twitched.

'I can't manage on my own like this. They keep asking me, "But don't you have anyone who can come and help? Isn't there *anyone*?" And I keep telling them, well, it's really hard to remember. I know I had mates, because I was with some of them in the pub that night. But I've been away on business a lot over the last few years and lost touch with most of my contacts in England. "But there must be someone else, a family member?" they asked and I wracked my brains. And then I said no, as matter of fact, there isn't! "But your girl-friend," they said. "The one who came to visit, surely she wants to help. Surely she would give up a little time to sort you out, just until you adjust." I asked them who they meant, and they said, "The small, dark, wavy-haired girl," and I asked when you had come, and they said the day after the accident.'

He was looking at me intently through his blue eyes, as if seeking reassurance. It must be terrifying to be so lost, without memories to help you navigate.

'So that's when I rang you, when I realised you were the one – if anyone – who would be there for me.'

The sun sinking outside shone directly through the window, colouring everything amber.

'Retrograde amnesia, they called it,' he went on. 'I can remember, you see, bits and pieces before and after my accident. And I can form new memories. But there are bits around the accident that have gone. Just gone. So when you came, I didn't remember you! But it's OK because they reminded me. And I thought, I have a beautiful girlfriend to get better for. Nothing's going to stop me performing the way I used to for her!' He twinkled.

It was warm and quiet beside his bed, and it occurred to me how very isolated from the outside world we were, how cocooned in this ward from my real life. There seemed no point in worrying any longer about what part I had in his accident. I was here now. I had to follow it through.

I thought of Fay, my yoga teacher, telling us to stay in the moment.

'I do remember now that we had planned a weekend sailing in Southwold when all that stuff happened in the pub. That it was going to be our first full weekend together. I think. Is that right?'

All that mattered was here, now. I wouldn't think either about what I had done, or about where this was taking me. I would just do whatever I could to help him.

'You're the biggest incentive I have to get up and get going,' he said. 'But I can see it's a pretty big ask for you to be patient with me. For you to wait while I learn to walk again, when you're so busy with – you see, I've forgotten. What's your work again?'

'I'm a painter,' I told him, 'an artist. And a primary school teacher.' The New York commission seemed a superficial and paltry thing next to what Patrick was having to confront, so I didn't mention it.

'I have to teach on Mondays and Fridays. But I wouldn't put anything before your walking,' I said. 'I *will* be here for you.'

'Pull the curtains round my bed,' he said. I did as he asked. 'Come closer.'

It was as though I had been hypnotised.

'I need you,' he said. 'I've been starved of touch in here all this time.'

How long, I wondered, did he think he'd been here? It was only four days. Poor man, to be so confused.

'Here, closer again. Next to me.'

'Won't it hurt you? Is it allowed?'

'It'll be fine.'

And I was doing as he asked.

I lay down on the hospital bed, leaving a gap of just centimetres between his body and mine. This man I barely knew looked at me, as if he was reminding himself of who I was, examining me from the top of my head and every millimetre of my face, my eyes, my nose, and then his eyes came to a stop at my lips.

He didn't move.

This *was* the right thing to do. I'd heard somewhere that if a person was deluded, say, with dementia, it's much better to play along than to shatter their fantasy.

I was applying this notion to this man, since I no longer had the faintest idea what else I could do.

I ignored other thoughts that were pushing against my consciousness. Vague jumbled anxieties about who the woman he believed I was might be, my commission, the plans I had for May's house, how they had all seemed to be coming together.

I told myself I'd set everything straight as soon as I got all the facts sorted.

So for now I didn't say anything.

And I convinced myself I was doing the right thing.

CHAPTER THIRTEEN

I stayed with Patrick until the sun outside the window turned a fiery blood red, colouring everything. I would have liked to paint Patrick's face in this light, half of it in shade, the rest tinted gold.

Patrick murmured to me as I lay next to him, relating to me more details about what he had been doing that Friday evening when our paths were about to fatefully cross.

'What I do remember,' he said softly, his face just inches from mine so I could feel his breath on my cheek, surprisingly sweet-smelling, reminding me of the sugared almonds Aunty May sometimes gave us, 'is that we were on our way down to Southwold and we'd stopped for a drink in that pub in Blythburgh. I do remember that.'

I didn't speak. I wasn't going to lie. I would just let him relate to me what he thought had happened.

'And then there was this git who was insulting me. Wasn't there? And I was stressed at the end of a long week.

I'd been working my arse off. I knew it probably didn't sound stressful to you, an artist – second-guessing the markets, building the portfolio, keeping my eye on the competitors. But by God it can wear you down. I was so looking forward to our weekend by the sea. Getting away from it all. Sailing. Chilling. A couple of rounds of golf. And those guys, the big bloke with the thick neck and his sidekick Mikey, they were laying into me about something. It was the old drink talking but I decided the sensible thing to do would be to leave. Scott gave me a lift to the road. You were going to come on later. I said I'd walk from there. I don't know why. It was dumb of course, much further than I realised, in my inebriated haze, but I didn't want to drive over the limit and thought I'd go back for the car the next day. And then. Smack!'

'What happened? Do you remember anything?'

'I remember an almighty thump, then . . . no, nothing. Lights, yes, that's right, there were lights that flared up, white, then everything went black. A pain in my knee, spreading to my lower leg, a searing, as if I'd been burnt alive, and the red tail-lights of a blue car disappearing into the night.'

'It was blue?'

'Silvery blue. I remember the colour because it was just light still, and I remember getting a glimpse of it. A small car, like a Corsa, a Micra maybe.'

My car was blue. Silvery blue. A Nissan Micra.

'How hard was the impact? Did it throw you in the air?'

'Things are a blank, then, until the ambulance came. I remember being lifted into the back but then I must have blacked out again, because the next thing I knew I was in the hospital, tubes coming out all over the place, the hideous smell of nitrous oxide. And this appalling, indescribable pain. I tried to move my leg, Ellie, to wriggle my toes. I remember an intense itch on my shin, and it took me some time to realise there was nothing to scratch. Just ... a gap. So fucking weird. How can a vacuum itch?'

I wondered whether he would hear the banging of my heart. I didn't need to know any more, but I had to, I had to work out where my responsibility began and where it ended.

'Ellie,' he said. He reached his hand out to me, took mine, and I felt how large his hands were, how much strength there was in them.

I couldn't bear to think I'd damaged – maimed – this perfectly healthy man, that I was the one responsible for his losing his lower leg! It was too huge to take in. If I'd done this then I wasn't safe to drive! I ought to give up my licence – it would be taken from me anyway when the police knew what I'd done, before they did whatever else they did to prosecute a hit-and-runner.

I couldn't look at him as I spoke.

'Your life's been ruined. You won't be able to work any more, will you? To sail, play golf, all those things you've been mentioning.'

The ward was dissolving now behind a veil of tears.

He spoke in a whisper.

'Hey, don't cry! We can get through this together.'

'But I'm . . .'

'Look. I'm not going to let this beat me. Every setback is a challenge, that's what I've always believed. Every problem is really a learning opportunity.'

When at last the tears began to dry up I looked at him. He'd kept my hand in his and now he squeezed it tightly. His was warm and dry. Comforting. I didn't want him to let go.

'What are you going to do? You should get some kind of compensation, shouldn't you?' What kind of coward was I? I should confess. Now. But the words wouldn't come.

Patrick was looking at me, his head tilted on the side of the pillow. He licked his dry lips and he said, 'No. I don't have to say anything. It's up to me. It isn't up to anyone else in the world. I've decided to ask the police not to pursue this. My choice.'

He was gazing as if right into me or even right out the other side, as if he was far away and thinking of something quite distant from here and now.

'Why, Patrick? Surely you should get them to find who-ever did this ghastly thing to you?'

'I don't have faith in the cops,' he said, dropping my hand, turning his face from me. 'To be honest I'd rather not have them involved any more. What's happened, has happened.'

I wanted to press him. Why wouldn't he want to find the culprit, claim compensation? And wasn't there a duty to report it, to prevent whoever did this from doing it to anyone else? If he decided to, I could – would have to – face the con-sequences even if it meant losing all I'd been working towards. But he went on.

'It's my decision. The ambulance guys informed the police when I was found, and they must have put it out on the radio, but I told the police when they came here to fire daft questions at me to drop it. How could I remember the colour of the car, I asked them.'

'But you said you saw it, it was blue?'

'Did I? I keep getting so confused. Anyway, how could I explain what had happened when I was only just coming round? I said look, it was an accident, and I choose to leave it at that and concentrate on recovering. What's done's done. I want to move forward. Take action and you get results, dwell on negatives and they simply multiply and obliterate your way ahead. I'm not interested in going over and over what might or might not have happened. I want to grasp the future by the short and curlies! I'm going to learn to use a prosthetic. I want to move forward.'

He sounded so sure, so convinced. Then he spoke again.

'Ellie,' he said, stroking my cheek with the back of a finger. 'I would understand if you didn't want to stay with me now I'm so changed. We haven't known each other all that long. I would understand if you wanted out.'

'No, Patrick. I wouldn't just abandon you. But I'm going to have to go now. They won't let me stay . . .'

His beguiling blue eyes locked onto mine, the dimples deepened in his cheeks as he smiled gently up at me. His teeth were even and white.

I had no references, no way of knowing how to deal with this.

The raw, skinless, floaty feeling came over me. I needed a ritual, I needed a voice to tell me to do something. *Look back three times and it'll be OK. Tap the bed three times and it will turn out to be someone else who did this to him.*

He was speaking again.

'I'll need help, learning to walk again – if that's possible, and if it isn't, I'll need someone to push the wheelchair for me, just until . . . until I learn to do it myself. I won't be able to drive again. If it's too much to ask of you, I'd prefer you just said so. So I know where I stand.'

I couldn't help myself, I placed my hand on top of his where it lay on the blanket. He smiled up at me.

'I'm here for you,' I said. 'You know I am.'

'How could I ever have forgotten you?' he said. 'Remind me what kind of painting you do?'

I told him they were river paintings, semi abstract, with many different layers.

'I can help you too, of course. I probably already told you that. I've got hundreds of clients who are always looking for art for their offices.'

'Really?'

'Sure.'

'But, don't you . . . isn't there anyone else?'

He pulled his hand from under mine then, his lips turning down, stared away from me and my heart rate sped up again. I was afraid I'd offended him.

'I don't want to think about anyone else right now. There's only so much I can cope with at the moment. I only want to think about you, Ellie, your lovely gentle face, your sweet voice, your wild dark hair, like a scruffy angel's. Your intense – what are they? Black? Brown? Green? No, hazel. Your intense hazel eyes. Your funny crooked smile. I can hardly bear the thought of the night apart from you.'

'It's OK,' I said. 'I'll come back tomorrow, I promise.'

I pulled back, turned my head.

'I must go.' I had left Pepper in the car; I could see him from here. My car was out there, Pepper's little face was in the back. I'd left him far too long.

'You'll come back, won't you?' he said. 'Tomorrow?'

'Of course.'

'Come soon. Bring me fruit, please, something fresh?'

'I'll bring you anything you like, you only have to ask.'

He was gazing at me, and I realised I was trembling, though I had no idea whether it was with desire for Patrick, or terror at where I was heading.

'Kiss me goodbye then.'

I couldn't – it was, surely, crossing a line.

But there I was. I was leaning over him and pressing my lips against his cheek, and he was moving his face so our lips were touching and we lingered like this, poised, lips against each other, not moving, just sensing.

The oddest thing happened as we stayed like this for I don't know how long.

It was as if the world just fell away.

As if there was no one and nothing else, no time passing, no world turning. Just our two mouths, and a kind of buzzing in my ears, and an emptiness that was soft and perfect. A translucent moment, in this treacly light, as if we were trapped in a perfect piece of amber.

CHAPTER FOURTEEN

On my way out I stopped to ask the health care worker at the desk if anyone else had been in to see Patrick.

'He's asked me to get in touch with a few relatives and friends,' I said, 'but I don't want to bother those who have already been.'

Each untruth I let pass led to another. Lying – or at least, glossing over the truth – was an easy thing, after all.

'There were a couple of blokes, mates of his,' he said. 'Came in yesterday, brought him some bits and pieces. And the police have been in. But he asked them to drop the investigation, for some reason. It's up to him of course. None of our business. He's been mainly asking for you. You're Ellie, aren't you? His girlfriend?'

I nodded.

'No other women?' I asked.

He grinned, winked. 'Don't worry! No one else. It's you he's been asking for. You're his number one. And if you're going to be caring for him we'll have to get the physio to run through some exercises with you, things he'll need to do once he's been discharged,' he said. 'But you'll no doubt be in again soon?'

'Yes, of course.'

I wondered if he watched me sympathetically as I walked back down the corridor.

I would help Patrick recover. It was absolution of a sort. All I had to do was make amends by helping him in the way he'd asked me to. I couldn't do more than this if he didn't want the police to pursue the investigation.

'I'm doing the right thing, aren't I, Pepper?' I said as I opened the car door and he looked up at me, his tail wagging ferociously, his tongue hanging out, panting.

I glanced up at the hospital as I got into the car, wondering which window was Patrick's.

There was a figure at the window of a third floor ward. Silhouetted against the lights that had gone on, stretching up. Probably a nurse, releasing the blind which slithered down and hid the room from view.

I woke up early, in May's bedroom. I should get back to London, work on my painting, but I had promised to visit Patrick again, and visiting hours weren't until midday. At least now I had a role to play.

Patrick's girlfriend's role!

It was obvious the woman he thought I was, was having no more to do with him. Then I would – should – take her place until I could explain the weird truth about how I'd come to visit him.

I leant on the window and watched a brisk wind send compact clouds racing across a pale blue sky. The sea glittered over the sand dunes in the distance, blond sea grasses against a bleached backdrop of sand. I did my salute to the sun, a yoga ritual that woke me up and put me in a good mood for the day. I had a sudden violent urge to see Patrick again. I'd take him fruit as he'd asked, soothe him, be the woman he believed I was, the one who cared. I could barely wait.

I pulled on jeans, boots, a jumper and my parka, called Pepper and walked out onto the shore, restraining myself from tapping the gatepost. The horizon was a dark line, the sea softened by the white cotton grass leaning away from the wind. I walked briskly, throwing pieces of driftwood for Pepper, licking the salt spray from my lips, the wind stinging my cheeks. People were out already, walking their dogs and stopping to ask me about Pepper - what breed was he? How old? And I trotted out my answers - a Norfolk terrier, at least fourteen, quite old for a dog, yes, at least ninety in people years.

As I walked, feeling the wind blow away all the anxiety of the last few days, I gave rein to the feeling that I'd been trying to fight since I'd visited Patrick last night. A yearning to have his blue eyes looking into mine again. A longing to feel his lips. I thought of the way they had rested against mine. His almondy smell. His strong hands. In my fantasy I obliterated the fact he might never walk again, ignored the fact it might all be because of me. He was fully recovered, tall and strong. When he was better he would come and stay with me here, in May's cottage.

Or, as seemed likely, in his own flashier place somewhere along this coast.

I let the fantasy develop. We would drive down here in a convertible – he was bound to have a nice car – and he would take me out on his yacht – he'd said he'd been on his way to a weekend of sailing – and we would make delicious meals of fresh seafood and drink the best wine. I would paint, and he would sell my paintings to up-market businesses all over the world. New York was just the start of it!

In this fantasy, everything *was* changing. Not in the way I had planned as I drove down to the seaside the night before my Private View. But an even more exciting and unexpected phase was unfolding. I was going to change more dramatically than anyone had ever expected.

Patrick was probably richer than anyone I'd ever met! I thought of the pictures of him on yachts on his phone. He had mentioned he had contacts who bought art, expensive art. I craved a new life, new experiences. And he had the capacity to provide them. I thought of the green dress I'd bought for the Private View, knowing Finn would never have wanted me to wear such a thing. Well I was going further than that – putting on new clothes wasn't the half of it! I was peeling off an old self and on the brink of putting on a new one.

At some point I would have to tell Patrick that we had never actually met before I came to the hospital. That I now believed I *was* the one to have bumped into him on the road that night. How I had meant to tell him, but that it was too much to dump on him while he was coming to terms with his atrocious injury. That since he didn't want the police to pursue it, I had realised the best thing I could do to atone for the appalling thing I had done was to help him recover.

He would see how hard it had been for me to carry this burden of guilt, but seeing how willing I was to stand by him when no one else would, he would forgive me.

I wondered about the woman he thought I was, the one who had decided to get out before the relationship had even begun.

How hard-hearted of her, to abandon Patrick when she realised he'd lost a leg. But then it was also understandable. They had by all accounts only met recently, there had been a fight in the pub, he had suffered this life-changing trauma. How many women would be prepared to stick around to deal with the repercussions of such a dramatic turn of events, unless they were as entangled in them as I was?

And then I was racing ahead, imagining what people would say when they saw me with this handsome new man, so different from Finn. Finn had been stopping me from moving forward, but Patrick, with his positive philosophy, would enable me to face the fears that had held me back over the years. I'd become ambitious and successful.

I would no longer be controlled by the compulsions that made me touch things or look back, to prevent something dreadful happening to someone I was responsible for – Timothy, Ben, Aunty May.

Pepper ran up to me then, jolting me out of my daydream. One or two hardy people were making their way over the shingle to the sea for an early morning swim, their flesh glowing white in the sunlight, their costumes drooping off their shrinking elderly bodies.

Perhaps – and the idea was like a whirlwind rushing through my mind – perhaps this was *meant*. You did hear of such things, elderly couples describing the extraordinary way they met, all those years ago, as if fate decreed they should be together. Perhaps the hit-and-run had happened that night for a reason.

Patrick and I were meant to be together!

I got to the beach café – a hut on the promenade, with windmills and buckets and spades piled outside. I ordered a fried egg and bacon bun from the girl serving up tea from an urn, and asked for a dish to put some water in for Pepper. Then I sat at a white plastic table sheltered from the wind between the café and the beach huts and drank my tea and shut my eyes and let the sun beat down on my eyelids, listening to the gentle sigh and sizzle of the waves on the shore.

Bliss.

When I'd drained my tea I got up and walked up the steps to the town past the brewery and the lighthouse, the Sailor's reading room, and the pub. I bought oranges, a punnet of early strawberries, and kiwis at the greengrocer's on the square.

As a student when I'd come to visit Aunty May, I had often walked about the little town, peering in windows and dreaming that this place, this kitchen, this courtyard was mine. Now having my own place here had come true! I let myself spin up on a high again, breathing the sea air; the headiness of knowing I was going to see Patrick again today, the thrill of owning a house by the sea, it all gathered until I thought I might explode.

I found myself crossing the grassy playground behind the church, where I used to come to as a child. The old swings I remembered but the tall metal slide had been replaced by an assortment of coloured plastic climbing equipment, in grotesque shapes. A woman sat texting on her phone while her child in a pink quilted coat swung to and fro on the swing, calling for her mother, who ignored her.

A memory nudged the corner of my mind, of me and Ben and someone else? And May calling, 'I'm leaving you in charge.' Pushing two younger children on the swing. Being pulled in two different directions, as the vague child I couldn't put a name or a face to vanished across the park to climb the steps of the tall slide. Knowing I couldn't just abandon my little brother to tell her to come down at once. Pulling him out of his seat – he was so small he still went in the ones with the safety harness – and carrying him across the park to the slide. Feeling like an adult, not the six-year-old I must have been. Then looking up to see May coming back, hurrying, treading a cigarette out underfoot.

I pushed through the swing gate into the graveyard. Wandered about looking at the graves. Reading the epitaphs and wondering about the people whose names were engraved. Then I stopped. It was a small, blackened grave in the corner but it was the words that caught my eye and made me stand stock-still.

'A piece of you.'

The very same words that appeared on the box containing a lock of hair in Aunty May's kitchen.

I peered more closely. The engravings had faded and were covered in some kind of lichen. I scraped the lichen away and brushed my finger along the stone, clearing the lettering.

Daisy 1985–90
Much loved and cherished and never forgotten.

I shuddered. So a child *had* died! And that old sense of darkness underlying the happy memories of this place washed over me.

The sun had gone in and it looked like rain, so I pulled my parka tighter around me. I'd quiz Mum next time I saw her. Make her tell me everything she knew about Aunty May's past. Now I was inheriting my aunt's house I was entitled to be party to the truth.

The sky was growing darker now. I'd take Pepper back to the house the other way, over the marshes. The wind buffeted us as we went across the exposed flatland where the circular water tower was silhouetted against the lowering sky. It was a desolate landscape, me and Pepper the only figures for miles around. Up to our right, the creek was a slate-grey expanse of water.

We reached the humpback bridge over the stream and went past the fishing huts. These ramshackle buildings hadn't changed for years, with their heaps of rope and netting coiled underneath and their smell of salt and fish and weed. Boats were moored along the quay. There was the clanking sound of metal ropes against masts, and the slap of the water against the makeshift jetties and landing stages. The other way, the sea sparkled, still lit up by glimpses of sun between the gathering clouds.

I was almost back at the house, when a voice startled me out of my reverie.

'Hey there! You!'

I looked up. A shock passed through me when I realised it was Larry, waving a hand up and down, his bike dropped at an angle between his knees.

I don't know why it made me shudder seeing him, why I wanted to run.

I controlled this impulse, however – the poor man was harmless. Instead, I waved back, hoping he'd move on.

'Larry! Anything I can do for you?'

'Where May gone?' he said, puckering his face up childishly.

'May doesn't live here any more.'

'May dead,' he said. 'May not coming back no more.'

'That's right. I'm here now. I'm Ellie.'

'You killed May.'

I laughed. 'No I didn't, Larry. May died. But you're right, she's not coming back. I'm sorry.'

He turned his back and was gone without saying any more.

Why did I get the impression he hadn't forgiven me?

I put the key in the lock, trying not to let his accusation take hold. I had to fight the compulsion to let his words germinate, begin to haunt me. May had died. She was depressed. Her suicide was carefully planned. There was nothing anyone could have done to prevent it. *'You killed May.'* I thought again, with a jolt of guilt, how I hadn't come down to see her that weekend. How I hadn't tapped the gatepost three times.

It wouldn't have been tapping the gatepost that would have saved her, my rational mind told me. But perhaps I could have cajoled her out of the depths of a despair that had convinced her she couldn't face another day?

Inside the house, I pulled out the kitchen drawer. There was a notebook in which May had listed the children she had fostered, but I put this aside for now and held up the bib. It contained a memory, I wasn't sure what of, more a series of impressions, a vague troop of images that I could barely put a name to. Childhood in all its fleeting intensity. The Crooked House had been the name of a shop on the high street, as well as featuring in the nursery rhyme. I remembered loving that house with its Aladdin's cave of beautiful trinkets, of jewellery and fridge magnets, of incense and bead sets and things to hang above your bed that swirled and caught the light.

I opened the tin next and again felt myself shudder looking at the lock of hair and the note 'A piece of you'. The very words that were engraved on the stone in the church-yard? As if she wanted to keep part of the child who had died. Then I noticed the matchbox, and opened that. The passport-size photo of a girl, not me, blonde, the name Daisy scrawled on the back.

Inside were six milk teeth, tiny and with little pointy ends and stippled with dry blood.

CHAPTER FIFTEEN

I left May's house as soon as I could after this. The physical mementoes of Daisy were making me feel nauseous. Anyway I couldn't bear to wait any longer to see Patrick. If I left now I should arrive just in time for visiting hours.

Patrick was sitting up, watching some film on the screen hooked up on an arm over his bed.

He held out his hand as I approached, took mine in his and kissed my palm, and I felt my insides collapse.

'I'm being discharged soon,' Patrick said. 'Back into civilian life. You'll get to see me with my clothes on again.'

I laughed.

'When?'

'Sometime this week.'

'Would you like me to come and drive you home?'

'Would you mind? Aren't I asking too much of you?'

'No, of course I don't mind. Where do you want me to take you?'

'To the flat. The one in Wapping. Matt and Suki said they'd leave some beer and bits, so it'll be ready for me. I just need a lift.'

Wapping! Blimey, I knew that area. It was highly desirable, mostly inhabited by City types, with its converted warehouse apartments right by the river near Tower Bridge.

'OK. That's fine. When do I come?'

'They haven't said which day, but they want the bed. And anyway I've had enough. If I stay any longer I'll get institutionalised. I'm on a processed carbs and sugar-only diet in here! I've started craving tinned peaches and plastic cream!'

'I've brought you some fresh fruit.'

'Aha! I said you were an angel.' I put the paper bag of oranges down on his locker and handed him a strawberry.

He ate it from my hand, taking my finger into his mouth and sucking it.

'Lucky I just disinfected it.'

'You couldn't have germs,' he said. 'You're too exquisite. Anyway, it's time I was up and about and back to sushi. And learning to use this damn peg leg.'

'I'm not sure if I'll be much help – I haven't dealt with anything like this before.'

'It doesn't matter!' he said. 'Together, we can be strong. When the going gets tough, Ellie, the tough get tougher.' He smiled, waved his hands over his poor damaged leg. 'I've just got to work at it. You will be an incentive! As long as you're sure about this?'

'I am. I'm sure.'

If they were discharging him later this week, then it was sooner than I had imagined it might be, given the extent and seriousness of his injuries, though I knew the NHS, short of beds, got people up and about as quickly as they were able to.

'I'm still amazed I forgot your beautiful face,' he said, gazing up at me. 'I can't tell you how glad I am to see you each time you appear in the ward. An apparition of loveliness. Come here. Pull the curtains around my bed. Just for a minute.'

And so it was happening. I was getting drawn further and further into his life and it gave me a curious, heady kind of energy.

It was two o'clock by the time I got in the car. It would be too late to do much work by the time I got home anyway so I decided to do the detour I hadn't done last weekend to see my mother. She wrote about complex relationships, maybe I could get some perspective from her about what was happening. And anyway, the teeth I'd found at Aunty May's had made me feel ill.

Who was the little girl? Why did I feel as if I remembered her, yet when I tried to grasp where I'd seen her she slipped out of my reach? She was the one whose name was on the gravestone, so what had happened to her? I would ask Mum to tell me about it.

I was wary of taking the smaller, prettier country route since the hit-and-run. But it was light, no chance of half-visions of possible victims of my driving. The countryside opened out as I got beyond Bury St Edmunds, flattened into large fields of rape, lurid yellow to either side, and the sky grew wider and murkier. I was at the junction to Cambridge in just over an hour and a half, driving down its leafy streets, along the river past Jesus Green, where students sprawled on the grass. My mother's house was in a narrow street off the road that ran along the river. I found a parking space, walked back down the terraced houses, negotiating my way between bikes propped up against the walls blocking the narrow pavement. I knocked on the front door, which opened straight off the street, and when there was no answer, used my key.

There was a vase of bluebells on the table in the front room.

'Mum?'

Her desk under the window was covered in heaps of papers and books. Photos of women cut out of magazines, and chiselled handsome men, were pinned onto a notice board. My mother churned out two romantic novels a year, sometimes three, and was in a constant state of anxiety that she wouldn't be able to come up with another complicated relationship to untangle in time for her deadline.

I called out again.

'Hi, it's me!'

No answer. She wasn't here. I went upstairs, Pepper at my heels, to the little room in the back where I always slept when I came, and dumped my bag.

I ran down the stairs, Pepper behind me, turning around three times, performing my stupid rituals before I'd even realised I was doing it.

I put the kettle on in her kitchen area which adjoined her open-plan sitting room at the back of the house, and strolled over to her desk. She'd scrawled notes above the photos on her board: 'Sabine begins affair with her sister Marcia's lover,

132

Bella tries to attract attention of sales assistant at Apple Store to no avail.'

'Hello?' Mum came through the front door, her arms full of carrier bags, her hair, which was just greying, a little wild and unkempt, her brow furrowed. She looked older, and her face had thickened, almost imperceptibly, but it gave me a tiny shock.

'Darling! I didn't know you were coming! Grab a couple of these bags for me, will you? I'm parched, let's have a cup of something.'

'You've been shopping . . .'

'I had an appointment at the Apple Store.'

'The Apple Store?'

'They run free workshops. Been there all afternoon. And before you say anything, let me tell you, I bloody needed it.'

'What is it, Mum? You look stressed.'

My heart sank. I needed to consult Mum about Patrick, to see if she might throw some light on the moral dilemma and vague feelings I had for this injured man that weren't even coherent but shimmered in the back of my mind, all mixed up with the confusion about his thinking he knew me and the accident and whether I'd caused it. Her own life had been complicated enough – she of all people would be able to give me some pointers as to what I was doing, where I was blindly heading.

'Stressed doesn't come near it.'

'Oh no. Nothing's wrong, is it?'

I looked her up and down, fear that she was keeping something from me coursing through me. She looked healthy enough.

'Nothing major. Just Life. With a capital L. Don't do that, Eleanor.'

'Do what?'

'That looking over your shoulder over and over again. I thought you'd grown out of that. Come on, let's talk.'

We went through to the kitchen area – an extension off her sitting room with a glass roof and French windows onto a small walled garden. She'd had the extension done quite soon after she moved in with Miriam.

'Use the tea temples, will you?'

'*Tea* temples?'

'Those Teapig thingies, whatever you call them. I'll have Peppermint and Liquorice. I've given up caffeine. And there are some soya bean whatsits there we could have. You're probably on a diet. Are you?'

'I don't do diets, Mum. You should know that. And why soya? Ick. Haven't you got cake? I haven't eaten much today. I've been down at May's cottage, Mum, and I want to ask you—'

'Soya's good for imbalances.'

'Imbalances?'

'Hormonal ones, darling, of course. Help me unload?'

I took the carrier bag from her and pulled out industrial-sized brown jars of magnesium, Evening Primrose Oil, Black Cohosh and Red Clover.

'I thought you were sceptical about these things?'

'I was,' she said. 'Now I'd try anything. Look,' she said, picking up a pot of cod liver oil. 'For my brain. Red Clover for mood swings, St John's Wort for depression, fish oil for my nerves. Calcium for bones and Black Cohosh for the hormones. It's got desperate. My flushes are catastrophic – if I could I'd peel off my flesh and walk out of it.'

'Ouch.'

'My body's a disaster zone. Eruptions, earthquakes, tsunamis, droughts, you name it.'

'Mum, while I was at May's—'

'*And* I'm on an emotional roller coaster – euphoric one moment, in the depths of despair and confusion the next.'

She paused, and looked at me, her mouth turned down.

'Not sure I like the sound of that,' I said. 'Are things OK with Miriam?'

'Oh, it's nothing to do with Miriam, it's being a woman. No getting round it. Puberty, menstrual problems, pregnancy.' She stopped and looked at me oddly when she said this. 'If you get through those, you're lucky to escape postnatal depression. Before you know it you're hitting peri-menopause, which I hasten to add is like a second adolescence – blushing, sweating, wanting to hide from the world. No wonder I need the Apple Store. It's the only place I feel sane.'

She shook pills into her hand as she spoke.

'Why the Apple Store though? Shouldn't you be going to the gym? Or a therapist of some kind if you're feeling like this?'

'NO! I want hard knowledge. Apple men with clean fingernails. Apple men with their patience, explaining about Siri and how to download an app. They're what give me respite.'

'Respite from what though, Mum?'

'From inner turmoil! They're so calm, and cool, and

smooth-skinned. And young. So sure. They do what they love and they know how to do it. You can go to as many workshops as you like and they never grow tired of showing you. Or maybe, maybe what I love is being taught again by people who have a greater knowledge than I do, yet who are so much younger, have so much future ahead of them. I find it rejuvenating.'

'You sound like you've found religion.'

'Actually, sometimes I wonder if it perhaps *is* a kind of sect. But that's my imagination running away with me. The fact is, those hours in that clean room among handsome young men in blue shirts calms my mind. They don't flirt though. I think it must be part of their training, not to flirt with the women who come to them in desperation. They listen, and they offer solace, and they have the patience of saints. But it is all strictly non-sexual, so in this respect it's definitely safer than therapy.'

'Mum, you're sounding cynical.'

'I'm going to use one in my latest novel. He's wedded to his Apple job, she can't make him notice her. She tries everything. So how's it all going? How's Finn? How's work?'

My mother was so behind with where I was up to I felt despair. And this, in fact, was typical. My mother had always been wrapped up in her work, her thoughts elsewhere when I needed her. Right back to those days in the school holidays when she'd packed us off to Aunty May's instead of taking time off to spend with her two children. Yet I always hoped, against all evidence, that this time, at last, she would tune in to me, give me her full attention.

'I wish you could have made it to the Private View,' I said.

'I sold quite a few. And some Americans have commissioned a painting.'

'That's fabulous, darling, but I knew you would. You're a star.'

'I wish you could've come. Especially as Dad couldn't.'

'I know, *I* wish I could have come too, but you know how my work can be. And I can't really face Southwold any more. That chapter of my life is closed. I don't want to keep on going over and over why May did what she did. If I'm not careful, it could haunt me. The only way I'll get over it is once we've sold that house and had done with it.'

I wanted to point out the house was mine now, and that she had no say in whether I sold it, but I sealed my lips.

My mother had lost her older sister and it was still raw for her. And lost her in such a painful, unnecessary way. This on top of the physical changes she was undergoing, did indeed sound bad enough to warrant an afternoon seeking the advice of geeks. I made her a pot of Peppermint and Liquorice tea and put some soya beans in a dish. I put a bowl of water on the floor for Pepper. Rummaged about in her cupboards looking for something vaguely sweet to have with my tea and finally made do with a handful of dried cranberries.

My mother had curled onto the sofa, her feet tucked under her.

'Mum, I want to ask you . . .'

'You're doing it again, Ellie! Do you remember when you were a teenager you had to turn the light off and on five times before you went to bed?' she said. 'I had to say night-night exactly the right number of times or you'd be distraught. But you're nearly thirty now, you must have grown out of it, surely? Oh, here's Miri.'

I looked up. Miriam had come in. The opportunity to talk shrank away from me.

'Hey, Ellie,' Miriam said, as if she was a teenager rather than a sixty-something woman.

'Hello, Miriam.'

'There's some herb tea in the pot,' my mother said. 'Now, go on, Ellie, what did you want to say?'

I wasn't going to tell her about Patrick in front of Miriam so I said, 'I found some things in May's house she must have kept to remind her of her foster children.'

My mother blinked. Paused, the tea halfway to her mouth. 'What things?'

'Kids' stuff. A bib, a lock of hair.'

'Tell me, what colour is the hair?'

My mother's face had gone pale.

'Blonde?'

'Oh dear! So she kept bits of her. How macabre. After all that had happened.'

'What do you mean? Did May do something? Something bad?'

'Look, I don't want to go into all this. It was done with and it was finished. That time spoilt my own love of that seaside town and now you're digging it all up again.'

'But I don't know what I'm digging up if you don't tell me!'

Aunty May had been a little wayward, a little wild at times, but at least she had been *there*. My mother didn't have time to spend with us. Even now I could feel that yearning for a mother who I never really felt was present.

'Your mother feels her sister's manipulating her from beyond the grave,' Miriam said.

I wished she'd go out again. She was hovering around, as if afraid she'd miss something.

'It's a shame. I wouldn't mind use of a house in South-wold. But Sandy's made her mind up and you know what your mother's like when she's made her mind up about something.'

I ignored her, and her blatant reference to what she knew full well was *my* house.

'Mum, I *need* you to answer some questions.'

'Don't, Ellie.'

'Look, I also found this.'

I held out the photo.

'Who was Daisy? What happened to her? I can sort of remember her but it keeps sliding away when I try to grasp the memories, and yet, and yet, the hair, and there was this label, "A piece of you" . . .'

'I can't go there now. It's better that you don't know. You've got your life to live, leave May's to pass away. I didn't want to tell you. I didn't want to tell you ever, Ellie, please let's let sleeping dogs lie. Talking of which, doesn't Pepper need a walk? He'll be wetting my floor.'

CHAPTER SIXTEEN

'Don't forget Othello on Friday,' she called as I walked back up the street, and I turned and waved goodbye. Maybe next time I saw her I'd get a chance to talk to her properly.

At least I had the New York commission to keep my mind occupied that week. George Albini, the man from the New York gallery, confirmed they wanted a river piece, but a London one, showing the same ambiguity I'd achieved in the Blyth painting, the menace beneath the apparently benign surface. They would pay me five thousand dollars. I reeled at this. It was more than I'd ever been paid for anything. I bought the canvas and a stretcher and worked on the sitting-room floor, placing my sketches and photos around the canvas, and planning the forms I was going to create.

I thought of Louise's description of what I tried to do. The sometimes nebulous line between light and dark, beauty and ugliness, life and death. I pulled out a sketchbook and looked at some drawings and photos I'd taken a few weeks earlier down at the river in Greenwich. I wondered if I could use these or would need to do more.

The delay I'd had while visiting Patrick and Aunty May's during the week had somehow galvanised me. I was brimming with ideas. I worked all day browsing images, thinking, sketching, working on the piece. I carried the knowledge of Patrick, what had happened between us, inside me, a kind of thrilling secret that intensified my work. I was waiting for his call, telling me when to go and fetch him.

I finished painting at five thirty, put my brushes in white spirit, cleared the floor of the rags and pieces of fabric I used on my collages. I looked back at my work. I'd put the shapes into place, and was building up layers. I tried to see if it was doing what I wanted it to do, reflecting the tidal changes of the Thames, the muddiness beneath the silver reflections of the water. The layers beneath what you actually saw, symbolising, for me, the layers beneath what we see in each other.

Working on something all day you could no longer see it. I needed to get some distance from it, to be able to view it objectively. Which meant giving myself time.

My brother Ben rang and asked if it was OK if he and his fiancée Caroline went down to the cottage. They would do any little repairs that I hadn't managed. Then George Albini rang again and said they were organising the shipping, could I give him measurements? They wanted to get the painting out there by the end of August. My heartbeat quickened. I must get on with it.

Then Patrick phoned.

'They aren't discharging me till Saturday now. I'm going stir-crazy. And I'm missing you like a mad person.'

'I'll be there soon, Patrick. It's not long till the weekend.'

'Can you come on Friday? Just to lie with me for a bit. I need to feel you next to me.'

So. I would have to cancel the play Mum had asked me to go to, I would remove all obstacles to seeing Patrick. To atone for what I had done to him. He and my New York commission were my priorities now.

I was packing my paints away when Chiara came in.

'Hi, babes!' she said, going to the kitchen with a bag of fruit and veg she had bought from a farmers' market. 'You've been rather elusive. Where have you been?'

I smiled.

'I popped back to May's cottage on Monday night,' I said. I didn't want to tell her about Patrick yet. It would involve too much explanation about my guilt over the accident that she was convinced I couldn't have caused.

And though Chiara was my best friend, and had my best interests at heart, I knew her loyalties lay with Finn as well. To introduce the idea of Patrick to her at this stage would be to risk a lecture which would simply muddy the waters I'd worked so hard to clear.

'And then I went to see my mum. She wants me to go down on Friday night to see a play.'

'Cool.'

'What's happening with you and Liam? Any news on the flat?'

'It's all so slow,' she said. 'We're waiting for a survey now. It's a pity you're away this weekend. I was hoping you and I might spend some time together. I wanted to ask you about birthing partners.'

'Sorry,' I said, barely hearing her. I had promised to give Patrick a lift home at the weekend. That was all I could think about.

'Oh, don't worry, Els,' Chiara said, stomping across to her room. 'We'll talk later. You're obviously preoccupied with your commission and everything.'

'How's my girl?'

I had driven with Pepper over to Dad's with his shopping, something I tried to do every week.

'I'm OK, Dad.'

It still pulled at my heartstrings to see him here in a cramped ex-local authority flat in the seamier end of East Greenwich when Mum had gone up-market to Cambridge. It still made my heart sink as I tramped up the concrete stairway and along the corridor past other front doors to his.

'How was the exhibition?' Pepper had run over to my Dad and leapt up onto his lap.

'It was great! I sold a few. I've got some exciting news.'

I told him about the Americans, the New York commission, and he sat, one leg crossed over the other in his old armchair, and listened.

'I'm so pleased for you, you know. As May would have been.'

'Mum's still got her heart set on my selling the house, you know.'

'I've told her I think we should back off. Leave it up to you. Now, what do I owe you for the shopping?'

Dad never went beyond the walls of his flat. The world outside had become too menacing to him. And I could understand it to a point, the panicky feeling I got when I ignored my compulsions must be how he felt all the time. It was his increasing withdrawal from the world that meant he'd had to give up his job as a curator at the Maritime Museum, and which meant Mum had finally had enough. She couldn't live with the restrictions his agoraphobia imposed on her, the fact he would no longer accompany her to parties, dinners, the theatre – anywhere. I could see how meeting Miriam must have opened up the world for her.

Or that's what I understood about their separation. I would probably never really know the whole truth. Dad's asking me what he owed me for the food was my cue to leave. I knew that. He reached a point where he needed to be alone, couldn't cope with company, even that of his own daughter. I leant over and kissed him, catching a waft of his Dad smell, damp washing, beer.

Friday came and my other day's teaching. I dropped my car off on the way into work to get the wing-mirror fixed.

Chloe arrived late as usual and handed me a soggy pink disc of minced meat. There had been a letter asking for contributions to an international food day, and Chloe, whose mother suffered from depression and was unable to get out of bed, must have taken the frozen burger straight from the packet herself. Six years old, caring for Mum, no one to show her that food had to be packaged, or bought fresh. Chloe was just one of the millions of hidden child carers out there, getting on with it because there was no choice.

I thanked her. 'You're doing a wonderful job, you know, Chloe?' I said, hoping she would understand my words referred to what she was doing day in day out, not just the burger. I exchanged a glance with Joyce, who took the burger from me and mouthed that she'd deal with it.

Billy showed a picture of Charles and Camilla at a refugee camp.

Chelsea-Lee pulled a louse out of her hair and held it out to me in the palm of her hand. Emmylou's mum came in complaining that Chelsea-Lee was on a higher-level reader than Emmylou. I made an appointment to speak to her the following week.

At three I got them to pack up early, and let them go as soon as I could. Timothy hung about as usual.

'Me stepdad's coming, 'im shouting at us again an' I don't want to go.'

'Timothy, it's home time. You need to go.'

I looked at the clock. I was desperate to get going, to see Patrick.

For once I wasn't going to give Timothy extra time. I was anxious to get on the road, I needed to get moving to keep my nerves at bay. I was going to visit him this evening then spend the night at May's cottage so I could be at the hospital first thing in the morning to take him home.

Nothing else mattered.

By three forty there was no sign of Timothy's child minder.

I felt on edge, impatient. I opened the classroom door and looked across the playground.

Ah. Timothy's sister was there – she sometimes came to take him to Westfield when the child minder was busy.

I left Timothy ambling across the tarmac towards the girl. She couldn't have been much more than thirteen years old herself – she stood by the playground gates, hair dyed a fierce black, in a black top that had had the shoulders cut out revealing her own pink shoulders. Plump legs in tight leggings, feet in pointed black boots, her thumb working her mobile, not looking up as Timothy ran towards her. Two small figures beneath the indifferent concrete walls and billboards of the inner city.

And I was heading off to pick up Pepper and my car and then to drive again towards the Suffolk countryside with only one clear thought in my head.

Patrick.

'Where will you stay tonight?' he asked me. The nurses said they had to run a few more tests, but that yes, he would be ready to come home the next morning.

I was lying on his bed again, letting him stroke my hair away from my forehead. I could feel the fingers of his other hand pressing into the small of my back and I moved closer to him.

'I told you!' I smiled into his eyes. 'I have a house by the sea in Southwold. Have you forgotten?'

'I remember now,' he said, pulling me to him, and I let him kiss me. His lips were dry and soft. It was the sort of kiss you want to go on forever, the sort of kiss where everything else in the world falls away, leaving just this soft pool of sensation.

At last I drew away.

'I need to leave before the gallery closes.'

'Do you have to?'

'Yes. I'll see you tomorrow.'

Valerie had phoned and asked me to pick up the paintings she hadn't sold.

'I'll be back for you in the morning,' I told Patrick. 'You mustn't worry.'

'There aren't many left at all,' Valerie told me. 'I sold another this morning. I'm loath to let you take these away, but this new show's going up and we have to make the space.' She handed me an envelope. 'That's the money for the sales after commission and the donations to Mind.'

'Thanks so much.'

'Keep in touch. We could think about a solo show sometime.'

She smiled, and I thanked her and left, not daring to look inside the envelope, but with a fizzing feeling inside me. A solo show! It was what all us artists dreamt of. I was on a high as I arrived at May's. Things really were working out for me – the commission, solo shows. The contacts Patrick was going to provide for me.

And the cream on the top, Patrick himself! I let myself forget about the reason I'd met him to start with.

Ben and Caroline had left the cottage immaculate. It was much nicer arriving to a place that had been occupied. They'd left a bottle of white wine and some cheese and bits and pieces in the fridge and a packet of oatcakes and a bar of organic chocolate on the sideboard. They'd also sorted through Aunty May's drawers of stuff, had emptied one out into a box with a note saying if I didn't want anything in it, it could be thrown away. There was a plastic box of toys they had dragged out from the cupboard under the stairs. Pepper lay down beside me and found a rubber ball to chew as I rummaged through them. A Fisher-Price pop-up toy with plastic animals that leapt up when you unhooked the lids. A wooden hammer and peg thing. A wobbly man. Old-fashioned toys. Things you didn't see any more in the nursery classes at school. A Fisher-Price garage, the kind with the winder that lets the lift down.

I got myself some cheese and oatcakes and poured a glass of wine and set about rummaging through the papers from the emptied drawer, chucking old postcards and bills into a bin bag and making a pile of things I thought might be worth keeping.

When in a tightly packed envelope I found an appointment card for the Maudsley Hospital, and a page torn from a small diary, I stopped, put my oatcake down.

I unfolded the page, written in May's chaotic handwriting that sloped one minute this way one minute the other.

It was dated 1990. At the top she had written, *My record as a foster parent. Written at Doctor Lipski's request.*

It was hard to read, the tight folds in the page had obliterated some of the letters, but I got the gist:

Daisy felt like the child I alwa-- wanted and yet gen---cally she --s quite dif----nt to ---- As if her bl- nde curls and her pale eyes t-unt-d me with how impossible this was. I have kept little mem--t-es of her, because I cannot bear to let her go. I will never get over -----.

Beneath this was some more writing, scribbled out.

I folded the paper and as I put it back in the envelope a photo fell out, a photo with a section cut out of it. The blonde child, Daisy, and next to her my little brother Ben, and then the shape of a third child who should have been there, next to them, slightly taller, standing on the shore. Me.

I stood up, looked about me. I was no longer happy being here alone.

I wanted someone to talk to, someone to explain. May had been my beloved aunt. She had left me her house. So why on earth had she cut me out of the photo?

CHAPTER SEVENTEEN

Patrick was waiting for me the next morning, in a wheel-chair beside the nurses' station. My heart skipped a beat at the sight of him in his blue shirt, with his blue eyes and black hair.

I'd spent the rest of the evening rummaging through May's things, trying to find the rest of the diary, with no success. I'd slept badly, haunted by the vision of the empty space in the photo where I should have been. I'd kept a light on through the night. I didn't like being in the house alone and was glad to have Pepper with me, who, as if by instinct, knew to sleep on the end of the bed.

'Here she is.' It was another young health care worker. He was addressing Patrick. 'She'll take care of you now the doctors have signed you out.' He winked at me and handed me a bag and some papers with diagrams of exercises on them 'from the physio', he said, and then I was pushing Patrick in his wheelchair into the lift, his crutches under one arm.

Seeing him in the chair, his left ankle dressed, his right lolling awkwardly in its prosthetic, I felt such tenderness, mixed with confusion about when I should confess about who I was and why I'd visited him. How long could I keep on deceiving him? Or rather, being economical with the truth, because I had never actually lied to him, had I?

His bright blue shirt smelt clean and almondy, as if all his health defied the antiseptic smell of the ward he'd been in. He did something to me. He exerted a forceful pull on me, as if I couldn't help but lean towards him. As I pushed him out of the foyer and across the forecourt, towards the car park, my senses seemed heightened to the sheen on the skin of his neck and arms as it caught the light. How badly I wanted to run my fingers over it. It must have been all that sailing I'd seen in the pictures on his mobile that had kept him so toned, healthy-looking.

'Have you got all your stuff?' I asked him.

'I hadn't packed for a three-week stay when I left the pub,' he laughed. 'So yes, just my pyjamas and a toothbrush, which the boys brought down for me.'

'So we're going to Wapping?'

'Yes. That'll do for now. As I say, the boys said they would leave some stuff out for me. And I've got work to get on with. It's nice and close to amenities for rehabilitation – they've referred me to a physio at the London Hospital. So London, please, if it's all the same to you.'

'You'll have to direct me to your flat,' I said.

'Of course!' He put his head in his hands. 'Stupid me! You haven't actually been there before have you? Look, just drive back to London and I'll navigate for you.'

'OK.'

'It'll be good to get back. I'm no good doing nothing. Got fish to fry, et cetera.' He rubbed his finger and thumb over his stubble. 'I could do with a shave as well – I've let myself go in there. I'll have to make an appointment with Bruno, for a haircut, wet shave, the whole works. There's so much to do. I've got to organise physio pretty pronto,' he went on. He waved towards his right leg. 'Got to get used to the prosthetic. The other one will heal, they say, but I'm not supposed to put weight on it so I need to get my new one working. You can't hang about in my world, Els. You've got to keep up with the markets. I can't afford to lose clients.'

I stopped myself asking him what markets he was talking about, in case I was supposed to know.

'Is this your car?' he asked, frowning.

I gulped.

I would have to say something now. I opened my mouth then shut it again.

There were hundreds of silver blue cars and his memory was still damaged. He was handing me his bag. It could wait. Now wasn't the moment. I unlocked the boot, my head down, putting his bag in.

'Let me help you,' I said then, opening the passenger door, holding out my arm for him.

'NO! I must do this by myself.'

'But don't you need a bit more time, to get used to the leg, to practise?' I asked.

'Been practising all week. It's driving me stir-crazy. I want to get home, get moving. Get my life back.'

'But . . .'

'It's OK! You're helping by being here. Take me home! And I want to know the latest about your painting on the way. We need to discuss what kind of prices we're talking about if I suggest to my clients to invest. And May's cottage. Where you're up to with it. I've forgotten what you told me. Everything's still a bit of a blur, you'll have to forgive me.'

I looked down at his black hair, finely cropped and dense as velvet above the smooth and tanned runnel of his neck, and as I helped him into his seat I had to fight the urge again to bend down and press my lips into it. I was discovering that the moral guidelines I'd always lived by could be subtly transgressed. Yes, I was being a little deceptive, was going along with his delusion that I was a girlfriend, but now it was happening I was finding it intriguing, playing a role, seeing where it would take me. And I realised then that my fear had metamorphosed from one of being discovered to a terror of losing him. Now the thoughts began to nag at me again. If I told him the truth about why I'd first visited him, would he still feel this attraction to me? Or would he reject me?

So could I just keep quiet forever? You couldn't conduct a whole relationship on the back of a lie. Could you?

I shut the passenger door, walked round to the driver's side and made a decision. I'd take him home, check he was alright, that he could manage, and then, at the pertinent moment, explain everything. I'd offer to do what I could for him, to help him rehabilitate. And I would just have to hope with all my heart that he would forgive me for keeping the truth from him, and admit that there was something developing between us so that we had to move forward together.

I would tell him I would stand by him, support him, be there. And he would pull me to him as he had done in the hospital bed and I'd feel again that powerful surge of desire I'd never felt before.

I had to push the passenger seat as far back as it would go to accommodate his long legs and the fact he couldn't bend the damaged one. I placed his crutches next to him and Pepper, who had been asleep on the back seat, woke up. His nose shot into the air as he spotted Patrick and he let out a low, menacing growl.

'Shshhh, Pepper!' I said. 'This is Patrick. Patrick's a friend.'

He sat down again, doubtfully.

Patrick was too big for my little Nissan Micra. He looked like the Fisher-Price pop-up toy Ben had found at Aunty May's – squished down into a container that he would spring out of if the lid was lifted! I smiled to myself, turned the key in the ignition and we set off towards London.

'When will you be going back to work?' I asked him.

'Oh, straight away. The containers need managing, and I need to check a consignment of fish for Malaysia. But it can all be done over the internet. There's a bit of a rush on glass eels.'

'Oh?'

'Never you mind, Ellie. No one who's not in fish gets it. Business probably isn't your forte, is it?'

'It certainly isn't.'

'All you need to know is I can manage the portfolio per-fectly well, one-legged.'

'What are these containers you mentioned?'

'Steel containers. Managing a shipment down at Trinity

Buoy Wharf. I'm letting them out, as offices and so on. Need to get down there, check them out.'

As we pulled away from the hospital I felt a kind of buzz, the like of which I hadn't felt since – since when? Since I was a child? No, it was more recent. It flitted in and out again. I'd felt like this on my way down to my cottage before the hit-and-run happened. When I believed my life with Finn was over and I was about to embark on something fresh and unknown, that there were vast expanses of uncharted territory lying before me. I was discovering you *could* go down different paths to the ones mapped out for you and it was exhilarating.

I glanced sideways at Patrick. He looked back at me with a kind of adoration in his eyes and my stomach did a back-flip. We drove in silence for a while.

He squeezed my hand periodically, and at one point ran the back of his hand down my face. I liked it. A lot.

As we got closer to London I looked at him again, and as I caught him unawares for a second he had a different look about him from the affectionate one I'd seen earlier. He looked tense, set, staring ahead as if he couldn't bear how slowly we were going – the traffic on the A12 was heavy, crawling along as we approached London, as the buildings reared up on either side.

He fidgeted a little.

'Try going in the fast lane,' he muttered impatiently at one time, and I pulled out, wanting to please him, or not wanting him to think badly of me. I wanted him to like me, I realised, not just the me he thought I was, but the real me as well.

Whoever I was turning into.

I wasn't sure any more.

At last we were passing the Olympic Park.

'It's funny, isn't it, how quickly a different landscape becomes familiar,' I said, wanting to fill in the silence. 'Do you remember the marshes when there were just dilapidated warehouses and worn-out storage units? Not even that long ago.'

'Yes, you're right. Seeing the Velodrome brings it home to me,' he said. 'It's not just walking, my cycling's a thing of the past as well.'

'Cycling?'

'I won't be getting on a bike for a while, will I?'

'You used to cycle? What, long distance?' I kicked myself. How much did he think I knew about him?

'Of course,' he said without suspicion. 'It's OK,' he added. 'I used to run, cycle, play golf and sail. But look at the Paralympics – you can still compete even without the right limbs.'

'Patrick . . .'

'So, it's OK.'

The frustration he was feeling must be overwhelming! No wonder he was irritated by traffic, he was someone used to working and playing hard, someone for whom doors opened. He wasn't going to tolerate them closing for him.

'How can you bear it, Patrick?' I blurted out then. 'How can you bear to face life without your leg when you were so active?'

'You know what I always say,' he replied, putting his arm

right round me now, his hand on my waist, under my top, so that concentrating on the road became an effort. 'Regard every obstacle in life as a chance to grow. Every problem as an opportunity.'

'That's amazing, to be so positive.'

'There's no other way to be.'

He was so different from Finn, who almost took failure for granted. His attitude was wonderfully fresh to me. An inspiration.

We turned into East India Dock Road, through the underpass, and headed for the narrower, older streets of Wapping. He directed me down towards the river. Up above, glimpsed between the towering walls of the buildings, the sky was a smooth and uncomplicated blue.

'Here?' We'd stopped outside one of those converted old brick warehouses that you can only get into via an entryphone and some automated gates. The kind of place only people with a lot of money can afford to live in. A high-end riverside 'des res' probably developed in the Nineties and redone in the Noughties and now, in the Teenies, it would have rocketed in value.

'There's a parking place just here, on the left,' he said.

It was good he could remember where he lived. He'd said it was 'retrograde amnesia' – that he could remember most things that happened a while before the accident, and could form new memories, but couldn't remember what had happened in the immediate aftermath and in the few hours prior to it happening.

'What's wrong?' He was looking at me, a half-smile on his lips.

'Nothing.'

I heaved the wheelchair out of the boot, unfolded it, pushing the seat into place and the footplates down.

He levered himself up and out of the passenger seat in a swift movement that showed again how powerful his biceps were and how hard he must have practised while he was in hospital, and I helped him into the chair. I left Pepper in the car. I shouldn't be long. Patrick held up a fob and the glass doors glided open. We were in a bare-brick vestibule, steel lift doors on the left, a vast window overlooking the river in front. The tide was in, and a boat had just passed, leaving an arrowhead in its wake; waves raced towards either shore, and the water was silvery beneath the spring sky. His fish business must be doing pretty bloody well for him to earn enough to live in a place with a view like this. It sent a little thrill through me. I'd never rubbed shoulders with the very wealthy before. My mother was comfortably off, true, but my parents had always frowned on 'new money' as if the only way to obtain it must entail some immoral activity. I'd grown up suspicious of it. But it seemed everything that was happening was teaching me to challenge my prejudices, the assumptions and values one is indoctrinated with at birth.

I would throw off all kinds of learnt restrictions, and strike out alone. I was thrilled to discover where he lived, right on the river. All the time I'd spent having to seek out spots from which to take photos, to capture its essence, and here was Patrick living in the perfect riverside location.

'Come up? Please?'

We were beside the lift and the doors were sliding open and before I knew it we were getting out on the fourth floor and he was opening the door to his apartment. I followed him into a massive open-plan room with a minimalist steel kitchen area at one end and a black wall at the other with a door in it.

There were views across the river to the Shard, its elegant pyramid of glass and steel rising to fine points over London like a giant's church spire. It took my breath away. It was my dream situation.

'What a fantastic view!'

I looked around. On the exposed brick walls there were enormous black-and-white photos of glamorous women, close-ups, arty in a way though too slick for my taste, the kind of thing corporate buildings often display in their foyers. Not much else on show at all. No books, no CDs, just the bare wood floor, brick walls, large windows, and a flat-screen TV.

Once he was installed and comfortable, I would blurt out my confession to him, then, if he wanted me to, I'd make an exit from his life for once and for all.

'Is there anything I can do for you before I go?'

'You're not going?'

'Patrick. Listen. I will get whatever you need, I will do whatever I can, but I need to tell you—'

'That you've work to do. I know, Ellie, I don't want to hold you up. But it's just that, now I'm here, I do wonder how I'm going to manage.'

For the first time he was letting his defences down, revealing some vulnerability about what had happened to him. My intention to reveal the truth retreated again as my heart went out to him. What else could I do but stay with him, make sure he'd got food in, drink, that he was comfortable and would manage with his wheelchair and on his crutches in the flat? Looking at him, sitting helplessly in the middle of the massive room, in the wheelchair, I tried to imagine what it must be like having to come to terms with such a devastating injury. To be restricted to a wheelchair after having been so healthy, so fit and sporty.

'How am I even going to unpack, sort myself out?' he said now, a small wail entering his voice. 'I'd only just got back from Corfu when I left that weekend. I hadn't even had time to unpack. There's my suitcase, look! Through there in the bedroom. How am I going to put everything away with these crutches?'

I wanted to say I would help, that I wanted to, but where were his usual friends? It was obvious the woman he believed I was, the one he had met in the pub, had left the scene – but what about his family? If they were to arrive, or to call him, how would I explain my presence?

'Patrick, look, I'll check you've got food and so on, but then, isn't there anyone else . . .?'

'There's no one else, Ellie.'

'But your family? Surely they must be beside themselves worrying about you?'

'I don't have any family,' he said.

'I mean your mother . . .' I said, remembering the thought that had come to me in the hospital, what a doting woman she must be.

'I haven't got parents, I don't even know my mother,' he said.

'Oh.'

I followed him as he wheeled his way across the vast floor

to the bedroom, instinctively knowing not to ask him any more, for now.

'Please, darling, would you open the suitcase? Help me put my things away?'

The bedroom was almost completely taken up by a huge bed with a view out of the floor-to-ceiling window over the river. On the opposite walls were sleek tall cupboard doors. I did as he said, still wondering when I should tell him I wasn't the right person to be taking out his clothes, some expensive, folded T-shirts – Ralph Lauren and Hugo Boss – and some fine linen pyjamas, putting them into the drawers, unable to resist the temptation to put them in my special colour order, a lifetime's habit that was hard to break and that became insistent when I was nervous. Then there were more casual clothes in the bottom of the case, sailing shoes, a wetsuit squished into a bag.

'Where do you want me to put your wash things?'

'They can go in the bathroom, over there.' I realised then there was another door disguised in the black wall.

I did as he said, laying out his things in the beautifully tiled en suite bathroom, dimly lit, with its stone sink and little lights around the mirrors. I went back to his room, fished the rest of the things out of his bag, putting his little alarm clock by his bed as he instructed me and then I stopped.

There in the bottom of the bag was a framed photo of a pretty woman dressed in white lace, holding a bouquet of flowers. And beneath it, a black leather album.

I swung round. Patrick was there, gazing at the photo over my shoulder.

And something seemed to descend over his face, a kind of loosening – the moment of recognition.

He looked at me, then back at the photo.

'Who is this, Patrick?' I asked. My voice had gone weak. It came out as a whisper.

'Oh shit,' he said. 'My memories are all topsy-turvy. I thought I'd told you, but I can't have done. Everything's gone so misty.'

'Told me what, Patrick?'

'That, Ellie, is my wife.'

CHAPTER EIGHTEEN

I left. I told him I was sorry, that there had been a mistake, and now I'd seen that he was OK I had to go.

I ran down the stairs, onto the warm riverside street and fell into my car. My hands were trembling. I clutched the steering wheel tight as I drove. I cursed the traffic lights – every one seemed to be on red as I crawled back up the gridlocked East India Dock Road towards Mile End.

My body was processing the new information slowly, like a drug gradually taking effect in my veins. A drug whose effects I couldn't predict.

Patrick had a wife!

Where was she? Surely he couldn't possibly have forgotten such a fundamental detail about his life, however bad his amnesia. But why hadn't she been in to see him? Come to collect him? Why hadn't the nurses mentioned her when I'd asked if he'd had visitors? And what about everyone else in his life – had he simply forgotten they existed too? Who did he think I was and what did he think I was doing, now he had seen the photo and remembered? It was one thing for me to be posing as a girl he had recently met, quite another to be replacing a wife who was out there somewhere, waiting to hear from her husband.

I needed to talk to Chiara.

The Mile End flat was empty and had the feeling about it that no one had been there for some time. It took me several tries to get Chiara to answer her phone and when she did she told me she was in the pub with the gang. I fed Pepper, kissed him and then ran down the stairs and along the Mile End Road to the Wetherspoon's where we always met.

I was so relieved to find Chiara and the others I almost cried. I squished up next to her on one of the leather sofas, and she leant across and spoke into my ear. But what she said wasn't comforting after all.

'We were supposed to be shopping together this afternoon. Did you completely forget? I've been texting and phoning you and in the end I gave up.'

I put my hands to my face.

'Shit!'

'When I realised you weren't coming I asked Louise instead.'

'Oh.' I felt a pang of juvenile jealousy. Louise wasn't her closest friend, I was!

'I completely forgot about shopping with you,' I said. 'I'm so sorry, Chiara. Things have happened, stuff . . .'

'*And* your mum's been on the phone wanting to talk. You mustn't leave your phone on silent! She's been ringing me since midday asking where you are. She wants to talk about your Aunty May's house.'

'I had to go down there this weekend. But my mum knew that, didn't she say?'

'Something's up,' Chiara said. She was looking at me with concern but I could tell she was still resentful that I'd let her down. 'Tell me what's going on with you. You look petrified. As if you'd seen a ghost. I haven't got long.'

Finn and Louise and Guy were on the other side of the large table, and with the background noise of the pub couldn't possibly hear our exchange.

I nonetheless spoke as quietly as I could.

'I'm honestly so sorry, Chiara. The fact is, I got a bit . . . involved with someone. I met him down at May's. I didn't want to get in touch with him, or tell you until it was well and truly over with Finn.' I was glossing over the truth again.

'I see.'

I told her he was a man who as it turned out spent weekends in Southwold but lived in Wapping but that it was far more complicated than I'd realised.

I wondered what Chiara would say if I told her, 'He's the one I ran over!'

I wanted to say, 'And I just found out he's married!' but that would put him in a bad light when it was me who had deceived him, while he, poor man, had had no memory about anything that had happened before I had appeared at his bedside.

He was the vulnerable one. It was me who had taken advantage of his amnesia! Me who had veiled the truth from him! What on earth must he have thought I was doing, visiting him in hospital, taking him home, behaving as if I was someone he was close to? I'd lain with him on the bed, for goodness' sake! We'd kissed! I'd let him believe we'd met before and were lovers. My deception was a thousand times worse than I'd imagined!

'Well that sounds exciting,' Chiara was saying, her voice clipped. 'You can fill me in when I've got more time. But I have to tell you' – she lowered her voice – 'Finn wants to speak to you again.'

'What does he want?'

'He wants to give you some advice about your commission. He's afraid it's a dog-eat-dog world out there in New York . . . that you don't quite know what you're letting yourself in for. With the commission you've taken on.'

'Chiara, I need to move on . . .'

'He simply wants to support you.'

'He thinks he's supporting me, but do you see why I find it stifling?'

'I can see he's a little over-protective of you, yes. I always have. But he cares. I said I'd let you know that he'd like to talk. There. I can't do more than that.'

'Thanks, Chiara.'

She looked at me. 'I've got to go. Oh, we're viewing the flat tomorrow. The survey's been done and Liam wants to measure up for curtains and so on.'

'Exciting!'

'Yes,' she said. 'Yes it is.'

But my heart dipped at the prospect of her moving out. All the heady fantasies of the last couple of weeks were proving to be just that – fantasies. Patrick was married. Finn didn't think I could deal with the New York art world. May's house was full of trinkets that gave me an uneasy feeling. I was still living in a stifling flat in Mile End and unless I pulled myself together and got on with my painting I wouldn't ever earn enough to move somewhere nicer. Worst of all I was possibly the culprit in a hit-and-run incident in which a man had lost his leg. I had told lie after lie.

'I'm going to miss living with you,' Chiara said. 'I'm a bit nervous, truth be told, to be committing at last.' She patted her swelling belly. 'It's all this little one's fault! I'll miss our chats. Our nights in.'

I hugged her. And felt her slipping away from me.

'How's the commission?' Louise asked, the minute Chiara had gone, shouting to be heard across the noise of the pub.

'It's going well, thank you.' I had hardly done any work on it.

'I hear you've been working on the sitting-room floor. Is that working out?'

'It has to, for now.'

'I'd love to see what you're doing sometime.'

She, Guy and Finn all shuffled round the table towards me. 'Have you been to the Turner exhibition?' Louise asked. 'Finn, Guy and I thought we might go next week. If you fancy joining us? It would be good for your inspiration.'

'Thanks, I'll see.' I didn't want to think about work now. I wanted to go home, nurse my misery. I was relieved when my mobile went and I could make an excuse to get away.

'I've just got to pop outside,' I said, 'I've got a weak signal in here.'

*　　*　　*

I stood on the hectic street, police sirens wailing and traffic rumbling past.

Patrick's name had flashed up on my screen.

I stood for a moment staring into the ringing phone. Had Patrick realised that I knew nothing about him? That I was an imposter in his life? I needed to know. I picked up.

'Hi.'

'Why did you run off like that?'

'Why do you think?'

'I've no idea. You left me so suddenly, I was afraid I'd offended you!'

'You've got a wife, Patrick!'

'I thought you knew. You must have known.'

'You didn't tell me you were married!'

'I thought I had! I'm dealing with such a lot. Please, bear with me. It was only when I saw the photo I realised I might not have told you before.'

'About your wife?'

'Yes. I'm sorry if I didn't, but I'm telling you now, aren't I?'

'Isn't it a bit late? After arranging to spend a weekend with me! After letting me kiss you and drive you home?'

'Oh, Ellie,' he said. 'I was sure I must have said. My wife's dead.'

CHAPTER NINETEEN

Although it was late, I found myself calling a cab and going back to Patrick's.

He let me through the main entrance when I rang the bell, and I pushed open the door to his flat, which he'd left ajar.

I found him sitting in his wheelchair looking out over the little balcony, a bottle of champagne in front of him, from which he immediately poured a second glass.

He looked up at me, held out his hand, pulled me towards him and kissed me on the lips. I felt my hand go instinctively to him, stroking his head, loving the feel of his short glossy hair.

'I was so afraid when you ran off like that . . .'

'I'm sorry. I was shocked. You're married . . . there's so little I know about you.'

'*Was* married, which I would have explained, if you hadn't bolted like that!'

I ran my hand through his hair again, no longer able to hold back. I bent down and kissed the top of his head.

'I'm back now though.'

'I know, and I'm glad. Here. Sit down, have some of this Cristal. You need it after that shock.'

We sat side by side, our fingers intertwined, looking out over the river.

'How did she die?' I whispered, after a while. 'She wasn't . . . she couldn't have been in the accident that night? Was she?' I knew this was a crazy question – it would have been mentioned on the news – but the thought would haunt me unless I asked.

He put a hand to his forehead, closed his eyes, frowned.

'No. No, it was two years ago. I was so sure I must have told you.'

'I don't know what I'm supposed to say.'

He shrugged. 'It's OK. You don't have to say anything. I've got over it now. More or less.'

'What happened?'

'Do you want me to tell you?'

'Yes. But only if it's not too painful.'

'It was an accident at sea,' he said.

'Oh! I'm so sorry . . .'

'I don't really want to talk about it too much.'

'Of course. I understand. How awful for you.'

There was a silence. I tried to take in what he had told me. I wanted to ask so much, what kind of accident, when, where. How appalling for him, to have lost his wife, then to be dealing with such a devastating injury.

'It must have been ghastly,' was all I could say.

'Yes it was,' he said. 'We both loved the sea.'

He paused, stood up awkwardly with his crutches, leant on the balcony and gazed out over the river. After a little while he turned and smiled at me, the dimples that I found so irresistible appearing in his cheeks.

'It's OK though, Ellie, it was a while ago now and I'm ready for a new relationship. Come here.'

I went to him, and he put his arm around me, pulling me to him, and kissed me again, long and hard, and as he did so I had an overwhelming urge to heal everything he'd gone through.

'The trouble with having this blasted leg to get used to is I won't be able to go out on the water,' he said at last. 'It'll feel like my wings have been clipped. I'm determined to get back out there just as soon as they've signed me off at the clinic. I'm no good without a boat to muck about in.'

'Even after what happened to your wife? What was her name?'

'Stef. But it hasn't changed how I feel about the sea. It's where I feel closest to her. Oh, sorry, Ellie, that's probably a bit insensitive of me, telling you that. Forgive me.'

'No, it's OK. It's fine.'

'Look, what you have to understand about me is that the sea's in my blood, it always was. Her accident doesn't change that.'

'What exactly happenned?'

I couldn't help it, I needed to know more.

Little lights had come on all over the river and high above it too. The sky was alight with a million tiny beacons like fireflies. Boats passed, lit up, music blaring, you could hear laughter from the decks where people were partying.

'I can't believe I didn't tell you. But then I guess we don't know each other that well. It's so hard to get it all straight in my head. How long we've known each other. What you know and don't know about me. It's ghastly. I still feel I'm sliding about on ice trying to get a foothold – that there are these fragments floating about in a vacuum that need putting together but just keep eluding me.'

'I hardly know anything about you,' I said.

At least this was true.

'No, it was one of our first dates, wasn't it?'

'Yes,' I said, hating myself for lying.

'That night in the pub in Blythburgh,' he said, 'was to be the beginning of the first weekend we'd spend together. We were going to go sailing.'

'Yes.' I wanted him to tell me more, without appearing to probe.

'When I first saw you, we fancied each other immediately, didn't we?'

'We did.'

'You know what though? You're much prettier than I thought at first. You are a million times more gorgeous than I remember. And sweeter. We were going to have such a romantic time in Southwold. But those guys in the pub didn't like the idea, for some reason, I think they felt they had some kind of hold over you, being a local girl. And gorgeous with it. And then that one got a bit heavy with me. And I remember leaving, and you told me not to. But the old drink got the better of me. You were right though, Ellie. Look where it got me, walking off like that!'

'It was a pretty big mistake.'

'It was.'

This was the moment I should tell him we'd never met before I came to see him in hospital. This was the moment I should say I was pretty sure now that my car had hit him on the road that evening. But that I intended to make up for it by being there for him.

'Patrick, I—'

'And you were the only one who came when you heard. Even though you hadn't known me very long. You have no idea how much that means to me.'

He took my face in his hands, and looked into my eyes. His own eyes were so intense. So full of feeling. Then he kissed me and the kiss was long and deep and lovely.

'You're the one I need, Ellie, you can't imagine how grateful I am to you,' he said at last, holding me close to him.

How could I disillusion him after all? When he'd been through so much?

He sat down again, and I leant over the wheelchair, wanting to leave, unable to, wanting to stay. He put his hands up and began to unbutton my shirt, peeling it off.

'You're so lovely,' he said.

His hands on my skin released a warmth that infused my whole body.

I knew now nothing mattered, nothing else in the world. Even if I found out after all that I had had nothing to do with Patrick's accident and owed him nothing, I couldn't have walked away any more.

I would stay with him whatever happened. I would help him learn to walk. I was mesmerised by him. His courage. His determination to get up and get on.

The tragedy in his past fascinated me. The vulnerability in him that was there, just beneath the surface, intrigued me.

I was falling for him.

I moved my hand down to his stump and caressed it, gently, through the bandage, asking him if it hurt.

'Not the way you are touching it,' he whispered. 'I think you're healing it.' And then he pulled me onto his lap.

I could still feel Patrick when I left, on me, in me, his hands, his mouth, I could still smell him. I could feel the way his bandaged leg grazed mine. I couldn't get him out of my mind.

'Come back soon,' he called as I left.

And of course I did go back.

I went back every night the following week. I learnt more and more about Patrick. It was becoming crystal clear that he was right when he said no one else had bothered to visit him. That I was the only one who cared. So I continued to let him think that I was a girl he'd arranged to meet to go sailing with in Southwold. It really seemed immaterial now since in reality we were getting on so well.

We found out we shared musical tastes. It was mostly romantic, mainstream. Ed Sheeran, John Mayer. He liked Beyoncé too, and Adele. I could hear Finn scoff, but it didn't matter. I hadn't realised how freeing it would be to break away from that relationship, how set in our ways we had become. How set in my ways I had become. There was another way, there were new roads ahead and life felt full of promise and a broadening-out that would encompass things I'd never done or dreamt of doing before.

I found out that, in addition to cycling and sailing,

Patrick had circles of friends for each of his interests, distinct groups who he had always met on certain evenings; his golfing buddies, his poker buddies, the guys he met for drinks. 'I'll pick up all those things again once I get used to the prosthetic,' he told me. 'For now, all I need is you.'

He told me that after the sea, his great love was for the Thames, that he had worked on it for a few years before he went abroad and made a fortune getting involved in fish futures, glass eels and other things which were, apparently, now fetching almost as much as gold in futures markets. He explained that he dealt these things online, it didn't involve actually touching or holding or even seeing any fish. 'It's like a currency,' he said. 'We buy and sell, watch the markets, do deals.'

'How strange. To get rich on fish.'

'Strange but true,' he said.

'So that's how you can afford a penthouse apartment in Wapping.'

'Indeed.'

'What did you work as, when you were on the river, Patrick?' We were lying on our fronts on his bed, looking out of the window over the Thames. Pepper was on the floor chewing his favourite rubber bone.

'I was a lighterman.'

'What is a lighterman?'

'A lighterman, my dear, is authorised to carry cargo on the river, whereas a waterman carries passengers.'

'Goodness. I never knew that distinction before.'

A light breeze blew through the windows.

'Anything you want to know about the river you only have to ask me.'

I found his cookery books and he revealed that he was a good cook and liked Pacific rim dishes which he made quickly and efficiently, sitting at the table in his wheelchair, or holding a crutch under one arm. He would text a list of ingredients which I bought on my way back to his after painting all day.

'Can't remember where I put the wok,' he said, one evening. 'Actually I'm not even sure I have one.' He sounded irritable. It sometimes affected him like this, the aftermath of his accident. He was in the kitchen rummaging through a cupboard, which was tricky for him with one arm on the crutch. I looked for it for him, telling him to sit and rest, but there was no wok to be seen and we made do with a frying pan.

'I'm sure I had one,' he shrugged. 'I've always preferred cooking in a wok.'

'It doesn't matter, Patrick, it's delicious anyway,' I said, scooping up mouthfuls of gingery stir-fry, wondering in what other ways his amnesia would rear its head.

'What I want to know about you, though you must have told me before,' he said, 'is, where do you do your painting?'

'Aha. At the moment I do it on the sitting-room floor in my little flat in Mile End.'

'On the *floor*?'

''Fraid so. I'm just a poverty-stricken artist, Patrick. You have to realise that. I don't have great assets.'

'You've got that house by the sea, why don't you go down there and use it?'

I shrugged.

'Maybe, one day. But I have friends and work here. Anyway. It's OK. I manage in the flat, on the floor for now,' I said.

'You need a studio, baby. I've got just the place for you.'

'What do you mean?'

'I told you I'm taking care of a load of studios over on Trinity Buoy Wharf. I'll take you down there and you can choose one. You can't work on the floor if you're going to be big in the art world. I want to see you selling your work for serious money. But first you need a proper place to work.'

Trinity Buoy Wharf, Patrick told me, was on the stretch of the Thames known as Bugsby's Reach.

I looked up into his lovely smiling handsome face and stepped towards him. I put my arms around him and my lips against his.

He really was too good to be true.

CHAPTER TWENTY

We made our first visit to Trinity Buoy Wharf the following week.

Patrick used his crutches as much as possible, rather than depending on the wheelchair. Sometimes, he didn't need the crutches at all, determined to manage on his prosthetic.

'You're doing really well, Patrick.'

'With what?'

'Your walking, of course!'

'Ah, yes! Well, I guess being in tip-top physical condition helps,' he said, grinning at my amazement. 'And a one hundred per cent positive attitude.'

'You can hardly tell you're using the prosthetic. I'm sure you'll soon be running, cycling again!'

'I hope,' he said, pulling me towards him, kissing the top of my head.

*   *   *

I drove, Patrick beside me, navigating. It was a warm May day, and the city was throbbing with music, and traffic and the promise of hot nights out after work.

Trinity Buoy Wharf wasn't far from Wapping, east past the Isle of Dogs then further along the river, over a busy junction.

'You must know it, you being an artist and a Londoner,' Patrick said as we waited for the lights to change.

'No. I don't know it. I never knew about it.'

'Hang a right here, then,' he said. 'It's just before you get to the ExCeL and the cable cars.'

We turned right at the next roundabout and drove between the tall walls of dilapidated brick warehouses, host to buddleia blooming madly through their walls. Then we were there. It was a very different view of the river to the one from Patrick's apartment. Here was an industrial landscape, warehouses, containers, the spikes of The O2 on the other side and the pillars of the cable cars pointing up to the hazy blue sky. Behind us, to the west, the towering blocks of Canary Wharf glinted in the sunlight.

The water looked browner, murkier here than upriver.

'There are whole swathes of the riverside that can't be developed,' Patrick was saying. 'They have protected status. So while you have areas that have been built on that are worth millions, other riverside locations are left to rack and ruin. These warehouses are gradually deteriorating. They are beside what are known as deep-water ports which have to be kept for ships to pick stuff up, ballast and sand and so on. And no one can do a thing about it. What a waste of space, don't you think, when property in London is at such a premium?'

'I'm amazed. I'd thought every spare square inch of the city had been bought up and developed.'

'I know. It's good for struggling artists though, isn't it? It means there's space available for containers. Now, we need to show you the studio. Turn left here.'

We parked in the wide yard flanked on one side by a block made of steel containers painted in vibrant primary colours. On the other sides were older brick buildings and warehouses. 'Those are all dance studios and prop workshops and stuff,' Patrick explained. 'The former Chain and Buoy Store where they made and tested buoys. And see that?' He waved over to the right. 'That's the only lighthouse in London.'

The river smell hit us as we got out of the car – silty mud, city grime and, faintly, frying from the nearby diner.

'The whole area makes you want to look up, doesn't it?' he said, taking my hand.

My heart leapt at the feel of his fingers, the way they curled around mine and squeezed them tightly.

He was right. In London I usually hurried along looking at my feet, deep in thought, hemmed in by buildings. I rarely thought to look at the sky. Here though, everything pointed upwards. The spikes on the dome of The O2 opposite. The columns that held the cable cars moving in a continuous stream like spiders crawling busily along a high-slung thread of silk up in the sky. Pylons marching across to the east in what might have been a perfect example of perspective, each apparently smaller than the one in front. The overcrowded city had, here, taken to the skies.

Things were in perpetual motion; the stream of traffic on

the A13, the red Docklands trains hurrying up and over the old wharves, the boats nosing their way through the surface of the Thames, planes droning overhead from City Airport. Beneath us the Thames water was a deep toffee brown, patchy in places with lighter cloud where the mud had been churned up.

'This is an old lightship,' Patrick said, showing me the vast hull of a red container ship with a construction like a lighthouse on top. Moored with ropes thicker than I'd thought existed, over a foot in diameter.

'And over there' – he lifted my hand and pointed to the other side of the river – 'is the marina where I keep a speedboat and one of my yachts. You can paint in situ here. Follow me.'

He pulled me by the hand inside the lighthouse and up the stairs.

When we got to the top we could hear the gentle sound of the circles of Tibetan Singing Bells.

'This piece of music is supposed to play for a thousand years with no repetition,' Patrick said. 'Composed for the turn of the millennium by Jem Finer – remember him? He was in The Pogues. He was commissioned to write this piece that would play forever. Lie down.'

We lay on the floor and listened.

'It gives you a sense of belonging to something bigger, more vital than our own little lives, don't you think?' Patrick said. 'You didn't know there was this side to London, did you? Bet you didn't know it had a lighthouse. Michael Faraday, the famous scientist, carried out experiments here. Funny, isn't it, there's a kind of symmetry between this little nook and your aunt's house in Southwold. They've both got a lighthouse, they both face east, they both border a body of water.'

I looked at him, trying to remember how much I'd told him about May's house and its position in Southwold.

'Only her house is a lot more salubrious than the tin box I'm going to show you in a minute.'

What had I told him? I didn't remember anything, other than mentioning that he could stay down there when he got better, that night in the hospital. And that was before he was conscious. I must have talked about it some other time. And May's house was after all quite distinctive, on its own as he said, facing the sea, to the east.

'That there is the old Chain and Buoy Store,' he said. 'You should see the size of the chains it used to store in there. Phenomenal!'

'It's certainly the perfect place for me to paint,' I said, hurrying after him back across the wharf. 'No more forays down to the river to take photos. I can sketch right here and collect debris washed up on the shore.'

He led me to a line of steel containers at the edge of the river, past an authentic American diner wagon selling burgers, arty-looking students standing about outside.

'They've been bloody clever recognising the potential of these metal boxes,' Patrick said. 'All they had to do was replace one end with glass doors to let in light, put a bit of cheap carpet on the floors and bingo – it's an office. But they're cheap enough for poverty-stricken artists like you to rent. I'm afraid my units are a little tucked away, over here beside the River Lea – the tributary once known as Bow

Creek. It's funny how once you've seen these containers they appear everywhere – on the backs of lorries, on ships down on the Thames, stacked up here into a whole micro-city tucked away in this enclave by the river.'

People were using the containers as studios and as offices and as recording studios. Some of the units were piled up into blocks with balconies, and had been decorated with pot plants and wind chimes. They had huge bolts that ran the length and breadth of the doors so they could be securely locked. Several had had porthole windows cut into their sides.

Patrick was going to help me take myself so much more seriously as an artist.

'How much?'

'I don't want to charge you,' he said. He held my shoulders, looked down into my eyes, the little lines at the side of his mouth twitching. 'It doesn't feel right.'

'But . . . surely . . . you have to . . .'

'I told you, I want to give you something in return for what you've done for me since the accident. You're going to produce your best work here, and I'll gain from that, once I get you new clients. I can charge you a little commission if it makes you feel better. But it's mainly because I owe you, Ellie, for being here for me. Come. Here we are. Your very own studio.'

He held his fob up and the door clicked open and I followed him into the space. A steel rectangle, lit at one end by a glass panel.

'What do you reckon?'

'It's perfect, Patrick.'

He came over to me.

'It's all yours,' he said, gesturing around the unit.

'I can't accept. Not unless I pay you the proper rent.'

'You have to accept.'

'Why?'

'Because if you don't you won't get your New York commission done.'

I wondered what twist of fate had allowed me to bump into him, literally – I felt a tiny shudder as I remembered again the odd way we'd met – just when I needed him most in my life. My secret sat coiled up in my heart, like one of the massive chains he'd pointed out to me, but I would leave it there. He didn't need to know. No one needed to know.

'Why are you doing this for me, Patrick?'

'Why are you asking?'

I couldn't reply. Then he pulled me towards him, pressed his mouth to my ear and whispered, 'It's because we're falling in love.'

CHAPTER TWENTY-ONE

Pepper and I spent most of the time when I wasn't working at Patrick's flat now.

I fetched Patrick his breakfast and prepared him his baths. I redid the dressing on his better leg, leaving the amputation for the nurses who visited while I was painting. I helped him to and from his wheelchair. I convinced myself I was doing more than enough to make up for the damage I'd caused. And anyway we were in love.

We sat on his small balcony and he pointed out things on the river while we sipped champagne cocktails.

We had the river in common. I painted it, he was a treasure trove of knowledge about it.

'Those things there, those wooden structures that look like rafts that appear at low tide, they are called passive driftwood collectors. Only sometimes they trap dead bodies instead,' he told me one night.

'Ick! Creepy!'

'Yes. You'd be amazed at how often they wash up. Suicides, horrible murders, drowned babies, foetuses.'

'Patrick, stop, I don't want to hear.'

'Sorry. Though I have to tell you, you always know if a corpse is a man or a woman, however decomposed, by which way up it floats.'

'Don't, Patrick.'

'A woman floats face up while a man turns over and gazes down into the deep after he dies. Funny, that.'

'How do you know?'

'It's a known fact among river folk. Stef – my wife – for example, after she'd drowned, even though it was at sea, and in salt water, she floated . . .'

'Patrick! Please!' How on earth could he talk so flippantly about his wife's death like this? It must be his macho way of pretending he could cope with it.

'Tell me something nice instead.'

'I'll tell you something historical then. See over there,' he said, waving downriver, 'that's called Cuckold's Point. And for good reason – when the men were at sea their wives slept around. That's something I would never stand for. I hope you are listening, Ellie.'

And I laughed, relieved he was being light-hearted.

But when I looked up he was staring at me, frowning. 'I mean it,' he said, quietly.

Now on my painting days, I took Pepper to the studio, and spent the day working on my painting.

My container was more secluded than some of the others, at the end of the wharf, facing the tributary, the River Lea, rather than the Thames itself, which meant it was comparatively quiet. I could work without being disturbed. If I left the door open I could look straight out onto the water when the tide was in, at other times, its walls and ladders exposed, right down to the muddy shore.

I liked my quiet corner away from the rest of the wharf. If I wanted company there was a hive of artistic activity around the corner, dancers coming and going to the big studio, people filming in the diner. Prop makers, artists, writers and musicans all bustled about, popping out of their containers to get a coffee from the café, or to chat beside the lighthouse.

It was the perfect place to work.

And one of the massive advantages of having a studio with steel walls was that I could fix my canvas up using the massive super-force magnets I'd sourced from an online provider. I had a superstitious abhorrence for using anything with a point, such as a nail, to fasten my pictures to walls. I also believed frames restricted or trapped my work and I had stopped using them.

If I felt any residual anxiety about being given this perfect workspace, it was due to guilt at the strange way it had fallen into my hands.

But I countered this by reminding myself that Patrick was benefiting from me too – I was caring for him, doing his shopping, looking after him. Making sure he did the exercises the physio had recommended (she had left a sheet with little diagrams).

And of course, at night, I gave him everything he liked.

'He wanted me to have it,' I told Chiara one evening when I'd gone back to the Mile End flat for clean clothes.

We sat in the sitting room while Pepper rolled about on the sofa tangling himself in the throw we'd put over it to disguise the grotty grey cover.

'He's given you a studio for nothing?!'

'Yup. He sees my painting as something to invest in, I guess.'

'Look at him!' Chiara laughed, as Pepper dropped onto the floor in the throw, making a funny wriggling sausage shape on the floor.

I went over to disentangle him.

'Mad little dog. By the way, Frank's nurse phoned and says he's being transferred to another hospital for a few more weeks. She asked if you were OK to keep Pepper longer. He's been worrying about him.'

'Of course I am. I'm very attached,' I said, fondling Pepper, who licked me on the cheek. 'Actually, Chiara, Patrick wants me and Pepper to move in with him. He wants us to do everything together.'

'He wants you to move in? Ellie!'

'What?'

'It just seems, I don't know . . . A little over the top. You haven't known him that long.'

'It's not to do with how long we've known each other. You're moving in with Liam, and I'd either have to move out of here or find someone to share with. This just feels right.'

What Patrick had told me about his wife, about his life before he met me, and the tiny snippets I was learning about his childhood, made me love him all the more. He had been through so much, but was determined not to let any of it hold him back.

'Doesn't it put you a bit in his debt? Accepting a studio from him? Living in his flat?'

'He doesn't think so. He's got plenty of money, and he wants to share. He's got contacts in the art world as well. He's not stupid, he's in business, he's probably seen an opportunity in me, and knows we're going to be of mutual benefit.'

'That doesn't sound very romantic.'

'Oh it's romantic alright!' I said, thinking of our nights together, nights of exhausting passion, exploring every millimetre of each other's bodies as if we simply couldn't get enough, staying awake until dawn and even then starting all over again.

I looked at her and she must have seen in my eyes how heartfelt my words were.

'Well, I must say you're looking well. You've got that lover's glow! I'd like to meet him one day,' she said.

'Of course, you will,' I said, and we left it at that.

I got to the studio early on my painting days, while the river was still waking, the sounds only just beginning. I drove, taking Pepper with me. Sometimes a mist, rather like whipped egg whites, lay upon the river's surface, softening all the outlines, the hard things only looming into focus as the sun began to disperse it. I learnt to love this time in the morning when I could feel alone in the big city. I'd stand, Pepper at my feet on his lead, before anyone else arrived, and breathe the acrid smells of the city, listen to the rattle of the trains on the Docklands Light Railway. Or the slapping of the river against the walls as a boat went past, invisible in the mist.

I couldn't believe how brilliantly meeting Patrick had turned out. It must have been meant, because now I had a studio to work in.

As well as a perfect lover.

It only occurred to me fleetingly as I let myself into my studio what an odd space it was – that you could feel like a commodity in these metal boxes when they were shut from the outside.

My painting was beginning to take shape too. I reckoned I needed another eight weeks or so and then it would be ready to ship to New York. The opening was in August. School would have finished for summer. I'd already booked my flight. If this thing with Patrick had never happened it would have been all I'd have been able to think about, a bright spot in front of me, not giving much consideration to what might come before or after, as it was such a massive achievement for me, a commission for a painting to be hung in a large trendy restaurant in the Meatpacking District.

As it was, I felt I was walking on clouds, on a high, dizzy with the euphoria of being in love.

I finished work at around five, then drove back to Patrick's, stopping to get basic things for our dinner from a corner shop.

I felt the future I'd been hoping for that night on the way down to Aunty May's open up before me. In spite of, no, *because of* the unthinkable thing I'd done that night.

It was all OK though, because it was meant.

*   *   *

'No! No!'

'What is it?"

I'd woken up in a sheen of sweat. It was night, though never completely dark in Patrick's apartment, with the lights of the city shining outside our window.

I'd been dreaming, reliving the thump on the car. In my dream, Patrick's leg had been sliced off below the knee and was flying through the air to lie on the verge in its black leather Converse trainer. I was out of the car, trying desperately to hold the severed leg in my hands and to fix it back onto Patrick's bloodied stump as he stood laughing down at me, leaning against the car as if nothing had happened, as if he was completely unaware that his leg had been sliced in half by my careless driving.

'What's up, Ellie? You cried out in your sleep?'

The real Patrick was leaning up on one elbow, looking at me with concern, his face lit by the neon lights of the city outside.

'Bad dream.'

'You shouted out.'

'It was horrid.' I buried my face in his chest and he put his hand in my hair.

'Ssshhhh,' he said. 'Everything's alright.'

I lay and tried to rationalise, remind myself there was no conclusive evidence that I had hit him. And that even if I had I was doing all I could to atone.

And he kissed me and we spent the rest of the night clawing at each other as if we couldn't bear the fact there was skin and flesh between us, as if we wanted to crawl inside each other's souls.

*   *   *

Often, over the first few days after I started working at the studio, Patrick would call me, unable to wait until I got back. Always when I saw his name flash onto my phone, my stomach somersaulted.

'Come now,' he would say, and I did, I dropped everything and went to him.

One day, as I was clearing up the studio he called and said, 'I want to take you to Oblix.'

'Oblix?'

'It's the restaurant at the top of the Shard. You won't get better than that. There's nothing to eat in the flat. So let's go somewhere we can eat haute cuisine and drink good champagne.'

'Wow. Isn't that expensive?'

'Ellie, money is the least of my worries. Come home immediately and get changed.'

And I did.

We must have given off some kind of aura, because everywhere we went people smiled at us, chatted to us, as if they wanted a little bit of what we had and were curious to get to know how we'd achieved it. Love is a very infectious thing.

'Let me get the door for you,' the taxi driver might say, leaping from his driving seat, coming round to help Patrick in. Or waiters brought us coffees and digestivos at the end of meals, saying 'On the house' with a smile.

In the more up-market restaurants waiters moved discreetly between tables holding ice buckets with white starched cloths over their arms. Patrick knew exactly which wines to order for each course, conversing quietly with the sommelier about grapes and chateaux and vintages and then plumping for something extortionate, as if money was no object.

Which it didn't appear to be.

'We'll have the Meursault with the starter and a bottle of Nuits Saint Georges with the main. And perhaps a Marsala with the dessert.'

He thought nothing of paying huge amounts for wine we didn't even finish.

Or he'd order bottles of vintage champagne, and if it wasn't chilled properly he'd send it back. Sometimes I felt embarrassed at his total confidence bordering on arrogance with the waiters, but he thought nothing of demanding the best service, and the waiters never seemed to mind. They seemed to like being in our orbit.

'We're paying for it. It's what they expect, Ellie.'

I ate things I'd never eaten before. Lobster, and langoustine. Monkfish and panna cotta and minimalist meals where everything was almost too pretty to put in your mouth. Patrick would press me to try things, urging me to change my mind if I did as I was used to and plumped for the cheapest thing on the menu.

'You don't want to go for that. Look, this will be good, the halibut with the truffle sauce.'

Sugar cages and crystallised flowers and purees and jus.

I wasn't really all that interested in the food. I was only waiting for the meals to finish so we could sit up close to one another in the taxi, or sometimes on what Patrick called his 'plebby days' on the Tube, and travel back to his apartment with him.

Patrick was introducing me to a whole other side of life I had never experienced before in my previous role as struggling artist and teacher. He pointed out that the most expensive restaurants also had art on their walls and suggested I collect their cards so I could invite them to my next exhibition, or make proposals for commissions to them. He knew about business and applied his knowledge to my art so that I felt it was something valuable, marketable as well as cultured.

The days passed in a blur, working, eating at good restaurants, lying with Patrick on his massive bed in his apartment, stroking his lovely, toned body. I marvelled at his bone structure, at his arm muscles, at the dips and rises in his back. I couldn't get enough of the smell of him.

And he made me laugh.

We were on our way to another meal in Knightsbridge on the Piccadilly Line. 'Have you noticed,' Patrick asked, his arm around me, so I was clamped to him, and never wanted to move away, 'how the Tube announcements get more refined the further west you go? She starts to say "alight" instead of "get off" and weather is suddenly "inclement" instead of "bad".'

'I never noticed before.'

'They tailor it deliberately to the clientele. The people who clean the tracks – fluffers, they're called – they say the stuff they sweep up gets more expensive the further west they go. So in the East End it's all man-made fibres, but beyond Hyde Park Corner it's cashmere and linen and silk.'

'Really?'

'No kidding.'

I laughed. 'You know such a lot about this city, Patrick. Did you grow up here?'

He stared at me, as if I was losing my mind, and for a second I felt ashamed, as if I'd asked him something that was crossing a line rather than a simple chatty request for banal information about his life.

'I grew up in Southwold, of course,' he told me. 'How do you think I knew your aunt?'

'*What?*'

I tried to remember if he'd told me this before, and if so in what context it had come up.

'Everyone in Southwold knew your aunt,' he said. 'With her posse of happy foster children.'

There was a clipped edge to his voice when he said this and I looked at him, but then he smiled. Pulled me to him so hard my mouth was buried in the fabric of his jacket. I pulled away and looked up at him.

'Don't look so worried, Ellie – in a small town, everyone knows everyone.'

'But . . . what do you know about my aunt?'

'She was famous, Ellie. Or infamous perhaps. The artist with the foster kids. She was always out on the beach or down on the jetties, surrounded by children, picnicking and giving the appearance of the perfect home-maker and surrogate mother. And then of course there was all that business, with the drowning, and her apportioning blame on some poor kid . . . and she ended up – hey . . . I'm not upsetting you, am I?'

I thought of Daisy on the gravestone and the note with 'A piece of you' written on it.

199

'I don't know. I don't want to have my memories tainted. I used to love going to stay with her.'

'I'm sure you did. That cute house right on the beach that everyone wanted to live in! But she ended up in a psychiatric hospital so it didn't do her all that much good after all. She was accused of stuff, Ellie – neglect, as far as I remember. But hey, stop looking so concerned. It was probably partly village gossip. You only have to be a little bit different in a small community like that and people have it in for you and drive you mad.'

'Where were you living then, while all this was happening?' I asked.

'Put it this way,' he said. 'We weren't all as privileged as you London kids who came down for the weekends.'

'But . . .'

'Shhh. Hey, we need to get off. Come on.' He tugged me out of my seat and we jumped down onto the platform.

Later, when we were back at his apartment, he went to get us glasses of something to drink in bed. I pulled out the leather album I'd noticed tucked into the bottom of his suitcase under the framed photo of his wife when I'd unpacked it. There might be clues about where Patrick had grown up in here. There was little else in the flat that retained any indication of his childhood. Little that indicated anything about Patrick's life. It was so male, so minimalist.

I opened the album.

'Birth Book' was scrawled across the first page in ink.

I began to flick through.

Bingo! Here were old photographs, colours faded, of

babies and children – I assumed one of them must be Patrick – and in the background the familiar landscape of Southwold with its groynes along the beach and the lighthouse towering above everything in the town.

So he *had* grown up there!

I began to turn the pages. There was Patrick in a pram. It was so obviously him, with his shining eyes and his black hair, it made me smile. We were meant to be together! We had probably played together on the sand as kids!

I began to turn the pages further.

And since he had told me he was two years older than me, it was quite likely we had seen each other down there, as children. This was extraordinary. I must tell him!

A shadow fell over me and I looked up to see Patrick in the doorway, his crutch under one arm, holding an ice bucket and glasses on a tray.

'Patrick, this is amazing . . .' I began. 'We probably knew each other as kids!'

'What do you think you're looking at?'

I stopped, stunned by the flint in his voice.

'I wanted to see what you looked like as a little child,' I said, taken aback.

He dumped the tray down on the table and took the album from me.

'Don't EVER look at my things without asking again.'

The next time I looked, the album was gone.

CHAPTER TWENTY-TWO

Louise was waiting at my studio when I arrived the next morning. She had a Styrofoam cup of coffee in her hand and she was sitting on a buoy staring at the men down on the Clippers preparing to carry boatloads of tourists up and down the river. Gulls were hanging around overhead ready to swoop on any unexpected pickings from the slurry that was being ferried onto barges waiting in the mouth of the River Lea.

'Hey,' I said. 'What are you doing here?'

I was still wrung out from the contortions with Patrick. After his outburst, he had apologised profusely, taken me by the hand, asked me to help him to bed where we had made desperate love as if we were both shocked, or wounded, by his outburst and needed to heal each other and console ourselves.

'I'm so sorry, Ellie. It's to do with my childhood, I don't want to be reminded,' he'd said to me as he worked his tongue down my body.

'I understand.'

'I should have burnt those photos, those reminders. I want to leave all the pain back there, not to have it uncovered all over again.' He reached my navel. 'Do you understand?'

'Yes!' I said. 'It's OK. Please don't stop.'

'You promise you'll leave it alone?'

'Oh yes, Patrick. Yes.'

I could still smell him this morning, even though I'd showered, a waft of fresh sweat and almonds catching in the air as I moved. I drew it in. I could still taste the tangy skin of his stump. The dressing had been removed now and I'd licked it, believing somehow that my attention to it would heal it, would take away the harm he had suffered as a child, and the awful injury he was enduring. I would make up for everything, the physical damage to his lovely body on top of any emotional pain he'd gone through. I'd never felt such a strong mix of passion and compassion for anyone before. I wanted to carry on feeling like this, I didn't want anything to distract me.

But I couldn't ignore Louise when she'd come all the way over here to see me.

Pepper, spotting her, began to growl.

'Pepper, Louise is a friend. Stop it!'

'Blimey,' said Louise, standing up. 'He can be quite vicious for a little dog. So you've landed yourself a neat little studio. This must be costing you a pretty penny?'

'Not really,' I said. 'It was a favour, from a friend.'

She raised her eyebrows.

'I came to see how the painting was coming on, for the New York commission.'

'Right.'

'Can I see what you've done so far?'

She was sipping from her cup, covering her face so it was impossible to see what she was thinking. But she must have known how uncomfortable she was making me. I didn't like showing people my work until I was confident I'd cracked what I was trying to achieve – she knew this about me from our art college days.

'I'm not sure, I'm sorry, Louise,' I said. 'You know what I'm like, I feel a bit superstitious showing my work before it's really taken shape.'

'I'm not going to rip it off if that's what you think!'

'I didn't think you would.' I wondered if she had any idea of the punch this delivered, the double whammy, the suggestion that I was so arrogant as to think anyone would want to copy my work combined with the stab that it wasn't worth plagiarising. I tried not to rise to it. 'It's not that, it's a creative thing. You know what it's like, you need things to germinate, sometimes having comments from other people before you're ready can throw you off course.'

'I came halfway across London! I wanted to check it out, see how you were getting on, see if I could help in any way.'

I looked into her face. Her tan had faded and there were dark shadows under her eyes and she wasn't wearing her usually immaculately applied make-up. Without it she looked older, more tired.

'Louise, is everything OK? With you and Guy?'

She shrugged.

'Since you ask, we're finished.'

'Oh Louise, I'm sorry.'

She drained her coffee, threw away the cup, sat back down and put her face in her hands.

'Look.' She held out her left hand. The beautiful ring had gone. 'He decided I was too "arty" for him. He bumped into an ex from Oz and they got back together. Just like that. So I'm alone again. And I'm trying to get my work off the ground and it's hard. Then when I heard you were struggling with the commission, I thought I might be able to help a bit with yours, since it sounds like you've been busy and haven't had as much time as you'd like to . . . Finn said he thought you were stalling a bit. He said you've been distracted by the cottage and all that.'

'Oh, that's so kind of you!' I gave her a hug. I'd misjudged her. 'It's OK though, really. I'm on track, I think.'

'Finn said you hadn't been at home for a while. He's been round to find you a few times but you're never there.'

'Poor Finn,' I said. 'I wish he didn't still worry about me.'

She shrugged. 'I guess he still feels a bit protective towards you.'

She said the word 'protective' as if it was compensation for something I would prefer him to be feeling. She was wrong. I didn't want Finn to feel anything for me any more. It was easier if we could have a clean break, hard though this was proving to be because our lives, our work, our friends had always been so intertwined.

'Well he's really no need,' I said. 'Honestly. I'm fine.'

'Anyway, can I see what you're doing?'

Louise was being nice. But it made me feel awkward. I should have been able to say, *thanks so much for your kind thought, Louise, but at the moment I don't need your help, though it's lovely to have your offer and I'll bear it in mind.* But I felt there was more to her interest than was apparent. You couldn't be clear with someone who was being murky with you.

And then she proved my suspicions correct: 'Chiara said you were traumatised by something that weekend. The weekend we all came down to your cottage. She said she hardly sees you, that you're avoiding things and you need support to get you through. So I've come to see what I can do.'

'*Chiara* said?'

Chiara was my most trusted friend. I couldn't believe she would have told Louise about the anxieties I'd expressed to her on the way back to London in the car.

But how else would Louise have this information?

I capitulated, opened the door of my studio, gestured at her to follow me.

'Come in. What did Chiara say?'

She followed me.

She stood for some time staring at my canvas. It was the biggest piece of work I had ever done and it had required two trips to bring all my materials down from the flat in the Micra.

I was pleased with it. I'd been building up the layers gradually, concentrating on the paint, on the surfaces. It wouldn't be anywhere near complete until I'd done several more layers, and worked on those, so what Louise saw now wasn't representative of the end product I was aiming for. I was glad of this in part – it meant she wasn't in a position to pass judgement, which might be off-putting, and if she tried, I could brush it off. I steeled myself for her reaction, but she seemed transfixed by the work, and didn't speak. She walked up and down, viewing it from different perspectives. At last she turned round.

'*When* did they say the deadline was?'

'August,' I said.

'That's pretty soon.'

She might not have known that I'd found it difficult, getting paintings into that exhibition when she hadn't. Or that I'd been embarrassed that I'd won a commission she and Finn would have killed for, but she was certainly making sure I suffered for it now.

I wanted to get on, but at the same time I had a burning curiosity to know what Chiara had said to her.

'It's OK,' I said. 'I have it under control. You don't have to worry for me.'

'You seem to think we're all in your way, Ellie. It isn't like that. I want to help you. Chiara wants to help you.'

'Thanks, honestly I appreciate it, but at the moment I don't need help.'

'You have to face facts: if you're charged with a hit-and-run, you won't get into the States. They will need someone else for the commission. The sooner they know the better. No point in burying your head in the sand.'

'I don't know what you're talking about.'

'The hit-and-run thing that happened when you were driving down to Southwold. Chiara told me you hadn't gone to the police –I guess you were afraid it would affect your chance of getting into the States, and now you haven't confessed, you're afraid it's too late, that if you tell them, you'll be done for whatever you call it, perverting the course of justice or whatever!'

I stared at her.

'That's all been sorted,' I said quietly. 'It was something I was worried about but it's OK. It's all been taken care of.'

But had it? My stomach contracted, the old anxiety. Would it ever go away?

'OK, hon. No need to sound so jumpy.'

Don't call me 'hon'! I felt like shouting at her.

'I really need to get on, Louise. As you've just reminded me, I haven't got much time left. I need to catch up.'

'OK,' she shrugged. 'But, Ellie, please don't take this badly, we all care about you.'

'Thanks.'

'And we all want to meet your new guy. Bring him to the pub, why don't you? You've kept him to yourself for too long. We're beginning to think you're hiding him from us deliberately.'

'OK.'

'See you around then.'

'Yes, see you.'

It took me a little while to regain my peace of mind after she had left. I went up to the café with Pepper and got myself a cup of tea and a muffin.

I sat outside on the wall beside the River Lea for a while, staring at the water. The tide was up. It was warm and there was a brisk breeze bringing with it the earthy smell of slurry. Cloud shadows raced across the surface of the river turning it murky grey, and then raced off, leaving it sparkling again in the sunlight. A radio played somewhere, 'We are stardust', and there was the clanking of building work and the rumble of trains. The cable cars moved steadily in a stream high up in the air. Out on the Thames, tourist boats passed on their way down to the Thames Barrier, sending a wash across the river and up the creek so waves splashed up the wall.

I tore pieces off the muffin and threw them up in the air for the gulls, who caught the pieces mid-flight. I tried to get the dreamy feeling I'd had when I left Patrick's this morning to come back. It was OK, I told myself. Patrick was the only person in the world who could pursue the investigation into the accident, if he wanted to. If he did, I would of course confess to the fear that I was the culprit. Even then, nothing would change how we felt towards one another.

I must not let Louise's comments bother me.

I remembered then something Finn once told me about the significance of the evil eyes painted onto the sides of boats in Turkey. They were not simply to ward off evil spirits, but specifically to ward off the vagaries of envy. People painted them on to their boats when they had had good fortune, because they knew that this good fortune was ammunition for other people's envy. Next time I was due to see Louise, I decided, I would need to wear an evil eye.

I went back to my studio and sat and stared at my canvas and could no longer remember what on earth I was thinking when I started it.

All I could think was that the hit-and-run had not gone away. Even if Patrick wasn't interested in it.

It was hanging around me the way the gulls were hanging around the slurry from the bulldozers on the other side of the River Lea, waiting for their moment to swoop.

CHAPTER TWENTY-THREE

Patrick was waiting for me when I got back to his apartment. I'd stopped and bought bags of provisions. I was going to cook for him so we didn't have to go out, and could move seamlessly from dinner to bed, or the other way round.

'You're an angel,' he said as I threw pasta into a pan and sliced smoked salmon, one of the few dishes I knew how to cook. With a little crème fraîche and some dill it would taste pretty good. It was deceptively simple. I chatted as I cooked, about my painting, filling him in on the visit from Louise, missing out the hit-and-run bit of course, but telling him how she had made me worry I wouldn't be finished in time.

'Who needs enemies when your friends behave like that?' Patrick said.

He was standing behind me, and he leant over, kissed me on the ear, took my earlobe in his mouth and nipped it gently.

I dropped the wooden spoon and turned to him.

'It's time you moved in here,' he whispered. 'Then you won't have to put up with them and can concentrate on your art.'

He took me in his arms as I buried my face in his chest.

'All you have to do,' Patrick said, taking my hand, and moving it towards the keypad on my phone, 'is ring the estate agents and tell them you're moving out. They'll have a waiting list of tenants desperate to pay ridiculous sums of money for a flat in Mile End, so they won't be bothered.'

'But isn't it a bit soon?'

I was remembering Chiara's reaction when I'd told her Patrick wanted me to move in. Yet, living with Patrick in his Wapping apartment was more than I could have hoped for – a dream come true.

'Ellie. You've just said, your friends have let you down. I always say better one you can trust than a million you can't.'

And he was right.

It only took a phone call to the estate agents who looked after the flat the next day, and I had done it. They said they would be able to find some new tenants keen to move in as soon as I wanted.

Chiara and Liam were moving into their new flat in London Fields at the end of the month. Chiara and I met at the flat one evening after work. She had already packed her clothes into suitcases that stood by the door and when I came she offered to make coffee.

I began to collect my bits and pieces together as she filled her espresso pot.

'So we're both moving on.'

'Yup.'

'You're decided, are you, Ellie?'

'Yes, I am.'

'But we haven't even met him.'

'You will do.' I still felt betrayed by her telling Louise a confidence. But I didn't want to bring it up. I continued to take things off the shelves, place them in the cardboard boxes I'd gathered from the Tesco Metro down the road.

'It feels odd you moving in with someone I've never set eyes on,' she persisted. 'Ellie, I hope this hasn't anything to do with that night in Southwold, has it?'

I glanced up at her.

'What do you mean?'

'The night you thought you'd hit someone in your car?'

'You shouldn't have told Louise about that.'

'I didn't tell Louise you'd hit anyone! I just explained why you were distracted that weekend! That you were having another of your irrational fears that you were responsible for something you couldn't possibly be.'

'Louise wouldn't understand that.'

'OK. Look. I'm sorry, Ellie. You matter to me. Let's please stay friends. Bring him to the pub at least, please?'

I stopped packing and folded my arms across my chest. Adopted my best teacher pose.

'I'm OK, you know,' I said. 'It's just perhaps difficult for you all to accept that I'm moving on, starting a new kind of life. I'm happy, Chiara, happier than I've ever been.'

'And I'm glad for you.'

'I'm happy for you too, of course, that you're settling

down with Liam. I would just like you all to be happy for me.'

'We are. We would be, if you weren't keeping us in the dark about this man.'

'OK, I'll bring him to the pub,' I said.

'Promise?'

'Promise.'

'Because it's important to me we stay friends.'

'Me too.'

'I want you to be godmother to my child.'

I stared at her, my mouth open.

'Oh, Chiara! That's so lovely! Oh! I don't know what to say. Really?'

'Really. Though of course not in a religious way, Liam wouldn't stand for that. Fairy godmother, he calls it. Will you be?'

'I am honoured. Totally.' And I was. The request had brought tears to my eyes.

And we hugged each other.

By the end of the month both Chiara and I had left the Mile End flat. She had moved into the London Fields place with Liam, who she'd been with for six years, and I'd moved in with Patrick, who I'd been with for just over six weeks. My painting things were in the studio and everything else I owned was in his flat. Including Pepper.

'Now I'm living with you, Patrick,' I said, 'I'd like you to meet my friends.'

'Why?'

'Because they are curious about you.'

'Why are they curious?'

'Because you are special to me, and they care about me, I suppose.'

'Who are these friends? Not the ones who let you down, I hope. Not the ones who poor scorn on your painting?'

'The ones who I was at college with – there's Chiara, my Italian friend, and Liam, her fiancé and soon to become father to her child. There's Louise who, well, she can be a bit complex. But I used to go out with them every week, and they miss me, and they want to meet you.'

He finally agreed to pop into the pub on Wednesday night for a quick drink – 'If you promise you'll come for dinner with me on Thursday. I want to take you to Moro's.'

We arranged to meet at Wetherspoon's as usual. It seemed a little down-market, now I was getting used to frequenting the high-end eateries of London, but it was important to me that my friends were comfortable with the venue, and none of them had much money.

Chiara and Liam were already there when I arrived, sitting hand in hand leafing through a baby clothes catalogue, and Louise was there with Finn sitting on the far side of an enormous table, which meant we were all far apart and would be struggling to hear each other's conversations.

I wasn't sure how Finn would react to meeting Patrick. I knew it would be awkward for him, but he would have to meet him sometime, now he was a fixture in my life.

I felt my heart swell with pride as Patrick swung in on his crutches beside me. He was looking disarmingly handsome in a deep blue shirt, one of his Paul Smith ones, which complemented his eyes, and an Armani jacket and trousers. He stood out among my bohemian crowd, who looked, in his presence, scruffy and thrown together in their eclectic outfits made up of vintage finds and bits and pieces from H&M or Primark.

Patrick smiled his beautiful smile, shook everyone by the hand and bought a round of drinks, and I could see them assessing him, wanting to work him out, wanting to understand how I'd pulled someone so different from our usual crowd. He came and sat next to me and put his arm around me and placed a chilled bottle of wine in front of me in an ice bucket, and two glasses.

'So tell me,' Chiara said. She was sitting closest to us and she leant over so we could hear above the noise of the bar. 'How exactly did you two meet?'

'We met through friends in Southwold,' Patrick said quickly. 'Ellie and I hit it off straight away.' He smiled, pulled me towards him. 'And when I had my accident she was the only person who came to see me in hospital. The only person prepared to put herself out to help me recuperate.'

'Your accident?' Chiara asked. She glanced quickly at me. 'Is that how you . . .?'

'Yes,' said Patrick, smiling. 'It's how I lost my leg. Don't worry, we call a spade a spade, don't we, Ellie, because there's no point hiding your head in the sand.'

'Of course,' I said. I could feel Chiara's eyes on me.

'Ellie's like my guardian angel,' Patrick said. 'She came to me just when I needed her. She's the first person I've really loved since I lost my wife.'

'*Lost* your wife? You mean . . .?'

'She died,' said Patrick.

There was an awkward silence during which even the bustle at the bar seemed to fade.

'I'm so sorry,' Chiara said. 'Was she. . .?'

'No, she wasn't in *this* accident,' Patrick said, waving his hand over his right leg.

He squeezed my hand under the table. 'It's OK. It was two years ago now. Babe' – he was looking at me – 'get me a bag of crisps, will you? I need something to disguise the flavour of this horrible wine.'

'Of course.'

I got up to go to the bar and left Chiara and Patrick chatting.

Later, after we'd had a few drinks and the conversation had moved on to more casual topics, Chiara made a gesture and I realised she wanted me to follow her to the loo.

'Are you OK?' she asked as we stood in front of the mirrors in the women's toilets.

'Of course.'

'He's traumatised,' she said. 'He's lost a leg. And a wife. Aren't you a little out of your depth?'

'I'm fine.'

'I hope you don't think you're somehow responsible for healing him emotionally, or even physically – it would be just like you . . .'

'What are you getting at?'

'He seems very needy. You quite often feel you have to rescue people. Like Frank, with Pepper.'

'He's not needy,' I said. 'He's incredibly positive and in control. And don't you think he's pretty damn hot?'

'Well, yes, he's nice-looking.'

'And buff.' I felt a little drunk. I felt as if I was the cat who had got the cream. Chiara was jealous. Everyone was jealous.

'OK. Yes, Ellie, he's nice. He's fit and he looks like he's got money. And if you're sure you're happy, that's all that matters.'

'I am. I am happy.'

'Good.'

'So let's get back. You wanted to meet him, so let's go and talk to him.'

I started to walk away from her out of the loos.

'It's just losing a wife to meningitis is shocking, so sudden, so unexpected,' Chiara went on, coming after me. 'He can't possibly be completely over it.'

We had come back into the noise of the pub now, the roar had got louder, it was hard to hear yourself speak.

'It wasn't meningitis!' I shouted. What on earth made Chiara think so? She must have misheard Patrick. 'What makes you think it was meningitis?' But she couldn't hear and was waving towards the door.

'Look! There's Ben and Caroline!' she cried. The noise of the pub halted any further conversation between us as she went ahead and I let the comment go. I felt the usual sense of grounding my brother Ben always brought with him and a kick of pleasure at the thought he would be able to meet Patrick, share my joy at meeting this amazing man.

We zigzagged our way through the crowds in the bar back to our table, and I put up a hand to wave to Ben and show him where we were sitting. Then I turned to tell Patrick he was about to meet my brother.

His seat was empty.

His crutches were there, leaning up against the pew. I looked around, but couldn't spot him. The crowds had thickened and the noise was deafening.

'Where did he go?' I asked Louise. She shrugged. 'He got up suddenly. Said he had to go.'

'Go? He hasn't got his crutches! How could he go?'

'Hey, Ellie!' Ben and Caroline had come up to me and Ben flung his big brotherly arms around me.

'Sorry,' I said, disentangling myself. 'I'll be back, just a second.'

I pressed my way through the crowds towards the door. He couldn't possibly be leaving. His crutches were here. We had only arrived about an hour ago.

But Patrick was outside, flagging down a cab, looking quite confident without his crutches.

'Where are you going?'

He swung round.

'I'll see you later,' he said, 'I've done as you asked, met your friends and now I want to get home.'

'Hang on. I wanted you to meet my brother and his fiancée, they've just arrived.'

'Leave me alone, Ellie. I'll call you later.'

'OK. Well I'll come with you.'

'NO! There's no need. Drop it!' There was the same hard edge to his voice that he'd had when he found me looking at his photos. His eyes had gone hard too, his pupils pinpricks in his icy blue irises.

'You don't get it, do you, Ellie?'

'Please, Patrick, I want you to meet my friends, my brother, I . . .'

As he sat down on the back seat of the taxi, he looked up at me and his face softened.

'Ellie, I can't sit there being pitied by all your friends. I can't let them see me so dependent on crutches. It's humiliating to me. You stay and enjoy yourself, and I'll see you later.'

He reached out for my hand and dragged me towards him.

'I need you,' he whispered in my ear. 'But I don't need pity from strangers.'

'They don't pity you, Patrick, they're not like that, and anyway you've left your crutches! How are you going to manage? It's nothing to be ashamed of, needing them.'

'Bugger the crutches. I can manage. I'm not hobbling around on them like some loser. I'll see you back at the flat.'

'Are you sure? I'll go and get them for you.'

But he was leaning over to tell the driver to take him back to Wapping.

He waved at me and winked and smiled and I had no choice but to go back to my friends in the pub. Disappointment mixed with hurt that he'd left so abruptly. But I was beginning to understand that there was so much more to his injury than the physical demands of having to learn to walk again. It had affected his confidence, his self-esteem, his sense of self and his pride. I was only just realising this. Only just taking in how vast the repercussions were for him.

*　　　*　　　*

'Blimey! That was a speedy departure,' Louise said. 'What brought that on?'

I sat down. Ben was at the bar, Caroline with him.

'He gets pain sometimes,' I lied, 'since the accident. Has to deal with it. He sends his apologies.'

'Hmph,' she said. 'He might have said goodbye. It looked a bit rude. I don't mind, but it was a bit hurtful to you, Ellie.'

'I'll see him later. He didn't want to spoil my evening. He was being thoughtful.'

Finn leant towards me.

'So that's the new man.'

'Yes.'

'Are you sure you know what you're doing?'

'What do you mean?'

'He doesn't look your type. Chiara says you've already moved in with him!'

'Yes, I have, Finn. But in a way, it hasn't anything to do with you.'

'You haven't known him that long. Are you sure it's a good idea, to live with him, so soon?'

'Finn! Please!'

'But look at him. Designer clothes, buying everyone drinks, calling you his guardian angel? It's not you, Ellie! It's all so superficial. You're deeper than that!'

I looked at my ex-boyfriend, trying to form a response that wouldn't sound defensive. This was typical of him, pigeon-holing me so there was no room for me to grow or change.

'And there's something fake about him,' Finn went on. 'I don't trust him. He might only have one leg, and a chip on his shoulder about it, but he looks like a player. You should be careful.'

'You want to watch out you don't start to sound bitter, mate,' Ben said, sitting down on the bench next to Finn. 'It's sounding a lot like jealousy. Looked like a nice guy to me.' Thank goodness for my brother. 'Where's he gone though?' he said.

I explained again.

'There was something familiar about him, I thought,' Caroline said. 'I only saw his back, but he reminded me of someone.'

'He's called Patrick,' I said. 'Patrick McIntyre. He sails in Southwold. Perhaps you've seen him down there.' Ben and Caroline had met in a pub in Southwold five years before; she had grown up in Halesworth, nearby.

'The name doesn't ring a bell,' said Caroline. 'Anyway, poor guy. Sounds like the accident was pretty serious. It's amazing he's up and about at all. Does he realise he's left his crutches?'

'He felt ashamed,' I told her quietly. 'He didn't want to be seen on them. I suppose that's part of it. Getting used to how people see you.'

'It must be hard. Especially when he was obviously so fit before – he's pretty athletic-looking,' Ben said.

I could feel something well up in me now my brother was here. A need to share my happiness, but also to shed all the anxiety I was still carrying about my role in Patrick's accident. I wished we could find somewhere to talk, on our own.

Ben put his arm around me.

'The cottage is looking great, Els,' he said. 'It's so nice now it's de-cluttered.'

There was no hint of resentment or hidden meaning on his face. How was it he accepted everything with so little complaint? Our Aunty May – our aunt, both of ours – had died and left me her house by the sea. Why wasn't my brother green with envy, or at least a little angry? It wasn't fair, even I could see that, but he didn't object. Aunty May and I shared our artistic interests, always had done, and I'd loved her, but so, I guessed, had Ben. I wondered what it was about Ben that must have convinced May she didn't want him to benefit from her the way I had done. Or what it was about me that meant she did. That photo came back to mind, the one I'd found in the cottage. With me cut out. Was May making up for something she'd done to me maybe? She'd left Ben in the picture so perhaps leaving me the cottage was some kind of atonement.

I shuddered.

Ben was three years younger and six inches taller than me. When he was little and ill, or frightened, or just unable to sleep, I let him crawl into my bed, wrap his hot sticky limbs about me, breathe into my ear. Now Ben lived in a kind of golden bubble, I sometimes thought, where bad thoughts and uncomfortable feelings such as envy, anxiety or guilt simply didn't penetrate. That was how it appeared anyway. So why had I been hounded by anxiety and a sense of guilt and responsibility all my life? I wanted to discuss all this with my brother, as well as my new relationship, but we were surrounded by friends – it wasn't the place.

Anyway, Ben had Caroline, who was smiling at him adoringly. She was like a thoroughbred horse – a Palomino, I thought, with her bronze skin and her blonde hair. Together she and Ben seemed to skim over the surface of life, partying, drinking, laughing, working at jobs they felt neither a great vocation for nor frustration with, earning enough for a mortgage on a flat in Clapham, spending their weekends throwing parties in their patio garden or going down to Caroline's parents' place in Suffolk to windsurf and sail.

'Hey, cheer up, Els,' Caroline said then. 'Look, let's finish this bottle of wine. You look glum. We'll meet your guy another time. Here.'

And she refilled my glass. I needed it.

'You and Ben,' she said to me, 'it's hard to believe, seeing you together, that you're brother and sister. Ginger Ben and Dark Ellie, did you get on when you were kids?'

'I did and she didn't,' said Ben, and Caroline laughed.

'What's that mean?' she said.

'It was just that I felt responsible for him,' I said. 'I was always made to watch him, even when I was quite little. I was terrified something would happen to him while I was looking after him.'

'It's damaged her irreparably,' said Ben. 'Look at her, she has a need to save people.'

'You were very lucky to have her,' said Caroline. 'I always wanted a big sister and I never got one!'

'Actually, Ben keeps me grounded,' I said. 'Ben's the calming influence now we're grown up.'

'I know what you mean,' she said, and kissed his cheek.

'Anyway, I'm so sorry, guys,' I said when I'd finished my drink. 'But I think I'd better go. Patrick will be waiting for me. I need to check he's OK.'

I couldn't bear to be apart from Patrick any longer. And I wanted to know the real reason he'd left so abruptly.

CHAPTER TWENTY-FOUR

'I didn't want to go to start with,' Patrick said when I got back to his apartment. 'I hate those dives. They're for losers. I need to drink in decent places. Luckily I've got some champagne for when you get in tomorrow night. We'll drink it before I take you to Moro's. Nowhere is too good for us, Ellie.'

'Patrick, I do understand how you feel, about being seen with your injury. . .'

'It's not an injury, Ellie. It's a life-changing bloody disability.'

'Yes, I know, but people aren't going to judge you, especially not my friends. Or my brother.'

'I was in top athletic condition before I was run over,' he said. 'You don't think it's easy for me to see people looking at me as if I'm sub-standard in some way? You have to let me deal with it, you have to let me be.'

'Of course. I wouldn't make you do anything you weren't comfortable with.'

'Well I'm not comfortable meeting your mates. They're a motley bunch anyway. You can do better.'

I looked at him, startled, but he was smiling, and I didn't know if he was joking or not.

I settled on the joking.

The next day I managed to make some advances on the painting, adding a layer of light, leaving gaps so that previous layers could be glimpsed beneath. I deepened the lower part of the picture, using thick paint here, and texture to suggest objects beneath, like the mud on the bed of the Thames when the tide was out.

I painted all day then went over to take Dad his shopping before driving back to Patrick's through the Blackwall Tunnel. He was waiting for me with the champagne already poured, on the balcony when I got in.

We drank while the world went on beneath us, doing busy stuff in the summer city, people hurrying hither and thither and texting and emailing and talking and tweeting, as if no one knew there was this other way to be, this blissful other world so close to their own.

We took a taxi to Moro's and ate fabulous Moroccan delicacies and Patrick ran his hand up my leg and told me he loved me. Then we got a taxi home again.

'Tell me something new about the river,' I said as we lay on his bed, gazing out over its rippling surface, lights reflecting up from its depths. 'Something nice.'

'I can't think of anything that nice at the moment. The river is a monster at times, Ellie, however benign it may appear.'

I looked at him.

'It looks pretty nice at the moment,' I said.

'Maybe. But it's deceptive.'

'Actually, I know,' I said. 'It's what I try to show in my painting. The darkness that lies beneath an apparently benign surface.'

'We've got so much in common, darling,' he said, tugging off my jeans and turning me over.

'What do you mean?'

'That we know that things that look benign can be deceptive. Now sshhh, while I kiss you, all the way down your back.'

Later, I awoke in his bed. Patrick wasn't there, but I could hear movement in the kitchen across the other side of the vast open space, could just see a soft light, hear the clatter of cups. A silvery light was pouring in through the curtainless windows from the city buildings all around us that meant it never grew completely dark outside. Lights flashed on and off at the top of tall buildings, and bright windows reached to the sky in towers of glass and steel while the spire of the Shard glowed tall and ghostly up to the sky.

On the cabinet on my side of the bed was the photo of Patrick's wife.

I picked it up, feeling a stab of jealousy that I tried to quash at the realisation he had put her right there. She was dead, for Christ's sake. You couldn't be jealous of a dead person – could you? I remembered he had told Chiara she had died of meningitis while he had told me quite clearly she had died at sea.

I looked more closely. She was wearing a white lace dress, flimsy, blowing back against her in the wind. Her wedding dress.

She was bending forward, holding the dress against her knees to stop it blowing up. Clutching a bouquet of flowers. Behind her was the sea and then, of course, I realised she was standing on a beach. In fact, it looked a lot like the beach in front of Aunty May's house. I squinted closer. It *was* the beach in front of Aunty May's house. There was the groyne, the one I knew so well, with the 'Danger' sign, and in the distance you could just see the great white spheres of Sizewell power station.

I shuddered to think she was dead. She looked so pretty, so alive in this picture. So full of love. She must have felt the same way towards Patrick as I did, and it gave me an odd feeling of sisterliness for her.

Patrick came back in then and I almost jumped out of my skin.

This time he didn't respond as I was afraid he might, the way he had been so angry when he'd found me looking at the photos of him as a child.

'I should have put that away,' he said. 'It must be upsetting to you.'

'Patrick,' I said, 'you told Chiara your wife died of meningitis. You told me she had an accident. What did happen?'

He came over to me, gently took the photo out of my hand and lay down beside me. I drew back from him, prised his hand off my breast where he had let it rest.

'Ellie, Ellie, I thought you liked this?'

'I do. I will when you've explained. Meningitis or an accident?'

He lay very close, his eyes shut. Was he going to speak? Or avoid telling me the truth?

'You told me she had an accident at sea,' I said. 'But how exactly did she die?'

'Speedboat,' he said at last. 'That's all I want to say at the moment. It's still quite raw. It's still very painful to relive it. I don't like telling people, Ellie. Especially people like your friends who I barely know. Because it wasn't pleasant.'

'No, I'm sure but . . .'

'OK. You're not going to let it drop. So I will tell you. She took out a power boat. I warned her it wasn't safe to drive, but she got it into her head and . . . oh no, I can't.'

'It's OK, if it's too painful, you don't have to talk about it now.'

'Look.' He got off the bed and stood up. He turned to face me. His expression had changed; he looked like a small boy who had been unfairly accused of something, indignant, his lips puckered.

'She was supposed to be there for me.' His voice had gone up a pitch. 'She *insisted* on leaving me. On going back to Dunwich without me, on taking that boat. She was so headstrong, always thinking she knew better than me . . .'

'Were you there?'

'Of course I was there, I was telling her not to go. I saw it all.'

'Now you're frightening me.'

'You asked me to tell you, so I'm telling you. Do you want to hear it, or not?'

I didn't, and I did.

'Go on,' I said.

'Exactly what I warned her would happen if she insisted on breaking up with me. The boat went out of control and there was no safety cord installed, which normally would have made the engine cut out. So. She shot out, and the boat cut her up into pieces.'

'That's terrible.'

'Stef died in a speed boat accident,' he said. 'And her family have given me strife about it ever since. They couldn't accept she had died in an accident due to her own head-strong nature. But that's how it is. How it was. That's it, Ellie. What else do you want to know?'

'Nothing. That was all.'

'Are you satisfied?'

'What do you mean?'

'You asked and I said I'd only tell you if you really wanted to hear. You insisted, Ellie, and now you're upset. So I'm asking, are you satisfied?'

'No of course not, Patrick. I'm shocked, not satisfied.'

'Then stop asking about it . . . she wouldn't want you to pry, and probe and insist.'

'But I—'

'Do you think she would want you, or your crusty friends, to know how her perfect body shot into the air, how the very boat she was driving walloped into her so her blood spilt onto the white froth of the waves, turning it all red? It was ghastly. And you're insisting on making me relive it.'

'I'm so sorry, Patrick. I really don't want to make you relive it. Let's stop talking about it now.'

'Ellie.' He moved towards me. He looked very tall, very big against the silver window, his face in silhouette, his broad shoulders tensed. His voice had gone back to normal and he spoke softly, gently.

'I think you ought to know that she let me down badly, the way EVERYONE seems to think it's OK to hurt me and then leave me. You're not going to do that, are you?'

'Of course not.'

'So I would like you to agree something for me,' Patrick said.

'What is it?'

'I don't want you ever to make me go out to meet your friends again.'

'Oh.'

I felt my heart sink. I had so wanted them to know him, to see how happy I was, how far my life had moved on. Though now . . .

'And I think I'd prefer it too if you stopped seeing them as well.'

'What do you mean?'

'Just what I say. You don't need to hang out with that bunch of hobos any more now you've got me. Do you?'

'But . . .'

'Ellie, Ellie.' He had come over to where I was sitting on the bed and he was holding me close to him, pressing me up against him, squeezing me so the breath was crushed from my lungs.

'You're mine and I'm yours, and that's all that matters. You can paint at the studio, that I have given you specifically for the purpose, and for now you can go and teach if you must, you can take your poor old dad his shopping, but then you're to come straight back to me, OK?'

His tone changed again, to the seductive one I had first been so attracted to.

'We're building the perfect life between us. You with your painting. Me with my contacts. We're both on the cusp of such exciting things, we don't need people who will hold us back. Sometimes I simply can't believe we met! Can you, Ellie? I want to share everything I've got with you, and for you to share your whole self with me. It's what's meant. But I don't want to share you with anyone else.'

And he began to kiss my face so gently, so slowly I didn't think I had any strength left to object.

CHAPTER TWENTY-FIVE

Although my teaching job was hard work I always found it grounding after the art I did in the week, which was solitary and about ideas. But today it also came as a welcome escape from thinking too much about everything that Patrick had said the night before.

I had awoken in the small hours in a cold sweat. There had been no covers over me. I'd sat up. Looked around. For quite some time I had no idea where I was. It seemed to be dark, but I could see a pink streak in the sky visible through the window and the usual lights blinking on and off across the city.

Then, it came back to me – I was in Patrick's apartment, *my* apartment now I'd moved in. I could see now the shapes were his strange, spartan industrial furniture, the white faces just the blown-up photos he kept on his walls. Then the sensations of earlier began to slide back into my mind, the drink he'd kept on pouring, saying it would make us both feel better, that it was too painful reliving that day, the day Stef died, that he hadn't meant to get angry with me. At first, I'd been so taken aback by the switch in his character I had considered leaving then and there. But as he apologised, his face a picture of remorse, I softened. It's OK, I had told myself . . . I can always run. He can't. After this I'd forgiven him and told him I understood. He'd repeatedly filled my glass, apologising, telling me I needed the drink to soothe me after his outburst. I accepted drink after drink from him. Then the vague awareness that I would no longer be able to run, and anyway, where would I run to? That I could barely stand up, but that it was all fading, everything was fading and I must have fallen asleep.

I felt parched and ill, and watched through the vast window in Patrick's bedroom the soft peachy light creep up over the Thames, the shapes of ships and pilings and the buildings on the other side gradually solidifying.

I thought of Chiara telling me I barely knew him, was I sure I should move in with him? Finn saying, '*But he's not your type, Ellie.*'

Were they right? But they didn't know him, didn't know what he'd been through.

I rolled over, threw my legs over the edge of the bed, but then I felt Patrick's strong arms hauling me back towards him.

'Patrick, I need to get to work.'

'I'm sorry, Ellie, if I upset you last night. I'm going to make up for it.'

Later I got up and pulled on my clothes. It was Friday – a teaching day and I couldn't be late.

I went into his bathroom to tidy myself up as best I could. I washed my face, took a toothbrush out of a holder and cleaned my teeth. My knees felt weak and painful, my eyelids heavy as if I couldn't open them properly. It was an effort to think, to put one thought coherently in front of another. I would put my teaching clothes on. I would brush my hair and then quietly I would leave and go to work. I needed time to assimilate what Patrick had told me last night. To think about what I was doing. Where my sense of responsibility for Patrick's injuries had seeped over into passion, where my passion had seeped over into obsession. Whether my obsession had led me to a place of entrapment?

Should I have left last night when all he told me about Stef and the demands he had made had made me feel uneasy? But where would I have gone? The flat was let. Finn was angry with me. Chiara had run out of patience with me.

Stupidly I must have accepted more and more drink from him until I lost the will to think for myself.

Now in the sober light of day, I rationalised. Patrick had violent mood swings, that was clear. But they were part of his frustration with his injury, the outbursts a form of fury with all that had happened to his wife as well as to him. Of course he was afraid I might leave him. Of course he was afraid that my friends might try to pull me back into their world. All I had to do was hang on in there with him, tend to him, and he would recover both physically and emotionally. I was perfectly capable of looking after myself if he got stroppy with me again. But I owed it to him to stand by him. I owed him more than he would ever be aware of.

As I ran my fingers through my hair, trying to make myself

look presentable for work, I considered his saying he didn't want me to meet up with my friends any more. In the sober light of morning this seemed ridiculous, there was no way he could enforce such a demand. I wouldn't make *him* meet up with them, while it felt humiliating to him with his fresh injury. I would just keep my two worlds separate. He didn't need to know.

I got into school early and said hello to Jim, the caretaker, who as usual lurked in his storeroom looking for staff members to swoop on so he could regale them with his latest football stories. I stopped and he asked me if I had heard the latest news of the Hammers and I reminded him I didn't follow football and he reminded me that my new studio was on the site where the team was founded and I should therefore take a certain pride in them. In the middle of a sentence, he paused and frowned.

'You bin in a fight?'

I'd absent-mindedly swept my hair up as I talked and now I let it fall.

'Sorry, luv, probably shouldn't mention it.'

'It's OK.' I could feel myself blushing. He must think I had a hickey – how undignified! We moved on, discussed the likelihood of the Hammers ever reaching the top of the Premier League. There was something comforting about this chitter-chatter: I wished all I ever had to occupy my mind was whether West Ham were going to win their next match. I left him counting replacement packs of toilet paper and passed the kitchens where I waved to Pauline, a warm woman whom the children adored – this school had more children on school dinners than any other; even kids whose parents were willing to make them packed lunches went for the hot dinner option because Pauline laughed and chatted as she served them up her lovingly cooked old-fashioned nursery dishes: shepherd's pie, toad-in-the-hole or macaroni cheese, culinary miracles when you thought of her restricted budget.

'You OK, Ellie?'

'I'm fine thanks. You?'

'You look like you didn't get much sleep last night. Out partying, were you?'

'You could say so, I guess.'

She smiled and winked at me.

I nipped into the staff loos and looked at my neck in the mirror. A pink mark beneath my ear which did indeed look like a lovebite. Then I remembered, vaguely, the pressure of Patrick's thumb on my throat as he spoke into my ear:

'You wouldn't leave me, would you, Ellie?'

I covered it up with make-up as best I could, and plastered some concealer on the bags under my eyes.

I dumped my bag in the staff room and went to the urn to make a cup of herb tea.

Very few teachers had arrived yet.

'Ellie. At last! Mrs Patel been looking for you – she's been wanting to talk to you.'

I turned. Betty, one of the TAs, was filling her mug with water, the label from her herbal teabag dangling over the edge. She'd lined up her Cup-a-Soup and her Weight Watchers crackers on the counter.

'You won't have heard about Timothy, it's ghastly. None of us can quite believe it.'

Betty was a gossip – every day she had some new drama to relate. I didn't feel like this now. I pulled the teabag out of my mug, looked around for the compost bucket.

'Timothy. It's unbelievable what that child has gone through.'

I turned. Caught her unawares. She was enjoying this, I could tell. There was a wicked gleam in her eyes. She was dressed as usual in bright turquoise, with her trademark costume earrings dangling from her ears. The colours felt too bright for my delicate head this morning. I felt uneasiness crackle up through me. Fear about what might have happened to Timothy on top of my own worries. I couldn't bear the thought of his coming to any harm.

'Last Friday' – she crossed her arms over her bust, half closed her eyes so she avoided meeting mine as she went on – 'his sister was supposed to be picking him up, but she didn't turn up. Decides to walk home on his own. Gets home to find his dad drunk as a lord beating up his mum so bad she ends up in hospital. Has to witness it all. All by himself.' Betty was obviously relishing being the imparter of bad news.

'That's not right.'

She looked at me through tightened, triumphant lips.

'Timothy's sister *did* pick him up. I saw her.' Even as I spoke, doubt crossed my mind.

She shrugged. 'You were taking the class that afternoon so I'm sure you would know.'

'Where is he? I noticed he wasn't in on Monday – has he been in school at all this week?'

'Nope. Poor little chap, he's really struggling to get a word out. The speech therapists are flummoxed. They reckon it's a kind of elective mutism. Caused by trauma.'

'That's awful.'

'Yes it is. Everyone's asking who was responsible for letting him go home alone last Friday afternoon – I told Mrs Patel you were teaching. She wants to talk to you.'

'What do you mean?'

My mind rewound to last Friday. I'd been desperate to get away, to get back to Patrick. He had asked me to get home early so he could take me out of town to a new restaurant he'd heard of.

And Timothy had been trying to talk to me.

And I'd told him I didn't have time.

I went over the end of the afternoon, tiny detail by tiny detail. I remembered – of course I wasn't responsible. Timothy's sister *had* been there, on her phone, I could remember quite clearly because I noticed her funny outfit with those bits missing from the shoulders – I'd seen her before, that night I'd gone down to Suffolk, I knew what she looked like.

Timothy had wanted to carry on talking, and perhaps I had been too preoccupied to listen. But then most teachers were too busy to listen. Usually I was the exception. Last Friday I had wanted to appease Patrick. Get back quickly as he'd asked me to. I hadn't had time to hang around or to listen to Timothy, who must have wanted to tell me about his stepdad.

I didn't want to spend any longer in the staff room with Betty. I couldn't bear to feel her eyes on me, I needed to sort it out. I walked out of the staff room not bothering to take my cup of tea, a familiar sort of dread stirring in my belly.

*   *   *

241

The uncomplicated smiles on my children's faces and the funny things they liked to show and tell would be a welcome distraction.

I hoped to see Timothy's little pale face, his eyes fixed on me, searching for an opportunity to talk. But he didn't come.

Again I tried to relive last Friday's home time in minute detail. Timothy said his sister was picking him up and taking him to Westfield. I saw her.

Her back, only, now I thought about it.

I hadn't spoken to her.

Had I seen her?

But the children were coming in. 'Miss Stanley,' came their voices, one on top of another, 'can I show my stickers, miss?' 'Can I show my new trainers?' 'Miss, I got a picture of Charles and Camilla on horses', 'I got lollies to give out, it's me birfday', 'I've wet me pants', 'I spy wiv my little eye something beginning wiv ler . . . litter . . .' and I had to put all my anxiety aside, for the morning at least.

As I passed the head teacher's office after the school day had finished, she called me in.

'Ellie, we're not accusing you of anything. Timothy's version of events is of course unreliable, but I do need your account of what happened last Friday.'

I liked her, this motherly-looking Asian woman who you imagined might have loads of children of her own. Instead she had had none, and had once confided in me that she regarded her own childlessness as one of her life's tragedies. She made up for it, she said, by treating every child in the school as though they were hers. Or at least as special to her as if they were her own. But I knew she had a ferocious side when it mattered, when there was any hint of injustice. Either on behalf of the children or on behalf of her staff. I admired her. I wanted her approval.

'You were teaching last Friday afternoon, weren't you?' She looked at me over her glasses. I noticed she'd done her hair differently, she looked prettier than usual, she'd curled it or something, it fell loose to her shoulders where normally she wore it tied back.

'Yes, I was.'

'And you dismissed the class at three thirty?'

'Yes.'

'Martha Humphries was on duty on the gates. Making sure none of the children left without an adult. But she says she doesn't remember Timothy coming out?'

'He stayed behind for a few minutes to talk to me. He often does.'

She frowned.

'And you didn't tell him it was time to go home?'

'Of course I did. But it's hard to hear him properly in class. The others all have so much to say, and he can't get a word in edgeways. I like to give him a chance. It's become a bit of a routine on a Friday afternoon. He was telling me about his stepdad. He doesn't like him much by all accounts.'

'Yes. It didn't occur to you to report that to Paula? The Child Protection Coordinator?'

My mouth had gone dry.

'I'd already talked to Paula about it. She was going to report it.'

'Right. I'll chase her up. Now, what I need to get to grips

with is exactly what happened on Friday afternoon in as much detail as possible, if you can, Ellie. Why didn't Martha see Timothy leaving?'

'It was about three thirty-five. I remember looking at the clock. No later. I saw the other kids had all gone, the playground was empty. Martha must have left the gates assuming everyone had gone. But I checked Timothy's sister was waiting for him. She was there.'

'Did you speak to her?'

I felt myself getting hot and uncomfortable. I'd only seen her back.

'No.'

Because I'd wanted to leave.

I was desperate to get away.

To see Patrick. To keep him sweet.

'Because as far as we can tell, Timothy walked home by himself that day. Which might not have been a problem, though of course it isn't sensible to let a child with his needs go home alone . . . if he hadn't walked in on the scene he found when he got there.'

I waited for her to elaborate. She didn't, she left me envisaging something horrible, Timothy cowering as he witnessed whatever unthinkable things he had seen. Perhaps even becoming a victim himself.

'Ellie, it's a fair assumption I make of all my staff that they put the welfare of the children before everything else. It seems you were in rather a hurry to get away last Friday.'

I could feel my palms grow hot. The raw, skinned feeling. I had the urge to look behind me three times. To find something to tap. I wanted Timothy to be safe.

I tried to swallow.

'Is he OK?'

'Timothy? Not really. Social Services are involved. My only concern at the moment is to clear your name – I could do without a disciplinary hearing. I value you, Ellie, I just want to get the facts straight in case I have to put it to the governors.'

'I left as soon as I saw his sister.'

'You didn't talk to her? Ask if she was with anyone? She's only eleven herself.'

Eleven! The girl I saw looked older than that. But then they matured early these days.

'Ellie?'

'His sister often picks him up. Mum's got five of them. She can't always be there.'

'Timothy says his sister didn't come that day. That you'd gone off in your car, so he'd walked home alone.' She was looking at me intently. 'I'd like to feel I could trust my staff to stay until they know every child is accounted for.'

'I know, of course . . .'

'It didn't occur to you to go back to the classroom to tidy up, to be there in case there were any further problems? Children leave things behind sometimes, you can't just assume that because they've gone, you can rush off.'

I couldn't speak.

'Well I think I've made my point.'

There was a silence. I wished I could be anywhere but here. I wished I could turn back the clock, reverse time, do things differently. Again!

I'd not only put Timothy in peril, I'd let down one of my favourite colleagues.

'We'll let it pass for now and if there's any questioning of your conduct by the governors I'll stand up for you, Ellie. I know you would never deliberately jeopardise a child's safety. Perhaps though, try to hang around till four in future? Have a chat to whoever is picking up? However exciting your weekend is going to be.'

She winked at me.

I blushed, stupidly, thanked her and left, to go and finish up in the classroom.

What I'd do, I decided, is I'd pop over and see Chiara, she finished work at six in an office near Covent Garden. I'd apologise for being a bit snappy with her when I'd moved out, and explain to her that Patrick was sensitive about his disability. That it might make him look unfriendly, but that he was actually a very sweet and passionate person if only she would take the time to get to know him.

Patrick needn't know I'd ignored his request for me to stop seeing my friends. And once he met Chiara properly he would see how lovely she was.

I needed female companionship, I realised. A bit of normality.

With this thought, I felt a little more relaxed as I got back to my classroom and pushed open the door.

Inside, someone sat with his back to me at my desk.

Instead of the usual delight I felt at the sight of him, I felt the blood drain from me and a lurch of alarm.

It was Patrick.

CHAPTER TWENTY-SIX

I opened my eyes, screwed them tight shut again. The sun was blinding, streaming straight in, light from above, light from below. It was white light. It pounded against me, making my head throb and ache. There was the smell of ozone, dizzyingly clean, and I remembered we were at Aunty May's. I felt Patrick's big strong hand on the small of my back. I opened my eyes and looked up into his. I felt my pupils contract, everything come into focus. He was laughing down at me. Leaning over me, his weight on one elbow, his shoulder muscles bulging. His old self.

And I found myself dragged towards him, I could smell the tang of him, as he sank his teeth into my shoulder. He moved his hand between my legs, pressing hard, so it almost hurt, but at the same time he was lifting my hair tenderly with his other hand and kissing my neck under my ear.

'Patrick.' I tried to push him away, surprised by how very strong his hold was.

'Please . . .'

'Ssshh.'

He clutched me tighter, and I gave in. He wasn't hurting me, he was being firm, but gentle. The more I tried to wriggle away the tighter he held me. Protesting was pointless, I realised. I'd come too far down this road. I could do nothing but give into him, let our bodies meld with the bright white sea light and the warmth of the room. Part of me liked it. Part of me knew instinctively it was safer to go with it.

We'd driven down to May's the night before.

When he'd turned up in my classroom I'd challenged him. Folded my arms across my chest.

'What are you doing here?'

He grinned. 'Oh, so this is you in teacher mode? You look fierce. I like it.'

'Really, Patrick. I mean it. Why are you here?'

'We're fetching Pepper from my apartment. You're to get some clothes, and then we're going to Southwold, to Aunty May's cottage for the weekend.' It was as if we'd discussed all this the night before. As if it was a plan.

'Hang on, Patrick! I need to think about this, you haven't given me any notice. And I still feel rough. We drank far too much last night! Things got . . . out of control.'

'I'm sorry, my darling. We were both a bit carried away. I got a bit carried away. It was shame. Pride. About my body. The fact it's not as . . . whole as it was. It was silly, I can see that now. But I've given myself a talking-to.'

'Really?'

'Yes. And I realised what my problem was. It was that I need the sea. I get so stressed when I'm landlocked for any length of time. So I thought, it's the weekend, what's stopping us? The air will clear our heads. After you left this morning I thought, bloody hell! What am I thinking? The date we were originally going on, before the accident, remember? It was supposed to be down there, in Southwold! Eating seafood, sailing, shagging our arses off . . . and we never made it! And I thought, we'll do it now. This weekend.'

I hesitated. He'd put me on the back foot again; I was the one deceiving him about that weekend. I had to broach this carefully.

'Patrick – you know, you never did tell me where you were intending to stay the night of your accident. Where did you use to stay when you went sailing?'

'Oh! Here and there. I didn't know then, of course, that you had your own place. You kept it from me, you little minx! But now I know you've got somewhere we can stay, for free, we should take advantage, eh?'

'Look. What you said about not wanting me to see my friends. I hope you didn't mean it. Because I can't promise you that.'

'Oh, you don't want to worry about that now, baby. What I meant was, your friends can wait. Because I want you to myself this weekend. We're going to have the time of our lives together. It will be healing, Ellie, to get out on the waves. Come on, let's go.'

As he stood up, he stumbled a little, and my heart went

out to him. I handed him his crutches and he looked at me with that sheepish grin I loved.

I didn't need to be afraid.

As he limped across to the door, I followed him, filled with tenderness.

We fetched Pepper from the Wapping apartment. I'd had a text saying Frank, Pepper's owner, was being kept in for further investigations. The little dog's enthusiasm when we clipped on his lead infected me, and Patrick waited while I put clothes in a bag, swimming things, towels, some food.

As I drove, the anxiety about being accused of abandoning Timothy played around my head. I had to get it off my chest.

'What?' Patrick laughed. 'You left school before checking one of your kids was safe? You're bloody lucky social services haven't come after you.'

I didn't reply. How could I tell him I'd left early to get to *him*?

It wasn't Patrick's fault I'd let my obsession with him – what I'd done to him, hiding what I'd done to him – override everything. So what would be the point in burdening him with it?

'I don't understand people who don't put children's safety first,' he said. 'Neglect is the worst form of abuse.'

'Oh I agree! But please, Patrick, don't imply I'd neglect a child. I feel bad enough already.'

He was frowning. This was something he felt more deeply than I would have imagined.

'What's his name? Timothy? Poor kid! I think you know what the right thing to do is. You have to hand in your notice. You have to leave that job.'

'No, it's OK. I've talked to the head teacher about it and she's going to deal with it. She was very understanding. I might get a warning but it'll be OK.'

'Ellie,' he said. 'Ask yourself. Are you fit to teach children when you are so distracted by whatever it is that you neglected one of them?'

'It's the first time I ever—'

'But is it going to be the last? Look what happened. Timothy survived. But if he hadn't, could you live with yourself? You're very sweet, Ellie, but you are also very scatty – naturally, you're artistic, the two traits go hand in hand – and from what I've seen, easily distracted. But these are children we're talking about. Not grown men like me who can look after themselves. Your little lad – you've traumatised him, and he's unable to do a thing about it.'

I had the sudden urge to perform one of my rituals, to look behind me three times to keep Timothy and me and Patrick safe, but I didn't want to risk another accident by taking my eyes off the road. So I drove on, towards May's cottage, with the uncomfortable unfinished feeling I was always left with if I didn't obey my compulsions and with the increasing suspicion that Patrick might be right. Had I put the safety of a child at risk?

Should I leave my job?

'Children can't tell you when they are being neglected. They don't know,' he went on. 'They only know when they are being actively abused, and even then they don't always know. They've got nothing to compare it with, no perspective. I should know, I'm one of them.'

'What do you mean?'

We had turned off the motorway and were driving through
the Suffolk fields now. The late afternoon sun was still high
in the sky and creamy cow parsley grew tall in the hedgerows
and the horse chestnuts were laden with white candles. It
was beautiful, but it didn't feel it. It felt like driving into a
frothy white web to a place where the harder I fought to get
back, the more entangled I would become.

'When you've been brought up in care, as I was, you have
no say in who they foist you on to,' Patrick was saying. 'I had
a succession of foster carers. Some better than others.'

I looked at him quickly. 'Did you?'

Had he told me this? He'd said he'd been brought up in
care. But he hadn't mentioned foster carers. And my own
Aunty May had been a foster carer in Southwold. But he
couldn't have lived with her – the link was too weird – too
much of a coincidence.

'I told you.'

'No, I don't think you did tell me you were fostered. You
only said you'd been brought up in care. I assumed you
meant a kids' home . . .' Actually I had no idea what he'd
meant.

'My mum couldn't look after me. I dunno. She was a
junkie or something so I was taken into care, and then I was
passed from one family to the next.'

'But, Patrick! This is odd! My aunt, the one whose house
we're going to, she was a foster carer. Did she ever take you
in? No, it sounds mad!'

'No, it doesn't sound in the least bit mad. May's blue clapboard house by the sea. As I told you, everyone wanted to
live there.'

I looked at him, trying to work out whether the threads that were tying us together were more intricate than I'd ever realised. It seemed impossible. But then Southwold was a small town. There was only one road into it. Only one road out.

'And did you? Live there, I mean?'

'No. I didn't. And then I heard what she was really like! Your aunt was the most famous foster parent in the area. Or perhaps infamous is more accurate.'

'What do you mean?'

He shrugged. 'It's probably just malicious gossip, Ellie. From small-minded small-town folk.'

'I need to know! Why was she infamous, and what happened that drove her mad?'

'Hey, calm down, babes.'

He took my hand and squeezed it and I pulled mine away. We were turning into the road into Southwold, where Patrick's accident had happened.

Was he going to say anything as we reached the spot?

It was warm. I was wearing a summer dress and sandals. The seat against my bare legs was sticky. My hands on the wheels felt sweaty. We passed one of those macabre collections of flowers that people place where someone has died. Most of them were wilting, and there were some cards with scrawled messages of condolence and love.

This benign-looking country lane must be a black spot for accidents. I shivered.

'Christ!' Patrick said, sitting forward. 'This is where I was run over! It's coming back to me! This section where the road winds and bends. Ellie, look. Flowers. Someone else must have been hit on this road as well.'

253

I clutched the steering wheel. My palms were dripping now.

He was bound to remember, now we were passing the place. We were in the very car that had bashed into him!

Why hadn't I ever confessed?

But every time I'd tried, the words had slithered away and then it had seemed too late, too complicated to explain why I hadn't said straight away.

'I'm sorry,' I said, my voice weak. 'There isn't another route we can go, it's the only way into Southwold.'

'I know. Phew! It's OK,' he said, his voice calming. 'I can't avoid it forever. It gave me a bit of a shock though.' He frowned. 'And a memory.'

I kept my eyes on the road. I mustn't panic.

'That's right,' he said slowly, 'I remember the car that hit me, I think, though as I said, I only saw the back of it. I think I'm beginning to remember more details now. A numberplate, or at least, a couple of the letters.'

I couldn't speak.

'No. It's gone,' he said.

I took a deep breath. Good! I could let it all fade into the background again and hope it would simply go away. I would never tell him. I was a coward. I knew I was. But what good would it do for him to know now?

A little further on he said, 'What were we talking about back there?'

'About my aunt,' I whispered.

'Oh yes, I remember now, what I was saying. There was a kid who drowned, who she was supposed to be looking after. Like I say, Ellie, neglect, which can simply take the form of turning your back at the wrong time, is the worst form of abuse.'

'But—'

'And the knowledge of what she'd done drove her mad. So she ended up in a psychiatric hospital. She had to come to terms with the fact she wasn't the wonder foster carer she was supposed to be. It caused her such conflict, she went doolally.'

'Patrick, please, she was my aunt! I can't believe she would have hurt a child deliberately. She was lovely. I loved her.'

'Yes, but they only section someone if they are a danger to themselves or other people.'

The silence hung between us as I drove on.

I tried to process what Patrick had said.

How could my aunt not have been watching a child she had fostered? I didn't believe it. But why would he tell me this if it wasn't true? And then doubts crashed in. A black feeling swept over me. The child had drowned while Aunty May was looking after her. And I had caused an accident I hadn't confessed to. Patrick had pointed out that I'd neglected Timothy. Was there something about my family?

We were coming into Southwold, past the cobbled fronts of the first cottages. Hollyhocks had shot up since I'd last been here, lining the pavements, and as we turned to cross the golf course the light turned soft and golden. I tried to relax, to get some perspective.

'And what about you, Patrick?' I said, trying to move the conversation on from the parallels he seemed to want to draw between my aunt and me.

'What happened to you?' I asked quietly. 'You said *you* had some bad experiences.'

'Well yes, I did. Not as bad as being left to drown. But there was the one foster parent who forced me to watch obscene films then locked me in her shower room for doing so. And one who wasn't quite as mad as that but who used to lose her temper with me and beat me.'

'What? You're kidding me! That's terrible abuse.'

He shrugged. 'It was a long time ago.'

'But it's awful.'

'Pretty fucking awful, yes. But you know, adversity is the root of development. Great things are often born out of struggle.'

'I'm amazed you've come through in one piece.'

Though I was beginning to wonder, had he come through in one piece after all?

CHAPTER TWENTY-SEVEN

I couldn't sleep that night. I got up and crept downstairs, leaving Patrick in a deep sleep in Aunty May's front bedroom. What Patrick had insinuated about May had disturbed me.

I wanted to find out more about the child who had died. I would rummage through the papers Ben and Caroline hadn't got round to sorting. I wondered now whether Patrick wanted to besmirch my aunt's name for some reason. I had to know. Because if she *had* abused or neglected a child, deliberately or even out of carelessness, then she wasn't the Aunty May I thought she was. Already my memory of May had had to adjust, when I'd found her diary entries, the grave of the child called Daisy. The photo with me missing. The hair and the teeth. My one constant, my one role model, would no longer be a guiding light in my memory but someone flawed. Not just flawed, damaging. Someone who had neglected the children with whose lives she had been entrusted.

And if Patrick had been thrown into my path, had I been handed, by some odd twist of fate, the responsibility for making amends for a different childhood ruined by another foster carer?

I opened the drawer in the sideboard where Ben and Caroline had left the things they hadn't had time to go through yet and rifled through. I wanted to find the diary she had torn the page out of.

Daisy, according to the gravestone I'd stumbled upon, had died in 1990.

It took me most of the night, going through her things until I found it. A small red pocket diary with tiny sections for each day.

I opened it. I flicked through, squinting to make sense of her untidy scrawl. Something caught my attention and made me stop and read on.

The little boy stayed with me for just three nights before I knew I wasn't the parent for him. Sweet though he can be, his troubles run deep and unfortunately Daisy has developed a kind of dislike/fear of him so violent she cries every time I leave them together. I'm afraid he's attacked her once or twice when my back was turned. Yesterday she wailed as if she'd been hurt when I went out of the room for a few minutes and though I asked the boy what happened he clammed up and Daisy was too distraught to explain.

I've told Social Services I think they need to find another home for the boy. It breaks my heart to send him away. But Daisy was petrified of him, and I have begun to suspect I can't leave the two of them alone for a minute.

I heard the floorboard above creak, snapped the tiny diary shut. I would tuck it away in a pocket and read the rest later.

For now I crawled back up the cold stairs and under the covers next to Patrick.

Instead of snuggling up to him as I would have done, I left a gap between us, afraid of disturbing him, frightened that if he questioned me about what I'd been doing he might react the way he'd done when he'd found me looking at the pictures of his childhood. I had to tread carefully with him, be on my guard so as not to upset him.

I lay next to him, and listened to him breathe, and tried not to make a sound, and I didn't sleep until the sun was beginning to rise again, over the sea.

I was leaning on the kitchen windowsill staring out at the dunes lit up by a bright sun against a perfect blue sky when I heard the clatter of Patrick's crutches as he came down the stairs and approached me across the hall.

'It's a beautiful day,' he said, 'and I need to get on the water.'

'The thing is' he said, 'as you know, I can only do it with assistance. You're coming too.'

My heart plummeted. He was going to find out I'd hardly ever sailed.

'Patrick, I'm not much of a sailor, I—'

'But we were coming down here to sail the weekend of my accident,' he said, frowning. 'You *told* me you sailed. I'm sure I remember you saying.'

'Yes,' I lied. 'I'm out of practice, though.'

He had his back to me, his elbow resting on the crook of his crutch, trying to spread a piece of toast with butter with one hand. I moved over to help him.

'Let me?'

He turned, smiled, the dimples I'd adored at first appearing in his cheeks, and in spite of my reservations I felt a pulse of desire for him, and wished the enormous deception that lay between us could just go away.

He handed me the knife. Kissed me briefly on the cheek. I buttered his toast, fetched him coffee and jam and he sat and ate hungrily.

'I'd love to come sailing with you,' I said. 'But not yet. You can't sail with one leg!'

'How do you think the long legacy of peg-legged pirates coped on the high seas?'

He slurped his coffee.

'Wait till you're better. Until you're more used to the prosthetic.'

'Ha-ha! I'm never going to be better though, am I?'

'You will be.' I sat down next to him, clutching my coffee cup.

'What we'll do,' he said, ignoring me, 'is we'll take the *Enterprise*, OK? It's smallish. Not the yacht, not yet, but you could manage the *Enterprise* single-handed if anything were to happen to me, couldn't you?'

'I'm not sure. I feel a bit queasy this morning, Patrick. I'd prefer to stay here.' He ignored this.

'We'll just have a sail round the bay, go down to Dunwich maybe for a pub lunch, and come back in time for dinner.'

Dunwich! That was where he'd said Stef was going when

260

her boat went out of control. The mouthful of coffee I'd taken refused to go down. I really did feel sick now.

'We'll be fine, Els,' Patrick was saying. 'The air will do you good. You can take over if my leg proves a problem. Remember' – he grinned his irresistible grin at me, dimples again, eyes sparkling – 'no obstacle is insurmountable when you put your mind to it. We regard every problem as a challenge.'

'I suppose this weather's safe for sailing?'

I peered through the kitchen window, out across the windblown grass, trying to see whether the white clouds that stippled the blue sky were moving, and if so, how fast.

'Of course it is. It's beautiful. Sunny, a light breeze, perfect, a little dull for me but what the fuck. I need to get out there, I'm going stir-crazy, Ellie, and I need you to help me.'

OK, so there was no choice. I would show Patrick, if I had to, that I was indeed the woman he believed I was, who liked sailing even though she wasn't as good at it as she might have given him the impression of being, and who loved the sea as much as he did.

And so I followed him out of the house and down to the harbour.

They looked small and easy to control, these sailing dinghies going about on the estuary, when you were standing on the esplanade. They looked no more than toy boats. What you didn't bargain for standing dry on the land was the force of the wind and the waves, the lack of regard the sea and the elements have for human frailty or fear.

And here, on the jetty, in the mouth of the estuary, a vague memory came to me, something long ago happening in this very place, or somewhere very similar. The swirling green beneath the duckboards, a child with a crabbing net, of screaming to no avail '*no, no, no!*' into the silence of the vast indifferent flatlands up towards Blythburgh, where the river lay silent and broad reflecting the grey sky. No one answering.

A couple of old seafaring locals – going by the weather-beaten look of their skin – looked on.

'There are storms forecast,' one of them said, watching me struggle as we got the boat in the water. 'You don't want to be out too long.' Patrick ignored him, his face hardening at the man's words. He issued orders. Although I didn't know what the hell he was referring to when he asked me to untie the painter or tighten the shackle key, I tried to look as though I was distracted by this talk of the weather rather than ignorant.

'Are you sure it's OK to go out in this weather?' I asked.

The wind had got up as I tugged randomly at various bits and pieces, things that screwed in and things that you had to wedge between cleats, with the boom and the centre-board.

'Of course it's OK. We're not wimps, are we, Ellie? Now, we're ready to launch. Get in.'

The minute I stepped aboard I felt small, the boat unwieldy as it bucked on the water that was hardly rough here in the estuary yet already made me feel as if I was riding a rodeo. I did my best, holding onto the side of the jetty with one hand as Patrick got in and shuffled to the stern to take the tiller. I could hear the water slap against the bows, the sails flap in the wind. Out beyond the estuary, the sea looked deep and dark and forboding.

'You know what to do, don't you?' Patrick shouted as he steered the boat out into the middle of the estuary.

'Yes,' I answered, but my voice was carried off in the wind.

The sails snapped rigid, straining, and the boat leapt forward, as the wind shifted so it was behind us. Spray hit my face hard and sharp as gravel and stung. I wanted to hold onto something stable. I didn't want to be on this boat at all. I wanted firm ground under my feet. I held tight to the rope that Patrick shouted at me to hold onto, the boat thrusting and rearing with the strength of a wild horse. I thought of Patrick's mottos, telling me every problem was a challenge, that you couldn't live life within tight, restrictive boundaries – how inspiring I'd found them at first. You have to step outside your comfort zone. I was definitely stepping outside my comfort zone.

'Christ, concentrate, Ellie! Pull that jib sheet in tight,' Patrick yelled above the flapping of the sail and the clanking of something against the mast. 'Or we'll be over and I don't fancy capsizing in this.'

In seconds we were out of the estuary and heading out to sea.

We turned about and the boat slowed down, and I relaxed a little. It was exhilarating, the wind in my face, the water slapping up on the sides of the boat, as we sailed out of the relative calm of the estuary onto the wild North Sea. The seagulls mewled above as the salt stung my face.

I began to understand the appeal of this total immersion in and interaction with nature. But then the boat keeled over and I was in the grip of new fear.

There was too much to deal with to give anything else

that much thought, however – a moment's loss of concentration and we'd be over, and the water was not looking too hospitable. I felt tense like the ropes I was clinging onto. I wasn't a strong swimmer and I prayed we wouldn't have to test my strength out here, where the waves were looking increasingly massive. Overwhelming. How capable would we be of righting the boat were it to capsize, me with my lack of experience, Patrick with his leg?

I couldn't think about it, must focus on keeping the boat upright. I tried not to think of what I knew about Stef, Patrick's dead wife.

Of course the more you try not to think the more a vision insists on filling your mind. I saw, though I tried not to, the white horses on the waves turning pink with blood, and I shut my eyes tightly. A vision of his wife in her wedding dress, the orbs of the power station behind her.

Patrick telling me that she had died in a power-boat incident, because she hadn't listened to his warning, his strange tone of voice as he'd recalled the tragic event. His outburst that she had let him down. The time he'd taunted me with talk of her corpse floating head up – or was it down – why had he done that? Was it just bravado? Or something else? NO. I mustn't think.

When I looked up, the shore had shrunk to a jagged line of pan-tiled rooftops, with the white lighthouse just poking up above them – a tiny group when seen from this perspective against the heath to one side and the long strip of sandy beach to the other, each building etched in a white outline of light. I felt the breath catch in my throat. The boat was keeling over, I was inches from the water. Patrick yelled at me that we must change tack and we went about, meaning I had to duck the boom as it swung across and shift myself to the other side of the boat.

Then the wind dropped and the sun caught my face, bright and warm through the blue sails.

The sea calmed and we were buffeted gently over the waves as we moved towards the shore.

My heart swelled. With relief, with triumph that I'd managed not to panic, and with something strong and as difficult to rein in as the boat on the waves.

Earlier, I had had a kind of out-of-control feeling, as if I'd relinquished my will to someone else and no longer had a handle on my own life. Now we were in sight of land, I was beginning to feel I could do this. I was feeling strong. If I could hold my own out on the sea in a boat when I'd never sailed before, I could handle Patrick's moods as well. If I played it right, Patrick would never upset me again. I could do it! I could handle him. If I stayed by him, I might, by healing him, change him too. His mood swings would stop.

We would be so good for one another, he would help me take new risks with my life and my work, I would soothe away his fear of being abandoned, show him I loved him and wouldn't let him down.

And then we were there, approaching land, the wind behind us, the beautiful blue sails perpendicular now to the mast, like wings spread to either side of the boat, the sun on them.

Patrick pointed up at the cliffs.

'That's where the cemetery has crumbled into the sea, due

to erosion. This was a city lost to the sea. Some people say you can see the bones from family vaults in the old church-yard, jutting from the cliff ledge as if they were begging for mercy. Broken legs and arms all exposed by the relentless onslaught of the elements.'

'Amazing.'

'Yes, this was once the biggest market town in East Anglia. Not much left of it now as you'll soon see. Now, chuck the painter, I'll moor us to the jetty.'

I helped Patrick out of the boat and he used his crutches to walk the short distance up the track to the Ship pub.

The lunch tasted better, I thought, than any lunch I'd eaten in my life. Something to do with the energy burnt out on the sea, as we'd trapped the wind, using all the strength in our arm muscles, confronting those waves, the invigoration of sea air in my lungs. It had all given us an appetite and we ate ravenously, both of us.

We had great crispy orange slabs of fish in beer batter and chunky hand-cut chips, and peas, and tartare sauce from a little bowl. We drank cider. We didn't talk. We didn't need to talk. Patrick ate as if his life depended on it, shovelling food into his mouth. The world began to look soft and muzzy.

We were scraping the last crumbs off our plates when a shadow fell over the table and I looked up into a face that sent a chill through me.

Patrick seemed to flinch too, a split second's doubt clouding his face.

The man had wide-set eyes, a broad nose, pale skin.

'I thought I'd seen the back of you,' he said, his eyes fixed on Patrick. 'I thought we had scared you off – a coward like you.'

The man was about fifty years old, balding, short and stocky. His face was red, but with weather, it looked like, rather than alcohol – it had that wind-roughened texture to it. He wore jeans tucked into short leather boots and a dark green fleece zipped up to his chin.

Patrick's fork stopped halfway to his mouth. He put it back down on his plate, wiped his hands with a napkin.

Slow, controlled movements.

'I don't know what you're talking about.'

'Don't bullshit me like you think you can bullshit everyone else. I wonder whose boat you came round here on today?' The man's protruding eyes swivelled to look at me. 'You can bet it wasn't his own,' he said.

I'd seen him before, I knew it.

But where?

Patrick wiped his hands again, took a sip of cider.

'If you don't mind, I'd appreciate it if you'd leave us alone.' He winked at me. The man took a step closer to our table.

'Not until you get the message. You're not wanted around here. I thought, everyone thought you wouldn't have the nerve to come back.'

'Give it a rest, mate.'

'Don't fucking call *me* mate.' He took a step closer, so he was right behind Patrick now, his fists balled up. He didn't look like someone who usually got into fights; there was a restraint, a nervousness about him, that reminded me oddly of my father.

Patrick placed his napkin in front of him, and put his

hands on the table, either side of his plate, as if in readiness to move quickly. But when he spoke his voice was calm.

'I don't have the foggiest what you're on about. My girl-friend and I are just having a quiet drink. I'd appreciate a little space, thank you.'

'Perhaps this will jog your memory . . .' The man pulled a piece of paper out of his pocket, a grainy photo, cut out of a newspaper. I couldn't see it clearly, but caught a laughing woman's face, alongside an inset of a power-boat type vessel on a rough sea.

'You got away with it, but we all know the truth. You'll pay for it. You haven't seen the last of me.' At that point the short man's voice cracked. 'You destroyed my family!'

People at the other tables in the restaurant were putting their knives and forks down, looking round at us.

'I could have you done for slander,' Patrick said in his best city-boy voice. 'I'd watch what you say.'

'You're lucky you're still putting food into that hole in your face . . .' The man's fist went back, his face reddening as he gathered himself awkwardly for a blow he clearly wasn't used to giving, and within a split second Patrick was standing up, his body tensed, his own arm retracting as if in preparation for a fight, his face hard, cruel, stony, the way he had looked when he caught me looking at his childhood photos.

'I'll eat where I like and with whom I like,' Patrick said, taking a step towards the man. 'You may think you can mess with Patrick McIntyre but you're mistaken. No one insults Patrick McIntyre.'

I flinched.

'Patrick, stop . . .' He was beginning to sound ridiculous now, I thought, and his face, contorted into one of menace, his teeth clamped down on his lower lip turning the flesh white, gave him a crazed look.

'Hey, hey. That's enough of that.' The publican had come out from behind the bar, grabbed the other man's white-knuckled hand mid-flight, stopped him from landing one on Patrick's face.

The other diners, realising the spectacle wasn't coming to anything, returned to their plates of food.

'This isn't the last of it!' the other man snarled as the publican dragged him away.

When he'd gone, Patrick sat down. His hands were trembling.
He stared down at the dregs of cider in his glass.
Then he stood up and swung on his crutches to the door.
I followed him, leaving our unfinished drinks on the table.
'Patrick?'
He didn't reply.
'What is it? What did he mean? What should you pay for?'
He didn't answer.
I was beginning to think I knew.
Of course I knew.

Outside, the man had reached a battered red van. He climbed in and revved it hard. It sent gravel flying up as he drove it past us. Its front was battered, dented, and it was thick with dirt. He drove it away up the track. And I knew where I'd seen that van before. Parked on the roadside in the dark. The night I'd gone back to see if I'd knocked a man over.

Knocked Patrick over. That man, with the wide-set eyes, was the one who had come after me as I'd got into the car. He'd looked in the window at me, and said something, and I'd driven off. What was it he had mouthed? I tried to visualise the way his lips had moved, what he might have been shouting. I'd assumed he was threatening me.

Now it occurred to me he might have been warning me.

Not to get involved?

Clouds had gathered while we were eating lunch, dark over towards the horizon, threads of lightning flickering in the distance.

'Is it coming this way?' I asked Patrick. I knew better than to refer to what had just been said in the pub, Patrick had that closed-off look on his face. A look that told me to tread with care. This tiny village by the sea was full of foreboding, the woodlands on one side, the sea on the other. The macabre remains of corpses waving from the cliff sides. We were marooned. But I was here with no means of getting home except on his boat.

At last he turned, took my arm.

'It's miles away. We'll be back by the time it presents any threat. But we'd better get going.'

'Patrick. I'm afraid of going back in the boat. Isn't there some way we could go by road?'

'NO! Get in. It'll be much quicker sailing round the coast.'

'But—'

'Ellie, have you any idea how far it is by road? We haven't got a car here and to walk would take you all night. Get in.'

*   *   *

270

I stood knee-deep in water helping Patrick re-rig the boat, fumbling with the soggy ropes, not knowing what to do with them, trying to look as though I did.

'Just hold the hull tight,' Patrick said after a while, realising how useless I was. I did as he said, fighting to keep it from running off without us into the waves. I could see it was urgent that we got the boat set up so we could get back before the storm got any closer. The sails beat so hard we couldn't hear each other. Eventually we were off, and I gave in to Patrick's superior knowledge and experience at sea. What choice did I have?

He was steering the boat further and further out.

We were heading towards heavy black clouds. Thin forks of lightning touched the sea in the distance. We hurtled along until the boat no longer seemed to be riding the waves, but was leaping up and slamming into them. I went into automatic, bailing water from the boat, my eyes screwed up against the salt spray, my fingers numb. When I looked up all I could see was the dark horizon dipping and rising before us. The photo the man had waved at us, of Patrick's wife, came in focus for a second, before fading away. We were going further and further out to sea.

'Can we turn back now, Patrick? I'm frightened.' I had to shout for my voice to be heard over the wind and the waves. It was as if he couldn't hear. Wouldn't hear. Patrick's face was screwed up, a yellowish blur in the lowering light, and his eyes were fixed on the horizon and I knew then that the man I had believed I might have loved wasn't there any more, this was someone I didn't really know at all.

Instead of fear, all I felt now was a dull sense of the

271

inevitable. There was nothing I could do but cling to the sodden jib sheet and clutch with one hand the slippery side of the boat as the waves sloshed over.

I don't know how long we were out on the waves before Patrick seemed to come back into himself, pushed the tiller right over and turned the boat back towards the shore. We rounded the headland and Southwold came back into view. I was so relieved to see the lighthouse, the beach huts, the terracotta-coloured pan-tiled roofs, I wanted to cry or whoop with joy. Patrick hadn't spoken or looked at me and I didn't know what was more frightening.

The storm or his silence.

CHAPTER TWENTY-EIGHT

We were back on the jetty. Patrick took the sails down and unhooked the mast and was packing the boat away, glancing about, though the esplanade was deserted now the rain had set in, apart from Larry, who was wobbling along on his bike past the fishing huts. He stopped, holding the bicycle between his knees when he came in line with us. He stood for a while, watching Patrick pull the tarpaulin back over the boat, his face lit by a lurid ray of sunlight that had slipped out from beneath the storm clouds, turning it a peculiar shade of green.

'That not your boat,' Larry said. 'Not your boat. That boat Arnie's.'

Patrick kept his back to him, ignoring him.

Larry shook his head and after a while lost interest and pedalled off towards the sea.

'Patrick,' I said, before I could stop myself, 'I just wondered why both the man in the pub and Larry seem to think this boat we were sailing doesn't belong to you?' The minute I'd spoken I wished I hadn't.

He swung round to face me, his face hard. My heart began to race. I had probed too far again.

'Are you telling me you trust a potato-head and a country bumpkin over me?' he said.

'Of course not.'

'Then why are you asking?'

'I just wondered.'

'Well don't. It makes me feel you don't trust me. Talking of which, I have to ask you something I don't understand, Ellie. You led me to believe you had sailed before. You agreed, that night in the pub before my accident, to spend the weekend sailing with me. You told me you loved sailing. What's going on? You didn't know what a jib sheet was, or a shackle key. You're confusing me – after my accident! Taking advantage of my amnesia to act as if you're quite a different woman to the one you led me to believe.'

He turned and began to limp away up the track towards May's house.

'Patrick,' I called after him. 'Please. Look! I'm not trying to confuse you. There are things we need to talk about. Things we both need to explain. Wait for me.'

I caught up with him at Aunty May's front door. I turned the big key in the lock and we fell in. Pepper rushed to the door and leapt up at us, wagging his tail, beside himself with finding we hadn't abandoned him forever.

I stood in front of Patrick, determined to clear the air.

'I'm here to help you, you know I am, and to get you back on your feet . . .'

He laughed a bitter laugh.

'OK, sorry, that was a bad turn of phrase. But you know I'm here for you. I would never *choose* to confuse or mislead you. It's just there are some things which have got over-looked since you lost your memory that I need to explain.'

He didn't answer, but stripped off his waterproofs, sitting to pull the leggings off his prosthetic, and flung them on a kitchen chair, then limped into the sitting room and began to pile logs on the wood-burner, his back to me.

'Look,' I said, following him. 'There are things you have to tell me too! Whose boat did we take out today? Was it yours or not?'

He didn't answer.

'And what really happened to Stef? Tell me that! Please, Patrick. We have to be honest with each other. You tell me stuff, and I can explain why I can't actually sail and why you thought I could.'

He wouldn't reply, wouldn't look at me.

'OK. I'm going to change.' I was shivering, my clothes were sodden. 'And then, we need to talk,' I said to his back.

I went upstairs, put the immersion heater on, wishing the house had constant hot water. I stripped off my wet clothes in my bedroom, which I still thought of as Aunty May's, my hands numb and raw. I pulled a towel out of the pile, rubbed myself down and stared out of the window at the stormy sky.

The picture the man in the pub had waved at us slid back into my mind's eye.

If Patrick had had something to do with his wife's death, as the man had implied, then was he more dangerous than

I'd let myself believe? I shuddered. And here I was, miles from anywhere, alone in a secluded house on the shore with him, a house that he had said all children wanted to live in – but I now suspected from what the diaries revealed – he had been rejected from.

Patrick was calling me from the sitting room.

I pulled on some dry clothes and picked up Pepper, gaining some comfort from his wriggling form.

'What is it?' I called out, trying to keep my voice bright and normal.

'Come quickly! My leg, it's hurting like hell. I don't know what I've done to it.'

I ran down, saw straight away the contortion of pain on his face.

'I must have strained it on the boat.'

'Can I get you anything? Paracetamol?' A plan was hatching in my mind. If I could get hold of the paper the man had cut the photo from, I could find out what they really thought had happened to Stef.

But how would I get hold of a paper from two years ago? There was no internet access here. I needed a library. There was one in the town. It would still be open if I hurried.

'Yes, please. And a strong whisky.'

My heart was pounding against my chest as I rummaged in the kitchen, my mind searching for an excuse to go into town without setting off his suspicions. I couldn't find any pills but poured a small measure of whisky and took it to him. He was sitting by the fire now.

'Ellie, I'm sorry about earlier. About being impatient with

you about your sailing,' he said. He was doing it again. Turning on the charm. It was so convincing!

'It's OK,' I said. 'I understand, you thought I was more experienced than I am.'

'Yes. But I was thinking that of course, we never actually got round to sailing the weekend of my accident! I made assumptions when you said you'd come with me and it was unfair of me. I've been thinking as I was sitting here and I'm sorry. I get a bit impatient when I'm out at sea. It's the sailor in me, we all get like that when conditions are hairy. When we're at the command of our superiors. You know who they are, don't you?'

'Who?'

'*At the command of our superiors* – it's a waterman's motto. It means the wind and the tide.'

'I see. Yes, I understand. I can see that when it's stormy like that you have to concentrate, that nothing else matters.'

'Exactly. Oouch! I've definitely pulled something.'

'Where does it hurt?'

'Here,' he said, taking my hand, placing it on his stump.

'It's so weird how sometimes I can still feel pain even though it's not there any more. As if it's being crushed all over again. Please would you massage it?'

'Like this?' I asked, taking his thigh between my hands, rubbing it, thinking all the time about how I might get away, get out of here, get home.

But where was my home now?

'The water should be hot by now,' Patrick said. 'Let's run a bath and take some wine up. And then we'll eat supper by the fire. I think that'll be enough to make me feel better.' He leant forward, took my face between his hands, pushed a piece of hair back behind my ear.

He was looking at me tenderly, his eyes shining, with his most disarming boyish expression, his head on one side.

'OK,' I said. 'Yes. That would be nice. But I need to get you some paracetamol. I'll nip into town with Pepper. You run the bath while I'm out.'

'There's no need.'

'No, it's fine, really.' I stood up and pulled on a coat then made for the door.

'Come on, Pepper.' Pepper sprang after me. 'I won't be long,' I told Patrick.

'Don't be,' he said.

I took the car.

I drove along the front and up into the square and parked on the high street.

The town was deserted, the shops closing apart from the Co-op, which was always open. I found the library, though it, too, was about to close.

I went to the young boy at the desk and told him I needed to see newspaper reports for a speedboat accident that happened two years ago.

He opened the big old computer laboriously and it clicked and whirred.

I prayed for him to hurry.

'Don't you have newspaper archives?' I asked. 'Perhaps that would be quicker?'

An older woman came over, and told him there were

copies of all the papers in a file downstairs, that she would go and get them and I should follow her.

'You'd better be quick though. It's almost closing time,' she said. I went with her, down into the dark basement, and she flicked on the fluorescent lights and hauled out some files of newspapers.

'I won't be long,' I told her, and began to rummage through.

Once I'd found the papers for two years ago it didn't take long to find reports on the accident. It was headline news in several papers in the May of that year, how the speedboat had gone out of control, just as Patrick had said.

One report stated that forensic evidence showed the safety cord had not been fitted. Again this tallied with what Patrick had told me. That Stephanie McIntyre, nee Gilligan, had died in a tragic accident.

I flicked through more papers.

Then I found a headline that took my breath away. Later the same year Patrick McIntyre had been arrested for the murder of his wife.

My heart banged, my head span.

Witnesses said they had seen him tampering with the boat he knew Stephanie was using.

The accident had happened shortly after some dispute between Stephanie and her husband Patrick McIntyre, when Stephanie had said she was leaving him. Friends said they had met up to discuss their relationship in the Harbour Inn and their meeting had ended in a fight where Patrick had lost control. Some people claimed they had heard shouting and crying and later seen Patrick fiddling with the boat just before his wife went off in it.

No evidence was found to prove that Patrick had tampered with the boat, however, and McIntyre had been released without charge.

On my way back to May's house the words played around my head: 'When Stephanie had said she was leaving him.'

The words Patrick had spoken when I'd first asked him about the photo of her in her wedding dress came back to me. They echoed in my ears as I drove down the straight road away from the town, the sea wall grey to one side, the sky lowering in front of me, towards my aunt's solitary house. I was filled with a sense of doom that dragged my heart down into my boots.

'I think you ought to know that she let me down badly, the way EVERYONE seems to think it's OK to hurt me and then leave me.'

Leaving Patrick was what I had to do.

Leaving Patrick was what meant Stef had been killed.

It occurred to me I could just keep on driving, not go back to Patrick at all. But Patrick was in my cottage, waiting for me, I couldn't leave him there. He would find me eventually. Perhaps I was over-imagining; after all he had never been charged.

I had to stay calm. Talk to him, adult to adult.

Patrick was still sitting by the fire when I got back.

'Ah,' he said brightly. He was in good-mood mode. 'Did you get the pills?'

Shit!

'They didn't have any,' I said.

'Then what took you so long?'

'Nothing.' I felt sick. 'I was just looking for a shop that might be open.'

'Oh, Ellie darling. There was no need to go to all that trouble. I was getting worried about you. Now, come on, let's get in that bath.'

He stood up and moved towards me, stroking my hair off my face.

Fear took over now. I could no longer control the adrenalin that was demanding I run for safety.

I spoke without thinking any more about it, trying to keep my voice as steady and as calm and teacher-like as I had to in class when a child was acting up.

'Hang on, Patrick. Listen,' I said. 'I think perhaps I should move out of your flat when we get back to London. It was all a bit rushed and I hadn't thought it through. I'll find somewhere else to rent for a bit and we can take it all a bit more slowly.'

'What are you talking about?'

'I'll drive us back to London tonight, and I'll go and stay at my dad's, give you some space, and then we'll take it one step at a time.'

'You're leaving me?'

'NO! No, not leaving. But it's all been too fast. I just want to take it more slowly for a bit.'

'But, Ellie, you can't. You owe me. Remember?'

'You can have the studio back, I'll find somewhere else.'

'NO, I'm not talking about that. Or letting you live with

me in a Wapping warehouse for nothing. You don't think I'd care about those, do you? Hardly! Money's no object for me.' He was smiling, his head on one side.

Then he took hold of my hair at the back and jerked it hard so I was looking up at him as he put his mouth back to my ear.

'You owe me my whole fucking leg.'

CHAPTER TWENTY-NINE

The moment swells and expands. His words ring in the air between us.

My instinct is to run, covering my ears, shutting my eyes, denying what he's known all along. But there is nowhere to turn. I want to protest but I can't speak. There's nothing to say. I'd like to shake my head, lie my way out of this. But I've been caught out. My face is immobile as I stare at Patrick and know he knows. Exposure and pure shame. I've known nothing quite like it since I was a child.

Patrick though, looked quite pleased with himself. He began to speak.

'I *knew* when you came to visit me in hospital, it was because you were the one who had bumped into me in your car.' He smiled. 'I knew you were the hit-and-runner!'

He was holding me tight to him as he spoke. I was afraid of moving an inch. I had been a fool! I should have gone to the police straight away, not let this thing ride on and on to this. The wood-burner was blazing, it felt too hot.

'I knew all along you weren't really a girl who was coming for a sailing weekend with me,' he said, chuckling. He had his hand on my thigh, pressing down. 'There was no girl! I wanted to see how long you'd keep up the pretence. Quite a long time, as it turns out!'

'I would have told you.' My words came out quietly when at last I found my voice. 'I wanted to. But then you said I was the only one who had visited you. I was worried it would be worse for you to know the truth than to go along with what you believed!' My protest sounded feeble even to myself.

'Do you remember,' he said, ignoring this, 'that while you thought I was unconscious, you promised me I could come down to your Aunty May's house by the sea when I was better? Because you wanted to make amends for what you'd done to me?'

'Yes, I do remember.'

'But now you're reneging on that promise! Surely all that hasn't just passed out of your mind now you're finding things a bit – how did you put it? "A bit rushed"?'

'It isn't like that, Patrick. We've got very involved with each other very quickly and I just think perhaps we should take it a bit more slowly.'

'NO!! You don't give up on me now! You don't walk out on me! Not now you've maimed me for life!'

'We aren't a hundred per cent certain it was me who ran you over, are we?' I asked desperately. 'What about that man at the pub . . .'

He pushed me off my feet, onto my back on the sofa. Held my hands against the sofa arm, above my head.

'Sweetie, your numberplate is branded on my brain.

NS08 NTJ. Your silver blue Nissan Micra disappearing into the night while I lay on the tarmac will never be erased from my memory.'

I stared up at him.

I struggled against his grip.

'What about – you know – compensation.' I could hear the fear in my own voice. I was breathless, panicky. It was too hot. 'Surely, if I was responsible for what happened, I must also be responsible for paying it somehow? And of course I'll do that, Patrick! I do understand! I have to pay. I should have gone to the police straight away. I'll go to them now, make amends.' I knew I was gabbling, revealing how panicked I was. But I couldn't stop myself.

'My goodness, Ellie, you're a clever girl but you're terribly innocent. You do know what you committed that evening, hitting me without reporting it, is a serious offence? All you had to do when you realised, was stop, call the police. The worst thing you did wasn't knocking me over.' He shifted his weight so he was bearing down on me even harder as I struggled again against his hold. 'It was driving away from it and withholding the information when the police appealed for witnesses.'

'Isn't there anything I can do? Now, I mean? Shouldn't we go to the police? Explain. Then I'll do what I should have done straight away and we—'

'I could sue the pants off you.' He laughed. 'Have you any idea what I'm worth? What my walking's worth? How much I could sting you for the leg you've destroyed?'

I couldn't speak. I was trying to process what was happening. What this meant.

His voice softened then, and he loosened his grip.

'I'm not asking you to do anything you've never wanted to do, am I? You *wanted* to help me, to care for me. You came to me, remember? Not the other way round. It's what you wanted too, isn't it? To be with me?'

'Of course. Yes, of course.'

'Then, Ellie, stop resisting. We're meant to be together, aren't we?'

'I don't know.'

'Yes,' he said. 'Yes, we are.'

I wanted to get away. I needed to go outside and breathe some air. But everything Patrick was saying was making me realise how trapped I was. I felt the heat from the wood-burner sear up my back to my neck, the back of my neck under my hair break out in a sweat.

We were here in Aunty May's remote seaside house, with nothing beyond us but the wild North Sea on one side, and flat countryside for miles on the other. A fear as familiar as my own hand, for it was the one I'd had as a child. I was alone, marooned in this village that was not on the way to anywhere, unable to get back to civilisation even if I wanted to.

Patrick could sue me to the bones. He'd seen my car. He'd remembered the numberplate. But he also knew that even if I were to pay money, compensation, a fine, serve a prison sentence, whatever, I would always have his injuries on my conscience.

I could walk away but I'd never walk away. I was trapped. With a man who had tried to kill a woman when she realised she had to leave him.

And it was a trap of my own making.

CHAPTER THIRTY

I handed in my notice to the school the following Monday. Patrick convinced me I couldn't be trusted to look after children, pointing out the ease with which I'd lied about his accident, on top of the way I often seemed distracted and had let Timothy go home on his own.

Mrs Patel, the lovely head teacher, reminded me my contract demanded half a term's notice, and if I broke it I would find it hard to be employed in schools again.

I told her nothing would change my mind.

She looked at me with concern.

'Are you sure you're doing the right thing, Ellie? I know your painting's going well, but it's hard to make it in the art world. Teaching is secure and you're good at it. I had plans for you to coordinate the art next year.'

I didn't want to bring up the issue of Timothy again, when she had so kindly overlooked it, so I said nothing, but thanked her and told her I'd keep in touch and let her know how I got on in New York.

I painted at the studio on Tuesday, Wednesday and Thursday and did my last day's teaching on Friday. It was the end of term, the children restless and excited, and the parents sent in presents: endless boxes of chocolates, soaps, biscuits from the corner shop. I donated all of them to the rest of the staff. I left the school for the last time with a heavy heart. Timothy was back at school, and speaking again. It was all I could do to stop myself from crying as I waved goodbye to him and he went off with his child minder.

The following week I worked at the studio without stopping, every day. I didn't eat anything. I worked like a maniac, only thinking of my commission. Convinced that once I got it done, if I got to New York, everything else would sort itself out somehow.

If I kept working, kept Patrick sweet, I believed somehow all the things I had done that had caused harm – to Timothy, to Patrick – would be atoned for.

As I worked I thought about the little child Daisy who had drowned and wondered again how Patrick knew so much about it. A horrible thought came to me about his possible part in her death. Hers, then Stef's. But then I remembered that I was the guilty one where he was concerned and I crushed the bad thoughts about him back down again and gave up trying to make everything fit together – it was pointless.

* * *

Patrick would come to see me when things were quiet in his work. He always came unannounced, arriving in a taxi, between jobs.

'I like to see how my artist is developing her work,' he would say and he'd sit and watch. He was a sentinel watching over me. His eyes wouldn't leave me. I wanted to tell him to go, but was afraid of how he would react, and so I worked on, and let him sit.

'Haven't you work to do, Patrick?' I asked him once, gently, so as not to anger him.

He shrugged. 'It's all gone a bit quiet on the fish front lately,' he said. 'I'm taking some down time, well earned, I'd say. And it's good to watch you work, to see what an artist actually does with her day. They do say, you know, that you should be able to churn out a picture in the morning, if you know what you're doing, and buy a Ferrari in the afternoon. But I guess you're not that sort of artist.'

'That's what commercial painters do,' I said. 'I like to think my work has more integrity.'

I told him how Matisse had once destroyed one of his works when he knew how much it was worth, to show this wasn't what his art was about.

'He was a bloody fool then, wasn't he?' Patrick said. 'You wouldn't be so daft, would you, Ellie? I told you, I've got people interested in taking a look at your work. That doesn't mean you're going to chop it up, does it?'

'No. I'm not quite in Matisse's position.'

'Yet.'

My painting *was* developing. It would be finished by the deadline. I was putting into it all the layers I felt lay beneath our surfaces, both mine and Patrick's. What else could I do with him there, watching, penetrating my creative thoughts? The painting might appear to be about the river, but it was about so much more. The darkness beneath, the depths, the unseen currents, the bodies it carried in the deep and deposited later on the shores, on the driftwood collectors.

I thought of Patrick saying, 'It might appear to be benign but it can be a monster when it wants to be.'

And my saying, 'It's what my painting's about.'

I was finding out just how true this was.

It isn't the people who are easy to be with who are the most sustaining to one's soul, I told myself as I worked. I could never have built such a painting about Finn. It is people who are complex, who stretch you to your very limits. The people who treat every obstacle as a challenge, who ask you to give 150 per cent to everything, as Patrick did.

Patrick hurt like a child when he felt he was going to be abandoned, and yet he gave so much – most of the time – when he was confident of my love. All I had to do was to stand by him. And be careful not to upset him. I had my antennae up all the time, trying to predict what might set him off, careful to avoid it. I reminded myself that I did owe him so much, that this was a situation of my own making. And I convinced myself that if I played it right, I might eventually change Patrick so that I no longer felt he was an explosive I was being careful not to ignite.

And in a way, everything he had given me, everything that had happened since his accident *was* what I had wanted, wasn't it? The high living, the meals, the beautiful riverside apartment. The sex.

At six o'clock each night I locked up the studio and drove us in my little Micra back to Patrick's apartment to spend the evening with him, either cooking there or going out to eat at yet another Michelin-starred restaurant. To care for him.

I avoided Chiara, and everyone else, and told myself it was because they didn't understand me any more or the new life I was leading. So I didn't ever suggest going to their gatherings in the pub. My old world, of friends, of chats about art, about our plans for the future, slid away and seemed unreal now.

'I don't want to share you,' Patrick said into my ear. 'I want you all to myself.'

And I went along with him. I couldn't see another way out. Only New York lay gleaming in front of me, a shining light, a chance of escape.

I moved between Patrick's apartment and the studio, painting, then spent the increasingly hot summer nights with him. I didn't tell Patrick, could barely admit to myself, that I was beginning to find eating in posh restaurants a little nauseating by now. I was tired of the minimalist food and, anyway, all food had lost its appeal, its taste. I was yearning to do things that were a bit more stimulating – visit some galleries perhaps, or go to the theatre, or the cinema, as I had used to do with Finn. But the only detour I dared to make now was to my father's to take his shopping, to check he was eating and looking after himself. I was walking on eggshells, afraid that if I took a step out of line, Patrick would lose his temper, set a trap for me.

*　　*　　*

One lunch time as I arrived back at my studio, I was sur-prised to see a familiar figure sitting on the wall staring out at the river.

It was Finn. I flinched. What would Patrick say if he found him here?

'Hi,' Finn said. 'I've wanted to see your studio for some time. And your painting. So I thought I'd pop in, since I was in the area. I've brought lunch.'

I looked around.

'You can't stay long, Finn. I've got to get on.'

'I don't intend to stay long. I know you've got to work.'

'It's just . . . OK, you'd better come inside.

It was one of those summer days when the dust hits you in the back of the throat. The bolts of my studio door had scalded my hands earlier as I pushed them back.

I'd flung open the doors and had been working with a pool of sunshine falling across the steel floor, the sounds of the river and its work tumbling in, a crane clanking, a lorry dumping its load somewhere, boats chugging upriver and cars and traffic on the roads a constant background drone.

'I prefer to work in silence,' I said to Finn, 'or as near to silence as it's possible to get round here. I often keep the doors closed. But today the sunshine's more important to me. I need light.'

I needed warmth to cascade in and fill up my aching mind with sustenance and goodness. I was happy to pay the price of peace to accommodate this.

Finn had brought bagels, and a pot of cream cheese, a knife, some posh crisps and a jar of Peppadews – something he knew I was partial to but which he used to consider an unnecessary indulgence. 'Three quid a jar, bloody daylight robbery,' he used to say. 'At least Dick Turpin wore a mask.' His tired old jokes had once been comfortingly familiar.

'You've pushed the boat out a bit, Finn,' I teased. He'd also bought tins of Stella – not a good idea at midday but irresistible on a hot day like this.

He stared at the painting.

'Blimey. It's quite something.'

'You like it?'

I realised how important to me it was to have Finn's approval. I probably valued his more than anyone else's opinion when it came to art.

'It's – well, it's beginning to take shape, and it's got depth, certainly,' he said. 'I love these marks, here. And the textures. Wow! Yes, I can see what you're trying to do. They're going to love it. They're bloody lucky to have you.'

We sat on the wall by the River Lea, our legs dangling over the edge, and he tugged at the ring pull and there was the satisfying hiss of the fizz from the lager. He handed me the tin and we passed it to and fro in the sun. The tide, which had been high when I first arrived, had been sucked away, leaving green algae up to the tideline on the walls. Ladders that had been hidden under water were exposed, running from the mud up to the top of the walls. Beneath us on the shore were unidentifiable objects, made uniform brown by their coating of mud, but revealing that the river was cluttered with stuff that only became apparent when it withdrew.

After a while I lay back and closed my eyes, letting the sun blaze down upon my eyelids, feeling it ease away the anxiety that Patrick might appear.

'You gonna tell me what's been happening?' Finn said at last.

'About what?'

'About you and this new bloke and why you won't see your old mates any more. What's going on, Ellie?'

'I can't say.'

He was quiet for a bit.

'Can't, won't, or are afraid to?'

I opened one eye.

'Ellie, all I know is when someone is being – controlled – by another person, they are often afraid to tell anyone in case that manipulation increases. They're afraid of being punished. They are afraid that person may attack them or' – he paused – 'something or someone else that is meaningful to them.'

Pepper yelped and pushed his nose into Finn's palm and Finn rubbed his back and fondled his ears.

I put out my hand and touched Finn on the arm, folding my fingers around his wrist. I'd forgotten how painfully thin he was. My thumb and forefinger met, where they didn't get anywhere near round Patrick's wrist. He didn't move, perhaps afraid to break the tension of the moment.

'OK. You don't have to tell me anything if you don't want to,' he said. 'I haven't come to pester you, just to let you know I'm around if you need me.'

'Thanks.'

'Here.'

He handed me a cream cheese bagel with Peppadews squashed into it. I sat up, took a bite. They managed to encapsulate in one mouthful sweetness and fieriness in almost equal measure, the perfect balance of bite and succulence. I washed the mouthful down with a swig of lager. I realised I hadn't eaten properly for days.

'It isn't as simple as you think,' I said.

'I didn't think it was simple, it never occurred to me it would be simple,' he said. 'I guessed for you to be so changed it must be pretty complicated.'

'Am I changed?'

'Christ, Ellie! Look at yourself. You're a different woman. You're so thin and pale and drawn-looking. Chiara says you left your teaching job, but without any good reason. And you've lost your sparkle. Anyway, if you can't see it then . . . but I guess that's all part of it. An inability to see what's really going on.'

'Have you been doing research?' I asked, teasing him, wanting to lighten the atmosphere.

He shrugged.

'I've been observing you.'

'That sounds a bit weird. I could get you arrested for stalking.'

'Observing what's been happening to you, listening to what others have been saying about you. Worrying about you. And as you know, my mother had to leave my dad . . . I have some unsolicited experience of abusive relationships. I spent my teenage years witnessing them.'

He was looking my face up and down as if trying to understand, to work out what was really going on inside my mind.

'It's nice actually, sitting here with you, drinking beer, eating crisps,' I said.

It *was* nice. I felt relaxed. As if I was getting back in touch with who I was. As if I'd lost myself over the last few weeks, had had no idea where I was heading. As if I'd been driving down a bendy road in the dark, unable to see round the corners, or to work out exactly what the shapes were in my rear-view mirror.

'Yes, well, champagne and la-di-da restaurants have their shelf life, I think you'll find,' he said.

'It isn't that, Finn. You don't understand.'

As I said the words I felt a kind of draining of my blood, as if someone had pulled the plug on me.

My energy sapped to my boots.

I took another glug of lager – it was beginning to make my thoughts feel all wrapped in a soft cloth. Padded thoughts. A relief. I knew it would go, that the harsher light would hit me later on, as the pleasant effects faded leaving only a raw-nerve feeling. But I needed this relief, I realised. I needed escape for a while.

I looked at Finn's sweet eager innocent face, and wished I could really tell him everything. But I couldn't. So instead I said, 'I've been there for him, Finn. I've been there for him ever since he was first in hospital, since he first lost his leg. He's come to rely on me. I can't just walk away.'

I considered for a moment my choice of words here – *can't just walk away*. Ironic, given it was actually Patrick, not me, who couldn't walk away. I could walk away, physically, but I felt chained to him by invisible links thicker and stronger than the enormous ones coiled before us on the riverside. I had run Patrick over that night, he was irreparably damaged and I was irreversibly involved. I was responsible for healing him emotionally and physically. I was stuck.

'Anyway,' I lied, 'I don't want to walk away from him.'

'I don't get it. I don't get what you see in him. Apart from the money. But you've never been materialistic, Ellie, so it doesn't seem . . . you.'

I needed Finn to go. Patrick might turn up at any moment, and I dreaded his reaction to finding Finn here.

'The thing is, Finn, Patrick is introducing me to things I would never have done if I'd not met him. He makes me push myself, extend myself, he expands my world.' I was trying to sound convincing.

'Expands?! But you gave up your teaching because of him.'

'Yes. Because he wants me to succeed as an artist.'

'You've abandoned your friends.'

'Because you don't understand my new world, you seem to want to hold me back all the time.'

I would have loved to have been able to pour out all my real anxieties. Anxieties that had become terror. But I couldn't. I looked at Finn, hoping he would see the layers I wasn't telling him. Hoping he would see the fear in my eyes. But then we were interrupted.

'Oi! What's the crack, you two?'

I looked up.

It was Louise. What was she doing here?

'Came to say there's a sale on at the art suppliers up in Brick Lane. You asked me to let you know, Finn.'

'Yes,' he said, 'thanks, Louise. I got your text. So d'you wanna come, Ellie?'

'No. I've got to work.'

Finn stood up.

'I thought perhaps I could make you see some sense,' he said. 'But Chiara was right. You've been brainwashed or something. Hypnotised. I give up.'

'Take the beer then, Finn.'

'No, keep it.'

'I won't drink it.'

'Whoa, Ellie,' Louise said, and I looked up at her.

'What have you been doing to yourself? You look really awful.'

CHAPTER THIRTY-ONE

When Finn and Louise had gone I sat and watched the tide begin to rise again, lap against the walls of the creek, thinking about the layers of deception that lay beneath the surface I'd presented to Finn. I would have loved to confess everything to him. Having him here had reminded me of the closeness we'd lost and I found myself stupidly yearning for it again. It was my own fault that I had gone too far down this new road with Patrick to turn back.

After a while, I packed up my things and got into my car. I left Trinity Buoy Wharf, unable to concentrate on my painting. I repressed the thoughts Finn had tried to make me confront.

I'd told Patrick I had to take some shopping to my dad. It was the one detour he allowed me. He would check up on me, I was sure of it, if I went elsewhere. He'd begun to appear at odd times to make sure I was only doing what I'd told him I was doing. I checked the car before I got in. I looked underneath it, unsure what I was looking for, but wary all the time now, afraid that something would catch me out when I was least prepared. The way the speedboat had caught out Stephanie.

I parked in a side road near the south side of the river, walked across to my dad's block and made my way up the graffitied stairwell.

I felt a pang of pity when he opened the door. He had put on weight, had no doubt been hitting the beer, his face traced with fine thread veins that gave it a harsh reddish hue, his greying hair long and brushed back in a way that seemed a little louche for a man in his late fifties. I wanted him to get it cut, and to shave. I wanted him to lose weight and treat himself with respect. I thought of Mum at the Apple Store, seeking solace from young computer nerds.

When did people ever reach a point of contentment? Of self-acceptance?

Was it *ever* possible to be a hundred per cent satisfied with oneself and fulfilled with one's life? You would have thought that by their age my parents might have reached some kind of equilibrium but they both seemed as lost as ever.

'Come on in, Ellie. How's my girl getting on these days? You still going up in the art world?'

'Sort of, I'm hoping so,' I said. His flat smelt slightly sour, of beer, and of washing that hadn't dried properly.

'Go on! How's the commission for New York going? Mum's thrilled about it. Can't talk about anything else!'

'Oh! You've spoken to her?' This lifted my spirits a little. And that my mum had remembered what I'd told her about my painting. I'd thought she'd been too preoccupied to listen.

'You were never one to tempt providence, Ellie, but I think you could allow yourself a little celebratory drink,' he said. 'I want you to tell me all about it, but first what would you like – tea or beer? I might even have some wine somewhere.'

'Thanks, Dad. I'm driving, so I'll have a cup of tea.' I looked over my shoulder, towards the door. I was on edge. Even here.

He put the kettle on, then went over to his old record player and put on a Lou Reed album.

'Still can't believe he died,' Dad said as the lovely piano riff for 'Perfect Day' came on.

We sat without speaking for a while, listening.

'Your mum's still cut up about Aunty May,' he said then.

'I know, she won't talk about her, or the house. I asked her about things I found there but she just avoided talking about it.'

'What things did you find?'

'A lock of hair in a box. Some milk teeth. A note saying "A piece of you". And I found a gravestone in the churchyard saying the same thing. And Dad, there was a photo of me and Ben and Daisy with me cut out!'

'You're putting me in an awkward position here,' he said. 'Mum and I agreed we'd never talk about this, let it pass out of family history.'

'But surely, now I'm an adult, and May left me her house, I have the right to know about her life, her past. I know May looked after a girl called Daisy who died. But what I don't understand is why May went into hospital. Was she accused of neglect? Was she in fact *guilty* of neglect? Were there other children she treated badly?'

I didn't want my memories of Aunty May sullied, but I had to know whether what Patrick had insinuated was true. Or was everything he had told me strategic? I had even begun to wonder if he had some kind of vendetta against May and my family. Patrick seemed to be everywhere. A shadow cast over my whole life.

Dad sighed. Stood up, ran his hand through his hair.

Then he turned and looked at me, his brow furrowed.

'Mum asked me to burn those pages from her diary, so you wouldn't stumble upon them by accident,' he said. 'As it happens, I kept them – in case. Now you've found other things so you might as well know the whole truth.'

He went out of the room and came back a few moments later with an envelope with some crumpled pieces of lined paper inside. I could see they had been torn out of May's diary I had found at the cottage.

'Perhaps I was wrong. I should have shown you, so you knew the whole story. Mum didn't want me to, but I can see now that half-truths are worse.'

I read May's handwriting quietly, sitting on my dad's sofa, the mug of weak tea he'd made me in one hand.

You asked me, Doctor Lipski, to write everything, to try and tell the truth and so I am doing.

Daisy's accident continues to haunt me. And my fury with my niece. That she disobeyed me. I told her to check on Daisy, and she chose to ignore me, to go with her little brother instead. Ellie is the reason Daisy drowned.

'Dad!'

I looked up. My heart was thumping hard. The picture of Ben and Daisy with me cut out was making sense, but the explanation was worse than anything I could have imagined.

I had been hated by my lovely aunty!

'I know,' Dad said, frowning. 'It's absurd that she wrote that. Do you think your mother and I believed you were responsible, Ellie? Of course you weren't! You were told to keep an eye on Ben, and then May asked you to watch Daisy. How could you be in two places at once? You did as we asked, stayed with your little brother. Daisy drowned.'

'So it was my fault?'

'Of course it wasn't!'

'But she's written that it was!'

'Ellie, listen, sweetie. May should never have left you all there unsupervised. It was outrageous of her to blame a six-year-old! But she was so traumatised by what happened, it was easier for her to explain it this way. A child should never be forced to choose between one responsibility and another. We never wanted you to know how May blamed you. You were six years old, Ellie! It was May's responsibility.'

'But I sort of half-remember the shame of it.' And I did. I remembered my face growing hot as it turned deep scarlet, the shame as she shouted at me.

'Yes, and we thought you must have picked something up, because you became obsessed with checking behind you – exactly what she'd accused you of failing to do.'

'But you never thought it was me, who drowned the child?'

'No. There were, in fact, witnesses, Ellie. You did nothing wrong. That's why, as the years went by, May became haunted by what she began to admit was her own guilt, and ended up in a psychiatric unit.'

'That's terribly harrowing. For her, for me, for all of us.'

'Yes. It is. Was.' He gazed at me then he said, 'Look. Read the rest. It might help to get it all out in the open.'

I began to read.

That September afternoon felt like another time of year. The wind off the sea was mild, the light pink and deceitful. It felt more like spring than the tail end of summer. The cotton grass sounded like a million people with fingers to their lips, hushing, lulling me into a false sense of security.

I would later feel that the landscape was out to fool me, to fool Daisy, that what happened was as inevitable as the grass growing in the spring, as the crabs coming out in the summer to be hooked onto bacon rinds and drawn out of the water and popped into buckets by excited children.

Daisy ran through the reeds towards Blackshore and the huts. Eleanor and Ben came slowly behind me. Ben was so small and couldn't walk fast in his wellingtons.

'Wait, won't you?' I shouted to Daisy. 'Wait for me when you get to the water's edge. She did wait. She was such a sensible little girl.

I can see her now, her hair finer than the cotton on the grasses, blown horizontal in the sea wind, her bucket in one hand, her crabbing line in the other. She's wearing yellow wellies.

I was going to paint while the children caught crabs.

The trouble was the colour. To get the exact shade of the

water that afternoon was virtually impossible. How would Turner have done it? The water was all light, all surface, an indefinable shade between silver and bronze and transparent and pure sunlight. I needed my tube of burnt umber, or my saffron yellow and my ochre.

The paints were in the beach hut.

Daisy was perched on the jetty, squatting, her crabbing line in one hand, her bucket in the other. I called Ellie, my big girl, to me, and told her to check on Daisy as well watch Ben.

'You must sit here, not lean, OK?' I instructed Daisy, fastening the bacon rind to the end of the string, letting Daisy lower it into the water. I told Eleanor to watch her. She was old enough to do this.

'Sit tight. And if you feel a tug on the string, just draw it in gently, and if there's a crab on the end you can drop it in the bucket. But you're not to lean over the edge. Sit tight. I'm running to get my paint.'

And I ran.

And I was only gone five minutes. And while I was gone, Ellie told me later, a crab took the bait and Daisy pulled. And the crab came up, an enormous one with three smaller ones hanging onto it at the same time. All greedy for that piece of bacon, and Daisy put them all in the bucket. A magnificent catch!

If she caught like that at the crab-catching contest she would win!

She watched the crabs crawling over one another in the bucket. All desperate for the meat, prepared to scramble over one another to get to it first. So desperate, the little blue bucket tipped and all the crabs went running out, all in different directions, so naturally Daisy went for the largest. The largest made for the edge of the jetty and over the edge and Daisy went after it.

Eleanor was watching all this, but she had strict instructions from me, and of course from her mother, never to let go of Ben's hand when they were near the water. So she held onto Ben, who was busy poking the mud under a boat with a stick, and she watched Daisy tip over the side of the jetty.

And when I came back, Daisy wasn't there any more.

I looked over the edge of the jetty, I could see nothing.

And Eleanor, I realised now, terrified she would be in trouble, shook her head when I screamed, 'Where is she? Where is Daisy? Did she go into the water?'

'No,' said Ellie, her little face frozen into a mask of terror.

I turned. Surveyed the quay, it was deserted, but Larry was there, watching, staring, with his bike.

I went back to the end of the jetty.

The blue bucket lay, dribbling seawater through the boards of the jetty. One small solitary crab, that hadn't had the temerity to move, sat there, motionless.

I folded the pages of the diary back up and looked at my dad.

And although I couldn't recollect the scene, the feeling swept back. The shame, the inability to defend myself. Screams and weeping and an angry face that was the one I had always associated with smiles and comfort and friendliness - May's - shouting into mine, shouting and blaming and then dragging me by the hand across shingle so my knees were all scraped, and Ben running sobbing behind me.

Then people in uniforms, and nurses, or people I thought were nurses, kneeling in front of me and asking me to tell them what happened.

And May's words, shrieking at me over and over again: 'You should have checked on her, like I told you to. You should have checked.'

Words that had got stuck on a perpetual loop in my mind, ever since, that carried with them the desperate knowledge that if I ignored them, I would make something truly horrible happen.

I had been a tiny child, trying to do my best, to look out for Ben. Trying to do the right thing.

My dad came over to me then and put his arms around me and I buried my face in his woolly jumper and smelt this Dad smell of wool and beer, and I wished I could stay there, protected by him forever.

It was making sense. Everything Patrick had hinted at.

If the little boy my aunt had referred to in her diary was Patrick, if he had been rejected by my aunt, of course he had a vested interest in sullying my aunt's name!

'Dad, who was the little boy May mentions in her diary? I read that she had taken a boy on who had frightened Daisy.'

'I don't know,' he said thoughtfully.

'It's important, Dad. I need to know.'

'There were one or two children she had on a trial basis. Sometimes she would realise it wasn't going to work out and she'd have to send them away again, which was painful for her, of course. And for them. But you'd better ask Mum, she went down there far more often than I did. She was

307

May's sister, after all.' He turned from me, his head down. 'How much do I owe you for the shopping?' And I knew it was time to go.

I wanted my dad to unravel everything that had happened to me in the past. And protect me from everything that was happening with Patrick. But he had reached that point of withdrawal that I knew so well.

It was time for me to get in my car and to drive back to the Wapping apartment. Instead of the excitement and joy this had brought me at first, it now filled me with a dull sense of dread. I had no choice. Patrick would be waiting for me, and if I didn't go straight back he would find me. I was sure of it.

I kissed my dad goodbye and went through from his sitting room to his hallway.

There was somebody outside the front door. A shadowy figure made indistinct through the wiggly glass.

My heart sank as I realised Patrick hadn't even given me time to get home. He had found out where I was again and he had come for me.

CHAPTER THIRTY-TWO

'We're going to Southwold for the weekend,' he said.

'Hey, hang on. You can't just decide without asking me.'

'I'm asking you now. Oh, sorry, no, I'm telling you.'

'But . . . I haven't got my things.'

'I've put a few bits in my bag for you.'

We reached my car and Pepper leapt up with joy as I opened the door.

'Come on,' Patrick said. 'Let's get moving. I need to get out of town.'

'Supposing I said I don't want to go to Southwold this weekend?' I said. His assumption was beginning to piss me off. There was an odd kind of anger rising in me at the knowledge my aunt had tried to blame me for Daisy's death. As if some kind of lava that had been bubbling beneath the surface, squished down, was about to erupt.

He shrugged. 'You won't refuse me though, will you? You want to spend the weekend with me, don't you?'

'What if I said no?'

'You won't. I want to spend the weekend in your house by the sea. So that's what we're doing.' His face had gone hard. I felt the fear again, the threat that if I disobeyed him anything might happen to me. For a second I wondered if he might already have set some kind of trap, arranged for something to happen to me in Southwold. I swallowed back my indignation. Revealing it would only put me in greater danger.

'Anyway, we can't go back to the flat. So drive, Ellie.'

'What do you mean we can't go back to the flat?'

'Craig's back,' he said. 'With a woman. So there's no room. He's only staying tonight, so we can go back tomorrow.'

'*What?* Who's Craig?'

I was turning off Greenwich High Street towards the Blackwall Tunnel.

'I told you about Craig?'

'I don't think you did, no, I don't remember anything about a Craig.'

He was silent for a few minutes. We came out of the tunnel and were heading up the motorway towards the M11.

'It must be that damned amnesia,' he said at last. 'Craig's the guy I've been apartment-sitting for, babes. In Wapping. While he was on business in Dubai. I must have told you.'

'The Wapping apartment's yours!'

'I never said it was mine. Did I?'

'You never told me it wasn't.'

'You didn't ask.'

'But, Patrick! I gave up my flat to move in with you! You own it.'

'Nope. I don't own a flat anywhere.'

I looked at him, but he was staring straight ahead. I must keep calm, I mustn't let him see how unsettling all these revelations were to me. The amnesia I knew, now, was a lie. He had deliberately kept these facts from me. But his mood swings were more real than ever.

'And Craig's coming back permanently at the end of next month,' he went on, 'so we'll have to get out of there. But it's OK, we've got your house by the sea. Luckily.' He began to hum 'Our house is a very very very fine house', a song I recognised from my dad's vinyl collection by Crosby Stills Nash and Young.

'I'll have nowhere else to go when he comes back, until I get another assignment,' Patrick said. 'So it's lucky we met, isn't it, even in such dramatic circumstances.'

'What do you mean, another assignment?' I asked. 'You work on things in the City? Fish futures and stuff.'

He laughed.

'That had you fooled! It was a joke. I don't even know what a fish future is. No. I get by doing the odd deal here and there. Sailing rich bastards' yachts back to ports so they can be chartered again. Hey, baby, keep your eyes on the road!'

'But where do you live? If you don't own the apartment we've been in?'

'Here and there,' he said. 'I sail boats from here to there and back again, and usually some guy lends me a place between jobs. But for tonight, we'll stay at your aunt's house. Aunty May's lovely house on the beach that she rejected me from all those years ago.'

311

'Patrick! I need to be in London. I've got the painting to finish, I have things to do! I have to work. I can't just drop everything.'

'I think you can, Ellie,' and he did what he always did now, waved his hand over his prosthetic, reminding me how much I owed him.

I drove on. We were heading up the M11 when something else occurred to me. 'My studio, the containers, they are one of your sidelines, aren't they? You do own those, don't you?'

'One of Craig's sidelines.'

'You mean I'm working in a studio that belongs to someone else?'

'It's OK, Ellie. Don't look so worried. He asked me to keep an eye on them while I was apartment-sitting and I figured it was better if they were used than sitting empty. That's why I suggested you use one. Keep going, Ellie. You've slowed down and there's a juggernaut behind us getting impatient.'

'But does he know? Does Craig know?'

'Why are you so worried about Craig? Isn't it me you should be worrying about?'

I glanced at him. He wore his little boy's expression again, a look of hurt, the look that said I owed him something. More than something.

Everything.

I must keep calm.

I mustn't stir him up.

'Watch the road!' he shouted then. 'Don't keep taking your eyes off it. I don't want another injury to get over.'

I clutched the steering wheel tighter, fixed my eyes on the road ahead, glanced in the mirror to check Pepper was OK.

'Then where do you get your money from?' I asked quietly, once I got my breath back.

'Ellie, too many questions for one night, darling. Now, like I say, why not drive rather than interrogating me? We don't want a repeat of what you did to me on that road all those weeks ago, do we? We don't want me to lose the other leg!'

I didn't speak for the rest of the journey. Patrick put music on through his iPod, and John Mayer accompanied us as we drove through the flat evening countryside. I yearned suddenly for Finn's music, something with a bit of instrumental variety. The sun was still high in the sky, though it was evening, and the fields had darkened since last time we came. The greens were deeper, richer, and the blossom and rapeseed flowers had all gone. It felt heavy and sultry out there.

At last we turned off the main road onto the single road into Southwold.

I felt sick.

'This is where it happened, Ellie, right here, do you remember now?'

Patrick took my hand and placed it on his thigh, where it was cut off at the base.

'This is where you were responsible for the loss of my leg.'

I couldn't reply, my jaw felt rigid. Jammed shut.

He had told me so many lies. Now I wondered, suddenly, could he possibly be lying about this?

There had never been any proof, other than his own memories, to say I had been responsible for the accident.

It was a hot evening, even the wind that came in through the car windows felt more like the hot blast of a hairdryer. It was growing dark when we arrived at May's house.

Warm air blew in from the sea.

I stood for a moment when I got out of the car, breathing the briny air deep into my lungs. It was OK, I told myself, it would all be OK. I would play this carefully, keep my wits about me. I had a car, I could drive away if I had to.

I moved round to the boot, about to drag our bag out, but then I felt Patrick's iron grip on my upper arm.

'We're not going in. We're going to swim.'

'No, Patrick. Not in the dark. It's dangerous, and I'm not a strong swimmer.'

'You'll be fine. And I want to swim, so you have to help me. You have to do as I say, Ellie. I feel as if you're somehow trying to slip away from me.'

These words frightened me more than any.

'No, Patrick. I'm not. Of course I'm not.'

And there I was, helping Patrick silently down to the shore, holding his arm, helping him hobble with his crutch to the edge of the water.

'Come here. You've had to do things for me, now I'll do stuff for you.'

He began to undress me slowly, without speaking, a tenderness in his touch that was utterly convincing, utterly overpowering. I flinched as his fingers brushed my skin, tried to make it look as though it was a shiver of desire.

His mouth was on my neck, his hands moving up over my back and under my arms, removing my clothes. I wanted to resist, my whole body shrank from him now, but, I thought, *it is better just to do as he says. It's safer this way.*

Patrick had removed his prosthetic. He was holding a crutch in one hand and he took my hand with his free one and pulled me, his strength and balance remarkable, so that I had no choice but to let him tug me into the water. Once he was in, diving through the waves, he moved so freely it made my heart ache.

The last rays of the sun disappeared over the horizon and the stars were thick in the clear sky above us.

I gasped at the bite of the water but quite soon the cold seemed to diminish, and felt almost soothing, a balm.

Patrick was a strong swimmer, no longer hindered by the uselessness of his damaged leg. He swam fast out into the darkness, beyond the end of the groynes. I followed at a distance. I was a slow swimmer, afraid of getting out of my depth, and used the groynes as a marker. If I kept within them, I would be able to get back to the shore easily.

The mist appeared with a swiftness that was shocking, rolling in over the sea, snatching away the stars, veiling everything in a thick white blanket.

'Patrick!' I was afraid. I could feel the beginnings of panic that I wouldn't make it back to the shore now it had vanished under the white mist and I turned, flailing my arms though they seemed to make no impact on the strength of the current. I turned, shouted again. He didn't reply.

'Patrick, I can't swim in this, come back!'

Pepper was on the shore, barking.

I needed to feel the shore. I pedalled my legs but the seabed had vanished beneath me. I moved my arms in breast stroke, though it felt as if they were getting me nowhere, until at last, when they ached with exhaustion, I regained the feeling of stones beneath my feet, and it was then that an arm grabbed me from behind and pulled me back out into the invisible water.

'Patrick. Please! Gently.'

He was turning me round and I was helpless as he positioned me so I was facing him. He took my hair in his hands and he was pulling it and my head was yanked backwards so I was staring through beads of salty water, my eyes stinging, and I had to shut them tight, and then my whole face was under the water. I opened my mouth and it filled so that I spluttered, struggling for breath. I pinched him hard and he let me go and I came up gasping for air. He was laughing. His arms clamped about me, looking down into my eyes. I could no longer feel the seabed beneath me again and gasped for breath.

'You know what, Ellie. We are now at the exact spot where Stef died.'

'Don't, Patrick.'

He was going to kill me!

He had somehow realised I had been thinking of leaving him and he was going to kill me!

I tried to swim back to the shore but he caught hold of me and turned me towards him again.

'It's true,' he said. His voice had that high-pitched tone it had adopted in his bedroom when he'd first told me that Stef had tried to leave him. When I first wondered whether he was completely sane.

316

'I remember which groynes she was driving between when the boat went out of control,' he said in his singsong voice. 'I remember she was parallel with that post! It was almost exactly here.'

The sea fret was dissolving as quickly as it had come, and the dark groynes were just visible now, waves smashing against them. My legs were exhausted with treading water.

'I don't want to hear about it.'

'There was such a lot of blood, the water changed colour. Oh, I already told you. They found her face up, floating like this—' And he turned me over so I was staring up at the sky, which had cleared again now. Water sloshed over my face.

'Please!' I was gasping for air. 'Stop it.'

'It's good to have you though, Ellie. It's good to feel a warm, live, body here now. It's so healing for my poor leg that you damaged.'

'Please! I don't like being out of my depth!'

'You're already out of your depth, don't you think?'

'What do you mean?'

And I was sinking beneath the water, struggling against his arms that had clamped mine behind me so I could only kick my legs to no avail.

'You're out of your depth getting involved with me, aren't you? Coming to visit me in hospital, letting me believe we'd already met, playing me along when I was vulnerable and had lost my memory.'

He yanked my hair again. 'Just say, "Yes, Patrick. I'm out of my depth",' he commanded.

'Yes, Patrick, I'm out of my depth.'

'So I'll do as you say.'

'I'll do as you say.'

'I'll live with you in the house where you always belonged.'

'I'll live with you.'

'I won't ever leave you.'

'I won't ever leave you.'

'Or I'll regret it the way Stef regretted it.'

'Or I'll regret it . . . please, please, let's go back now!! I'm here for you. I'm yours. You know that!'

At last he released the pressure, let me go, and I turned and thrashed my way back to the shore.

Pepper leapt up at me, barking, and I picked him up and kissed his ragged fur.

I dried myself roughly with the clothes I'd left in a pile on the shore, pulled on my knickers and my T-shirt and walked back up the dark beach to May's house. I was trying not to cry.

Patrick followed me in.

I was shaking with cold, or with the shock of his taunting me in the water with his wife's horrible death, the conviction he was about to kill me.

He said he wanted alcohol, and I went straight to the kitchen. There was still some whisky left in the bottle on the shelf. I took down two tumblers. I didn't usually like whisky but I needed it, to ease the shivers and to warm me up. May had an old spirit measure somewhere in one of the drawers. I rummaged about and as I looked my eye fell on the bib I'd found between the floorboards when I'd first come down to sort her house.

I lifted it and looked at the funny hand-painted picture

she must have done on the front of it for one of her children and the nursery rhyme.

'There was a crooked man.'

I looked at the picture, a tiny figure beside a stile. Lopsided, crooked.

I put it in my handbag.

I handed Patrick his whisky, then I found old flat towels in the bathroom and dragged them out of the cupboard and chucked one round Patrick.

'You're a good girl, Ellie,' he said. 'You work hard to atone for all the harm you've done, don't you? That little girl who died here when you were meant to be watching her. Your kid Timothy at school. And me. But you're making amends by doing all this. It's good. You're doing the right thing. Now, I need food. You cook and I'll build the fire. We can play at houses.'

He began to sing 'Our house is a very very very fine house' again, a song about home-building, about comfort. It felt wrong hearing the words coming out of Patrick's mouth, in my Aunty May's cottage.

Not a comfort at all.

CHAPTER THIRTY-THREE

'We've got another month here then we have to move on,' Patrick said. 'It's so lucky we've got your Aunty May's lovely place by the sea.'

We were back in London in the Wapping apartment.

My painting was almost complete. I didn't remind Patrick it was only a few days until it was due to be shipped out to New York. Or that I had booked a flight to go out there too.

'I'm going to the studio,' I told Patrick on Thursday morning.

'OK, babes. I'm making us bouillabaisse tonight. I'm popping over to Borough Market this morning, want to treat you. I'll come and get you this afternoon and we can drive back together. Work hard.'

And he leant over me, pulled me harshly to him and kissed me fiercely on the lips, taking my lower one between his teeth and biting it.

*　　*　　*

I was working extra hard at the studio. Powered on by the approaching deadline.

New York. There was always New York. Once I got there, I thought, I would be safe.

I didn't have long. Patrick was coming to pick me up from the studio at five, he said, so he could travel back with me. I knew what he was doing, he was keeping tabs on me. He was terrified I would do a runner. But where would I run to? Nowhere was safe after what I had done to him, and never confessed.

All I had was the little bib in my bag and the germ of a theory that was forming like a faint light glowing in the murk in my head. But I had to see my mother.

Ask her if she remembered a little boy who had stayed with Aunty May, ask if she remembered his name, what he looked like? If I took the train from King's Cross I could be in Cambridge in an hour, see Mum and be back by the early afternoon. Patrick was going to Borough Market, so he wouldn't be coming to the studio this morning. He would never know he'd lost track of me for a few hours.

I found Mum at the Apple Store, of course. She was sitting up on a stool at a large table among other middle-aged to elderly women bent over iPads and listening intently to the workshop leader, a man with golden skin and long bronze hair who looked as if he had been moulded out of metal like a football trophy.

'Ellie, sweetie!'

'Mum, I really need to talk to you. It's about Aunty May. Please, could I have some attention?'

'The workshop's nearly over, darling,' she said. 'Give me five minutes. We're just learning about this terrific app where you can scan in the barcode of a food and learn exactly what its nutritional value is. Look, poppet, you go over to the Eagle, get yourself a glass of wine and I'll meet you in the courtyard. Get me a large Sauvignon too. We can walk home, can't we?'

The Eagle was buzzing with tourists and students even at this time on a weekday morning but I managed to find a table outside, and sat waiting for Mum, May's bib in my bag, Pepper on my lap. My palms were damp; I was impatient to do this and get back – I didn't want to risk upsetting Patrick. I knew what he was capable of and I knew my life was in danger.

'Darling,' Mum said, her face already pink with the wine she'd knocked back in almost one mouthful. I wondered what good all her supplements were doing when she mixed them with such large doses of toxins. 'Now. I'm all ears. What is it?'

'It's this,' I said, pulling the crumpled bib from my bag. It was made from towelling material with a plastic back and the painting on the front was faded, but the words of the nursery rhyme were clearly embroidered around the edge.

'Now that's a typical bit of Aunty May artistry,' she said. 'She was always making things for the kids in her care. Actually,' she said, taking it, smoothing it out on her lap, 'do you know, this makes me really quite sad.' She wiped a tear from her eye. 'Oh no. I'm going to cry. Poor May. She tried so hard with you all.'

'Mum, the picture looks like a little boy, not an old man, but the words of the nursery rhyme are "There was a crooked man". It seems odd.'

'So it is. Yes. As I say, typical May. Look, come back to mine and we'll go through some photos and things, and we can talk a bit more about May. Dad rang and said you wanted to know the whole story and that he'd told you. So there are things you can see now, things I've kept from you over the years.'

She finished her wine.

'I think I might just have another glass. There's nothing else happening this afternoon and I need to oil the wheels a bit if I'm to get all this out. It's been under wraps for so long it feels odd to air it. Do you want another?' She had stood up, and was delving for her purse.

'No thanks. Mum, I haven't got long. I've got to work.'

'Paint, you mean?'

'Yes, but it's work for me. I don't have my teaching job any more and . . .' The implications of this were hitting me. No regular income, no flat. 'The painting's my only source of income now. I've got to finish the commission so I can get to New York. I need to hurry. I can't drink at lunchtime anyway. And I have to drive later.' I was feeling edgy.

'OK, OK. Relax, darling. The alcohol would have worn off by the time you get back to work. But you were always so very law-abiding,' she said. 'Unlike me.'

She came back with her next glass of wine and sat down again.

I looked at my watch. Mum began to talk.

'OK. I'm going to say it. It's true that May blamed you.

And Daddy and I were determined you shouldn't be allowed to find out. You were only six years old, a little girl. Doing what you had been told to do. What I'd asked you to do, to watch Ben, to guard him with your life. But May had *told* you, by the time I came to pick you both up after that weekend, it was all your fault! What a thing to tell you! You were so cowed by it. Such a changed child.'

I felt tears come to my eyes, tears of betrayal and dismay as we began at last to walk back to Mum's, through Cambridge's crowded streets and along the river. Mum talked as we went.

'It was after that you began to have those obsessions. Checking over your shoulder three times every time you left a room. It was understandable – you hadn't checked on the child and had been told you were to blame for what happened to her. But then it escalated, you started asking me to say goodnight the right number of times, switching lights on and off, tapping things, and other things, I forget what now. May never got over that child drowning, though she tried to blame you. And eventually the guilt, I think as much over the fact she had used you as a scapegoat as the loss of the child herself, drove her mad and she tried to take her own life and that was when she was sectioned. By the time she came out of hospital the first time, she had forgiven you and you and she were quite close again for a while.'

'Yes, I know.'

We had reached Mum's front door. She talked as we went into her front room.

'But I couldn't forgive what she'd done to you. So that's why, when she left you the house, I didn't want you to have

it. I felt it was a deliberate reminder. That might sound irrational now, darling, but all I could think of was how I wanted
to put that episode out of our lives forever.'

So! My mother's desire for me to sell May's house was her
way of protecting me. I wanted to go to her, hug her, but she
was speaking, rifling through her shelves.

'Listen, Ellie, now you know all about this, I have some
photos you might like to see. There are some of May's paintings too. I kept them from you, but now it's all out in the
open we may as well have a look at them and then I can
throw them away once and for all.'

I looked at the time. I had an hour and then I *must* get back
or who knew what Patrick would do to me? I thought of the
speedboat again, Stef not knowing what was about to hit
her as she set off in an attempt to get away from Patrick.
How it had come out of the blue, the trap that killed her.

We sat in Mum's courtyard garden, flicking through her
albums. It was soothing.

I wished I could stay forever, be a child again.

I wished I didn't feel the clock ticking away, my life
hanging in the balance.

Here was a whole book of my life that had been kept from
me. Pictures of me, a serious look on my six-year-old face as I
clutched Ben to me. A little girl who I remembered now quite
clearly, with blonde curls, sitting on the jetty over by the
estuary, where riptides and ferocious currents meant lifeboat
men had put up warning signs, and here she was sitting right
on top of a sign saying 'Do not climb on the gantry', laughing.

All three of us, Ben, me and Daisy, leaning over this structure with buckets and strings catching crabs. Days that were warm and glowing with summer, with freedom, with being children in an idyllic setting. Amber days. But the menace of those red 'Danger' signs, to which we were oblivious, all around us. The flies caught in the amber.

I turned the pages, feeling the past fall into place.

And then I stopped. I looked at the photo, and looked back at a previous one, and a previous one. In each of the photos, in the background, there *was* a small boy looking on.

A small, dark-haired boy with amazing pale blue eyes.

Wearing shorts. Just like the boy on the hand-painted bib.

A boy whose sweet face was so familiar to me that even seeing it here, pre-adolescence, slightly pudgy, sent a bolt of fear through me.

But the biggest shock was that he was holding crutches.

One of his legs was missing from the knee downwards.

CHAPTER THIRTY-FOUR

I felt numb on the train back to London.

'Who's that boy?' I'd asked my mum.

'Oh yes. He's the little boy who lived in foster care nearby. He was born with his lower leg missing. Look! He is definitely the one she painted here on this bib. I think May tried to foster him once but gave up. He was very troubled. Patrick, his name was. His mother was young, troubled herself, couldn't cope with his physical disability on top of her own drug problems – she rejected him. No wonder he was so full of anger. He went at Daisy with a knife one day and threatened to pull the tail off her pet mouse. What a thing for a child to do!'

I got back to East London at five, praying I had beaten Patrick to it. As I walked across Trinity Buoy Wharf, on this balmy summer's afternoon, people stopped to fuss over Pepper, to throw him the odd titbit as they made their way to and from the café, or sat about on benches chatting. Planes took off and came in to land at City Airport. The cable cars moved in perpetual motion up on their high wires, and far beneath them the river lay, barely moving, lit in places by streaks of reflected sunlight. There was nothing to be afraid of.

Bright daylight and a perfect blue sky above the heat haze of London. I got to my studio. No sign of Patrick. Yet. The studio walls seemed to have soaked up all the heat of the summer so far, and I had to throw the doors right back to let air in.

I stood and looked at my painting for some time. It was right, but there was something missing and I couldn't work out what it might be. I had booked the shipping company for Tuesday – the first day that they could do it – and they would expect it to be packed up and ready to carry to Heathrow. I would already have flown out to New York by then! I only had a day to add the last touches.

I felt on edge, unable to concentrate. I wanted to get away from Patrick *now*. He had let me believe, all this time, that I had caused his horrific injury – what else was he prepared to put me through?

The two days until I was due to fly to New York felt like an eternity. But there was nowhere I could go. I couldn't go to Aunty May's. Patrick would find me there – it was, after all, where he wanted to be. He believed, it was quite obvious, that he deserved to live in the house he was denied as a child. He felt my Aunty May owed him something. A life he perceived other children to have had, that had been denied him.

I knew what I would do. I would phone Chiara. She would

let me stay with her and Liam until I got on the flight to New York, and Patrick wouldn't find me there.

'Hi, Ellie! This is a surprise!'

'I know, I'm sorry I haven't been in touch lately, Chiara. How are you?'

'Good, I'm good.' Her tone was distant though, and I couldn't blame her, I had been a terrible friend.

'Chiara, I need to talk. I've things to explain.'

'Now isn't a very good time, Ellie. I've got the midwife here, discussing home birthing options.'

'Oh.' My heart sank.

'I feel a little hurt too, Ellie, that you've taken so little interest in my pregnancy since I asked you to be godmother.'

'I'm sorry, Chiara. It wasn't intentional.'

'Look, let's talk another time. I've got to go now.'

She put the phone down. I stared at mine for a few minutes. She was right, I had been far too preoccupied. But who else was there? Ben and Caroline were away. I thought about asking Dad if I could stay with him. Just until I could get on the plane to New York. I knew he couldn't cope with constant company but I could convince him that I needed him to look after me, and hope he was able to put his own demons aside for me just until I left. But Patrick had found me at Dad's once, he would find me there again. He would find me wherever I went!

It would be safer to stay with him, in the Wapping apartment, to continue to play along with him just until I could get away. It was only two days till New York, I told myself, and then I would be gone for good. Somewhere Patrick wouldn't be able to follow me.

I hoped.

There was no choice that night but to go back with him to Wapping.

Back at his apartment, I behaved as though nothing had changed. I smiled as much as I could at Patrick, and did everything he asked me to do. I acted as if I knew nothing about his childhood and the fact he had been born with his leg missing.

I tried.

But I couldn't sleep that night.

The picture of the small, lopsided boy on the bib haunted me, and the photos my mum had found, Patrick with a leg missing since birth. Then I remembered Patrick leaning over me hissing, 'You owe me a whole fucking leg.'

I owed him nothing!

Yet here I was, trapped in a relationship I no longer wanted to be in, with someone who had consistently lied to me. Someone who had wanted his previous wife to die when she realised he was dangerous and had tried to get away.

I couldn't bear it any more. I lay awake all night, in a state of paralysis. Terrified of the man who slept like a baby next to me.

I had to get away.

I got up at dawn, remembering the words that had come to me the evening I'd driven down to May's when I'd tried to finish with Finn, that loving someone and needing to get away from them was a paradox I couldn't explain.

Now the *needing to get away* had taken on a stronger, more urgent meaning.

I tore a sheet of paper out of my sketchbook and wrote a note to Patrick telling him I knew all about his leg. That I couldn't stay because he had let me believe I'd done this to him. Did he have any idea how distressing this had been for me?

That I wasn't telling him where I was going.

It was better this way.

That we had to split up.

He was sound asleep, and I tiptoed across the room to prop the note up on his pillow.

I took one last look round the apartment, picked up my bag, and gathered Pepper in my arms. I made for the door. I opened the main door quietly, and stepped out into the vestibule. Pepper growled.

I swung round.

'Where are you going?'

Patrick was in the doorway, in his boxers, no prosthetic, holding onto the doorjamb to steady himself.

'Nowhere, Patrick. Go back to bed.' I began to back down the stairs.

'You've got a bag with you!' he said. 'You can't go. It's not an option.'

'I can. This isn't your apartment. I can't live in someone else's apartment.' I kept my voice steady, firm.

'*I'm* the one to decide that. You're staying here until we move to your Aunty May's.'

'It's not going to happen, Patrick.'

'You owe me! You have to do as I say.'

333

'I don't. I don't owe you anything. I know that now! I've left you a note. Read it!'

'I'll go to the police, I'll . . .'

'You won't.'

I continued to move back down the stairs, talking to him up the stairwell. 'I know that you were born with one leg. You let me believe I did this to you! I didn't! And I've left my job, abandoned my friends. For you! Because you let me believe I owed you. Well, I can't take any more.'

I turned and began to run down the stairs towards the doors, and freedom.

I turned as I reached them. 'Please don't come after me.'

'You might not owe me my leg,' he shouted, 'but I can still tell the police you ran me over that night. I can still sue you. I can still demand compensation. I had head injuries! I was unable to walk because I'd sprained my other ankle! No one walks out on me unless I let them. No one disobeys Patrick McIntyre. I'll find you, Ellie.'

His tone changed as I pushed the button that released the main doors and they slid open.

'Come back, Ellie. Please. Please . . .'

And he began to sob.

But I was getting into my car, Pepper in front of me, slamming the door and driving away from him before he could catch me, and stop me for good.

CHAPTER THIRTY-FIVE

'Finn, it's me.'

'Where are you?'

'In my studio. I need to see you.'

'You must be ready to ship?'

'Yes. Almost. They're picking up on Tuesday. I'm flying ahead tomorrow.'

Tomorrow lay before me like a beacon. My flight to New York was all booked and I'd managed not to tell Patrick that I'd brought it forward. He wouldn't know that I'd gone! I would be thousands of miles away.

George Albini had said I could stay with them in their Manhattan apartment, help put the show up. Once I was on that flight I would be safe. Then, in New York, I would have time to plan my future.

The painting had what I'd intended it to: a sense of things lying beneath the river. The colours and light and shade captured this, and towards the top, where it faded to white to indicate the open space of the sky, I'd crisscrossed it with fine lines to represent the perpetual motion of the cable cars and the trains and the aeroplanes, the rhythm of the human landscape around the natural one.

The picture was meant to work on many different levels. But did it?

I needed Finn's objective critical judgement one last time. Only he could help me decide how best to know when to stop, when it was finished, only he had a deep knowledge of my work and would be able to reassure me I had worked on it enough.

He was in Mile End having coffee, he said. I could go and see him, but could I come quickly?

'You couldn't come down here?' I asked. The minutes were closing in on me. 'I haven't got long, I need to finish today – this morning preferably.' As long as I was still in the studio, Patrick would be able to catch me. He'd do something unexpected as he had done to Stef.

I was sure of it.

I had to get out. Disappear from his radar. I'd pack the painting and be gone.

'Not just now, no, maybe later,' Finn was saying.

'I need to ask you for some advice.'

'Come and have a quick coffee with me,' he said. 'Take a picture of the painting on your phone and I'll see what I can suggest.'

He sounded strange. He was nervous, I realised, his voice had a quake to it.

'It won't take you long to get here if you hop on the Docklands Light Railway and change at Stratford. There's something I need to talk to you about in any case. But I need to stay around here.'

I looked at my mobile. It was ten thirty. It shouldn't take more than twenty minutes at the most to get to him. And I could be back here in time to complete everything and leave my painting for the couriers. There was no point in driving as the traffic would be heavy. I'd parked my car on the far side of the wharf beyond the lighthouse, where I could leave it all day.

And so I did as Finn told me, wishing as I hurried away from the studio, Pepper under one arm, that I wasn't so dependent on his opinion as to let him drag me across London when my deadline was right upon me and my fear of Patrick's arriving unannounced, to show me I was his, hung over me.

The DLR came straight away but the Tubes were held up due to some engineering work further down the line. I stood on the platform, praying for the train to arrive. I remembered those nights I had first gone out with Patrick and how he had made me laugh about the announcements and how he had a theory they were tailored according to the social class of the passengers.

How in love I had thought I was.

It took me over an hour to get to the cinema coffee bar. But now I was on my way, there was no point in turning back. And something was propelling me, more than the need for his critique of my work, something else. There was unfinished business I had to sort with Finn – and this might be the chance to explain why things had gone so awry between us. To make amends somehow. Perhaps, if we could make up, Finn would let me sleep at his tonight. And I would feel safe.

*   *   *

I pushed open the doors of the cinema, went into its cool dark interior and looked about the high-ceilinged room with its bare brick walls and enormous film noir posters, its mismatched assortment of vintage furniture, sofas from the Seventies, school chairs from the Eighties or Nineties, Formica tables with metal legs and velvet cushions. I could see the back of Finn's head, his ruffled dark hair that I had loved for so long, over on the far side, on a bright green Ercol sofa, his back to me. He was with someone and it took me a moment to realise that the closeness of their two heads indicated something more intimate than a working meeting or two friends having a casual coffee. I cursed the Tubes for being late. No wonder Finn wanted me to come quickly, he was obviously meeting a new girlfriend.

I walked across, hesitated, unsure whether I should interrupt them. Pepper began to growl.

As I drew nearer, the back of the head of the other person seemed familiar, bleached curls cascading past her shoulders. My stomach plummeted. Finn was with Louise!

I considered turning around and walking away again. But I had to talk to Finn. I walked around to where they sat, hands intertwined, Finn's nose buried in Louise's neck. He was playing with her hair, just the way Guy had done that night at the cottage – what is it with men and curly hair? Pulling it out, letting it spring back into place, as if they regress into children when confronted with natural curls. I was thinking, *but Louise doesn't go for men like Finn. She goes for men with bronzed bodies and long blond hair and big biceps.* Finn, though he had a beautiful face, was hardly the type to model underpants in a glossy men's magazine, as Guy had looked as though he might, and Louise had seemed so proud of Guy. The way she had looked into his eyes as if no one on Earth would ever match up to him!

I felt awkward, standing there over the two of them as they smooched on the couch, their arms round each other, and wondered if I could make an excuse and leave. Then Finn glanced up and his face flushed. He had seen me.

He got up, took a step towards me and went to hug me but I shrank from his embrace. I don't know what it was. Pride, or hurt, or jealousy, but it wasn't a good thing to do.

'What's up, Ellie?' Louise looked up at me, frowning, as if she couldn't imagine I might be taken aback by their being together.

'You two!' I said brightly. 'Hi!'

I tried to look as if I wasn't in the least surprised to see them there together, that Chiara had told me, that I was fine with it. I didn't know what else to say. I ought to congratulate them but the words simply wouldn't come out of my mouth.

'Oh my God, you didn't know?'

Louise laughed, pulled Finn to her, and kissed his floppy hair.

He flushed again, and squeezed her hand.

'No, I didn't,' I said. 'So! How funny. I had no idea. Well . . .'

I shouldn't mind, I told myself. I had no right to mind.

'I'll get coffees,' I said. 'What would you like?' I needed a few minutes to assimilate this new information, and to deal with the ache that had come to my chest, that had no right to be there.

'We realised,' Finn told me, catching up with me at the counter as I ordered the coffees, their two lattes and my espresso, 'and ironically, it was through you, in a way, that we came to realise, that we'd always liked each other.'

'How was it through me?' I rummaged through memories of the previous few months, unable to identify a moment when I somehow engineered their liaison, but could only remember how wrapped up in Patrick I had been.

I'd thought I could run around with Patrick, and ask for Finn back the minute things didn't work out with him. How arrogant of me! How short-sighted.

I had to be big about this, grown up.

Back on the sofa, seeing the two of them together, everything fell into place.

The subtly exchanged glances, the discreet conversations I'd thought were about me. The time Louise had come when Finn was visiting me at the studio.

They were all about what was going on between *them*! Artistic meetings, swapping of paint and canvas and graphite and bitumen and the shared outings to the galleries.

I'd thought Louise was simply out to win the commission off me – it had never occurred to me that she might be trying to take Finn from me.

What was I telling myself? Finn wasn't mine! She hadn't *taken* Finn from me, he was free for the taking. I had chosen to end my relationship with him all those weeks ago. And then I had become involved with Patrick.

My old life, the one I had so determinedly left, but which I thought I could pick up and carry on with whenever I wanted to, had moved on without me.

*   *   *

'So, what's the problem with the picture, Ellie?' Louise asked. I didn't want to talk about it to Louise. Finn's criticism was the only one I valued and trusted. But I couldn't tell him in front of her. I felt weak and vulnerable, and helpless, and looked about for some talisman, something to make me feel safe again, failed to find one. I glanced over my shoulder anyway, three times, the urge to do so more pressing than the fear of looking weird.

'Finn said you were bringing a photo?' she said. 'Are you pleased with it? Can you show us?'

'I think I've finished,' I said, 'but it's at that stage, you know, where you are not quite sure whether to keep working on it, or to stop. To leave it alone.'

'Ah,' said Finn. 'Let's see the photo then, if you've got it.'

'I haven't.' I said. 'It needs to be seen in the flesh, so to speak.'

'Do you want us to come later and look at it?'

'Yes. No. I'm not sure, I . . .'

Louise moved closer to Finn, and spoke into his ear so I could just hear. 'Don't forget we're going to Gavin's film preview at the ICA this afternoon. Then we're meeting the others at the Coach & Horses.'

'Yes,' he said. 'I know. But there would be time if I went right away. If she wants me to.' He had said *I*, this time, not *we*, and I wanted to hug him. 'I could get the Clipper up to Embankment, in fact,' he went on, 'couldn't I, Ellie? From Trinity Buoy Wharf?'

'Yes. The Clipper goes from North Greenwich, you have to call the *Predator* to take you across.'

'The *Predator*?' This was Louise.

'It's an ex-police boat that runs a ferry service over to the other side,' I said. 'You have to call it up. It only runs when there are enough passengers to warrant a crossing.'

'Sounds very anachronistic,' she said. 'I thought the wharf was supposed to be ultra-trendy?'

'Anyway,' said Finn. 'I could do that if we left straight away. Meet you on Pall Mall, Louise?'

I felt Louise prickle and I knew what I had to do.

'No,' I said, 'It's OK. Thanks, Finn. I can manage. There's no need. You should go with Louise or you might miss the film.'

It was time I was able to judge my own work. It was what I had wanted all those weeks ago when I'd made the decision to end my relationship with Finn, to be independent, to stand on my own two feet both artistically, and in life. Patrick had interfered with the latter, though I was freeing myself from him, now. So I must deal with the former myself. I'd won the commission without Finn's help, without anyone's help. I could complete it on my own.

'I'll see you two soon,' I said. 'Have a good time at the ICA. Come on, Pepper.' And I left them, without looking over my shoulder once.

Finn caught up with me as I got to the doors.

'I found this the other day. But I was afraid you'd be angry with me for interfering.'

He thrust a printout of some local Southwold news into my hand.

'It was just, when Louise told me you'd caused an accident on your way down to Southwold, the weekend you didn't invite me' – he shrugged and pulled the corners of his mouth down – 'when she said you hadn't gone to the police, I knew it sounded more like one of your old obsessive thoughts about hitting something in your car. All those times you thought you'd knocked someone over! So after I saw you the other day, and realised how convinced you were you had to put up with Patrick when it was clear you were unhappy, I did a bit of research on the internet. Here.'

I read it on the Tube.

A local man has come forward to confess to the hit-and-run that happened in April. The man in question decided he preferred to confess than to have the accident on his conscience. He describes how he deliberately went after Patrick McIntyre in his van, knocking him over on the A1095 in April after a dispute in the pub. However, the victim of the accident, Patrick McIntyre, who suffered minor head injuries, failed to press charges and is no longer living in the area. The dispute was over the death of Stephanie McIntyre, the man's niece. Patrick McIntyre was arrested for the murder of Stephanie McIntyre after her speed-boat went out of control. Witnesses said they had seen McIntyre tampering with the boat. However, insufficient evidence meant he was released without charge. His wife had made previous complaints about domestic violence since marrying McIntyre and was said to have been living in fear. McIntyre has since been out of the country. He had had previous convictions for Grievous Bodily Harm and Actual Bodily Harm. Police say they are not looking for anyone else in connection with the hit-and-run.

CHAPTER THIRTY-SIX

I couldn't get the picture of Stef's smiling face out of my mind. Looking so happy in her wedding dress in the photo by Patrick's bed. She had had no idea what lay in store for her, that day she tried, for whatever reason, to get away from Patrick on the boat.

She thought she was leaving him . . . she had no idea she was about to die.

I tried to wipe the image from my mind as I made my way back through London's summer streets to my studio.

Finn, dear sweet Finn, had bothered to find proof that the accident had been another of my obsessions. And tomorrow I was going to New York! I would be far away, on the cusp of a new life.

I'd lost two and a half hours' painting time, however, by the time I'd dealt with the disrupted Tubes, ended up walking two stops, and finally decided to walk back between the high walls of the disused warehouses back to Trinity Buoy Wharf.

I had to finish the painting, but every time I thought I'd finished and was ready to pack up, I changed my mind. It needed a little more work here, another mark there. A layer in the top right-hand corner.

Every so often I checked outside, alert to the fact Patrick might decide to come down and find me. There was no sign of him. Only the usual bustle of the wharf, a crew filming beside the lightship, dancers sitting on old buoys outside the café, drinking coffee, chatting, calling Pepper to them, tossing him bits of panini. Reassured by the everyday activity all around me, I worked on. There was no way Patrick could hurt me here, even if he did turn up, with so many people about.

And soon I'd be gone.

I added a layer to the sky, hoping to give it a sense of the opaque, and then decided it didn't work and that I should change it back. I wondered what Finn would have said. Reminded myself I could use my own judgement.

The shipping company phoned and said they would come first thing on Tuesday morning and could I have the painting bubble-wrapped and labelled and ready to transport? I was to leave the studio key at reception. I could feel panic build within me, crippling my creative muscles. It would take some time to change the painting back to how it was before I'd fiddled with it, and then it wouldn't be exactly as it had been before I added the layer.

I should never have meddled with it.

Unable to make a decision, I went outside. The tide was

low. I leant on the wall. Counted the rungs on the ladder leading down into the red lightship. Twenty metal steps. Up above, the cable cars moved silently across the sky, passing each other on their wires. Sunlight glittered on the surface of the Thames. It was hot and airless and I wanted to get away. I had no more energy for the painting, or for anything.

In the end I changed my mind. I would leave the painting, hoping the new layer added nuances, and have another look at it after leaving it an hour or two, see what it was like when it was dry.

In the meantime I would pack up everything in the studio, make sure I left nothing for Patrick to use as an excuse to get in touch with me, and be on my way to Dad's. I'd persuade him to let me stay on his sofa tonight, reassuring him that tomorrow I'd be out first thing, and on a flight to New York. There was no choice, nowhere else I could go.

Lights were twinkling on across the River Lea by the time I had wrapped the painting and packed my things in my car.

I was ready. I could hear music somewhere, the beginnings of an evening of drinking and laughing in the pubs, and on the tourist boats on the river.

Behind me in the towers of Canary Wharf, lights were coming on; it was a bright checkerboard to the skies. Over to my left, The O2 was also lit up, ready for whichever big event people were gathering for. On this side, my container was the only one with a light left on. Once upon a time I would have gone off to meet Chiara and the others in the pub, Louise had said they were all meeting at the Coach &

Horses, in Soho, but that would be impossible now Louise and Finn were together.

I would simply have an early night at Dad's, ask him not to answer the door to anyone.

I walked across the wharf to my car, which was parked beyond the lighthouse. Before I got in I turned round to have one last look at the studio and realised the window in the back of the container was lit up. I'd left the lights on.

'Come with me, Pepper.' I hurried back across the yard.

I pulled back the bolts of the studio door, stepped inside to reach the light switch, flicked it off and turned.

Patrick moved so quickly I didn't have time to gasp.

I'd seen the look in his eye, the one where it was as if Patrick the charmer, the sweet-talker, was simply no longer in there. As if he was possessed by someone else entirely. Or perhaps it was that there was nobody there at all. Certainly there was no empathy. No humanity. A blank.

My mind did a quick scan of the situation. I was alone, everyone else had gone off, as far as I could see, wanting to get some air, or to a pub for a cold drink on a hot night like this. And anyway, the container was isolated, facing away from the yard, and over the River Lea.

Pepper was growling, low and fierce.

I spoke, words coming out without too much thought. Automatic, defensive.

'I've finished, I think,' I said. 'Let's get out of here, it's too hot on a night like this. Let's go for a drink.'

'You were leaving me!'

I made for the door.

He put his leg out and tripped me so I keeled over, banging my head on the metal wall. I grabbed one of the girders and just managed to maintain my balance.

'I thought you were better than all the others, Ellie. But you just picked me up to let me down.'

The blow was so sudden and forceful I stumbled back across the container, lost my balance and fell onto the floor, stars spinning around my head when I forced my eyes open. Instinctively I reached for my mobile but Patrick snatched it out of my grasp and hurled it at the wall where it smashed and clattered to the floor.

Then I felt something pressing down on my chest, and when the stars subsided I saw that it was his foot, not the real one, the prosthetic. I tried to move but was constrained by the weight of it and a searing pain that gripped my chest and shoulder where I had landed awkwardly. Pepper had sunk his teeth into the fabric of Patrick's trouser leg and was tugging at it angrily. But before I could sit up, Patrick grabbed him by the scruff of the neck and stuffed him into a bag of bubble wrap.

'Patrick, no, stop! Why would you do that to Pepper? He's done nothing to you.'

'He's annoying me.'

He kept his foot pressed against me as he ripped parcel tape from the reel I'd used earlier and wrapped it round and round Pepper in the bag. Then he tossed Pepper into the corner, where I could see him wriggling inside the polythene. The rigid plastic of Patrick's prosthetic foot pressed me back down harder.

I tried to kick my legs, to bash my heels against the floor

to alert someone, anyone who might be outside, but there was no chance of anyone taking notice of a thump inside containers that were surrounded by the sounds of the docks and building works, the almost constant drone of the planes landing at the airport, and police sirens wailing out on the A13.

'I really thought you were better than Stef. I really believed in you, Ellie, I thought you were the one I could trust. But it turns out you were just the same.'

He stood tall above me, looking down at me.

Then he knelt beside me. His hands, the ones I'd loved, with their black hairs and strong knuckles, crept up my chest and then exerted extreme pressure on my throat.

I could barely breathe.

'How could you walk out on me, Ellie? When you'd already run me over? When you had already driven away once, and left me without a leg?'

'I know all about it. I told you already.'

My words came out strangulated, followed by a coughing fit that made me feel my lungs were giving in.

'Patrick.' I could barely speak. 'It wasn't me, you know that! You used my doubt to control me.' His hands increased their pressure on my throat and I grew hot, felt the world vanishing until it was far away, just a speck.

'You came to the hospital. You led me on!'

He released his hold a little and I struggled to sit up but he pushed me back down.

I looked into his face, attempting to appeal to him, but I could see straight away that nothing would get through to him.

350

'When someone comes to find you, in the morning, or whenever they come looking, because it's the weekend, isn't it, and I suppose they will assume if this container's locked up it will be because you've gone off to New York with your painting. When they find you, I will be gone. I'm the one who's leaving you now, Ellie. I win.'

He kept his foot on me as he picked up my Stanley knife, leant over to my canvas, all beautiful and complete and ready to ship. He looked at it, then I heard his knife slit through the wrap, the crackle and pop of the bursting bubbles as it moved. A sad vain hope shot through me, that he just wanted to see the painting, that this was the only reason he was undoing all my careful wrapping.

'This was taking you away, it's all you cared about, instead of me,' he said, and again he lifted the knife.

'No, Patrick. No!'

'You used my studio, my flat to make your painting and then you dumped me!'

'It's not like that.'

'You thought you could just drop me and move into the New York art scene, you thought you were superior to me because I was a poor abandoned child brought up in care who your aunt wouldn't even take on as a foster child.'

'That's not true, Patrick.'

His eyes came into focus, too close up, cold as ice, almost white, his pupils pinprick dots.

'I really don't understand why you wanted to do this to me,' he said. 'Why you decided to come to me, and then leave me. Why would you do that?'

'I . . . never meant to. It wasn't a plan, it . . .'

'So now I'm going to have to show you how it feels. It's what I had to do to Stef. She gave up on me too the minute she decided I wasn't good enough for her. Decided to run off in the power boat! I couldn't guarantee the boat would lose control, but I knew if it did, she would be chopped into little pieces by the engine, and I chose to check it over before, in case she *insisted* on driving it. No one could ever prove one way or another that I had *arranged* for there to be no safety cord. But she deserved it. She deserved it.'

'Is that why those guys came after you? At the pub . . .'

'All the charges against me were dropped. They are so frustrated!' He laughed. 'So mad at me! They even tried to run me over! But they can't do a thing any more except watch me become more and more successful.'

'Successful? But the flat in Wapping isn't actually yours, is it? Where did you get the money from to buy all those designer clothes, all those dinners?'

'Successful at using other people's credit cards. It requires a certain kind of intelligence, don't you think? To use one, and move on to another. And not get caught.'

I stared up at him.

'Let me go, Patrick. Punishing me won't help. Someone will come, they'll know it was you. And then they'll come after you for everything else . . .'

'Got myself a job on a yacht out in Malta and no one will bother to look for me out there.'

'Look, if you let me go, we can talk. When I get back from New York, when things have settled down.'

'You still think you're off over the pond?' he said. 'Watch.'

And he took the knife back to the painting. Then he stood

back but with his heavy foot still pressing me down, and I watched helplessly as he lifted the knife and let it rip through my canvas.

All my hard work, all the feeling and emotion I'd put in since – yes, since I'd met Patrick, all the heightened emotion that in a way had been due to him, he cleaved in two with his knife.

And I saw my whole future, my career as an artist vanish in those few seconds it took for him to destroy what I'd spent months creating. He moved the knife through the painting with broad sweeps, each movement making another slash, and I saw the canvas curl apart, peel open, revealing the blankness behind.

'You led me on like everyone else,' said Patrick, his eyes bright with fury, and something else beneath, which I took to be sorrow. 'If you move, if you scream, remember, I have Pepper and I'm sure you don't want him to suffer.'

I thought of Frank, the old man who I had taken Pepper from, promising him Pepper wouldn't die before he did.

And now Patrick picked up Pepper– he was still wriggling – and all I heard as he walked away and slammed the door was Pepper's frightened yelps, and the bolts that kept the container door locked shut slam down into place outside.

CHAPTER THIRTY-SEVEN

I realised I wasn't so afraid of dying as I was of being in the wrong place when it happened. I wanted to have sorted things out first. I wanted to apologise to Finn. To my other friends. And I wanted to be in the right place. The way May had chosen where she was to die, and made it the way she had wanted it to be. Not dying of starvation or dehydration in a hot metal container. Not with Pepper struggling inside bubble wrap with Patrick in a state that meant he might do anything to the old man's little dog who I had promised to keep safe.

I lay in the stifling heat, in the dark, afraid of moving in case Patrick was waiting for me. My face throbbed from where he had hit me, and my arm was trapped uncomfortably beneath my chest. While I lay there, uncertain whether moving would hurt more or less than lying here and waiting for the stars to stop spinning round my head, I thought of my friends enjoying an evening in the pub. I thought of my mum at the Apple Store and Dad with his bottles of beer and Lou Reed saying what a perfect day it had been on the spinning vinyl in his flat. No one knew where I was. No one would miss me. Even Dad – he'd assume I'd changed my plans at the last minute, it wouldn't occur to him to find out where I was.

They all thought I was busy with my commission, getting it packed off and ready to be sent, busy with my new lover, my new ritzy life in Wapping.

My head began to swim, the container started to feel as if it was swaying, and then I must have passed out for a time because later, I woke with a start, no longer dizzy but aware that the world outside had fallen quiet. It must be late. It was still stifling, and my mouth was so dry I could barely peel my tongue from my palate. For the first time, I began to panic. If I didn't get out of here soon, I would become dehydrated. How long did it take to die of thirst? I began to feel breathless as well as parched, as if the air in the container was being sucked out.

I could lie here and weaken and slowly expire, and let Pepper suffocate in his bubble wrap bag, or I could show Patrick I'd had enough once and for all. That he wasn't going to get away with this, however much he felt the world owed him. The anger that had begun to erupt before, when I first learnt how Aunty May had blamed me and then again when I found out Patrick had strung me along, started to simmer again within me. I'd done all I could to help him, when he knew all along I was not to blame!

It was time to take action.

I tested my right arm to see if it hurt to lift it. Not too

bad. I shifted so I was sitting up. My head was throbbing, but I got onto my knees and hauled myself up, ignoring the pain that shot up my left arm and chest and shoulder as I did so.

I pushed at the door. It wouldn't budge. I swore at the metal containers, remembered again the fleeting sense I'd had when Patrick gave me this workspace for nothing – that I was like a commodity in this metal box.

I considered my situation again. I could make a racket. It was unlikely anyone would hear, but it was all I could do. And so I began to thump against the walls, with my hands at first, then with my feet. It didn't make any impact at all. I might as well have been hitting solid concrete with a wet rag. I needed a tool, something heavy to bash against the steel walls if I was to make any sound at all.

Then I remembered the magnets which I'd used to attach my painting to the wall. In my fear of piercing or spoiling my canvases with frames that jarred, I only ever used magnets to mount my pictures. The practical rationale had, as it often did with me, turned into an irrational compulsion – I had started to depend on these magnets to stop someone I loved coming to harm. Another silly superstition. But perhaps it would come in useful now.

The magnets were heavy and so powerful when held near anything metal, it was said they could make a blood blister if you put a finger between them. Now I lifted one of them high and walloped it against the steel wall, causing an almighty clanking sound that reverberated through my over-sensitised eardrums, but of course the magnet stuck fast and it took all my strength to pull it off again.

357

It was a relief to vent some rage. I began to shout as loud as I could, straining the muscles in my throat to scream, letting out all my anger and hurt and sense of injustice.

After several minutes of this I knew it was hopeless.

Then I realised. It wasn't impatience and rage that was going to get me out. If I stood any chance at all of saving myself from dying of dehydration, I would have to think carefully. I had these giant magnets at my disposal – surely I could put them to better use than simply bashing the walls with them?

The bolt was fitted at waist height outside: I should be able to manoeuvre it into position and open the door. I held the magnet to the steel door. Slid it up and down until I heard the rattle where the bolt handle must be, shook it until I could hear the bolt loosening. I moved the magnet up the wall, knowing by the weight that it was pulling the bolt with it.

The difficulty would be holding it up once I'd got it to the right position. I knew on one level it was a crazy idea. But I wasn't going to give in.

Persistence would pay.

It took several attempts. But then at last the door shifted. I pushed against it. It opened a crack and the bolt fell back into place with a clang.

Fighting the temptation to rush, I started again to work the bolt up.

This time, it happened more quickly than I had anticipated. The bolt slid into place, the door clicked, and when I pushed it hard, it swung open.

I gulped in lungfuls of warm night air.

Then I heard something that made my heart lift. A distant, muffled yap coming from the base of the lightship.

Pepper.

The tide was about halfway out, the ladder on the wall exposed.

I didn't wait. I got to the ladder and climbed down the steps into the hull, followed the sound of the yapping until I could make out the bundle of bubble wrap stuffed into a corner. I picked him up, felt Pepper wriggle against me. Luckily one end of the bag had been left open allowing Pepper some air. It took me a few minutes to peel open the tape and clasp Pepper to me. His breath rasped in and out as he gulped in more air, his tongue hanging out.

We sat, Pepper and I, in the lightship for some time. I was weak, and exhausted, and afraid that if I moved and Patrick hadn't gone he would spot me. I was desperate for something to drink. The lights of the city were all around us, thousands of beacons glowing in the dark, yet Pepper and I were completely alone, no one knowing what we had just gone through. But Pepper needed water too. I had to do something, for him. At last I stood up.

CHAPTER THIRTY-EIGHT

Climbing back up the ladder was awkward with Pepper under my right arm, and with the pain in my left one, onto the wharf. I summoned the strength from somewhere, however, and at last we reached the top of the ladder and I stumbled across to the containers. My studio door was swinging open.

My painting lay wrecked on the floor, my mobile in pieces scattered about the place. There wasn't time to register the sense of despair I knew I would have to acknowledge later at the sight of all my hard work destroyed.

'Come on, Pepper. Let's get out of here.'

I clutched him to my chest, and moved through the shadows of the buildings around the wharf, still wary of alerting Patrick to our whereabouts in case he hadn't gone off, as he had boasted he was going to, to Malta. I had no idea what time it was. The river was silent, no more boats running over its surface, and although the skies were lit up as usual, there was less noise, less vibration in the ground. Was it past midnight? I had no idea. I edged my way past the other steel containers, and then across to the little lighthouse Patrick had shown me that first day we'd come down here when I thought I was so in love. Its door was unlocked. I was so tired, I had an urge to push it open, to go in, to lie down and sleep there, letting the eternal music play around my ears, soothing me. But I had to keep going, get to my car, that was parked around the other side of the Buoy Store at the end of the wharf. I was about to step out of the shadow of the lighthouse when a movement caught my eye back near towards the steel containers and I ducked into the doorway. Pepper yelped and I put my hand over his muzzle to silence him.

My legs went to jelly as I moved swiftly with Pepper under my arm into the darkness of the lighthouse and up the stairs. I didn't think, just pulled myself, clutching the banisters with one hand, up to its dark chambers where the endless music played. And where, I half-imagined, I would have a better chance of protecting myself, since at least I would be able to see where Patrick was, if he was out there, through the small window that overlooked the wharf, while he couldn't see me.

I found a corner, squatted there and listened.

It was dark, and cool and protective, and the music, the endless music supposed to play for a thousand years without a break or repetition, played on. My eyelids drooped and I was afraid I would fall asleep to the soothing sound.

I would have to make a run for it soon, get to my car, get to Dad's or, perhaps better, drive out of town up to

Cambridge. Take refuge at Mum's until my flight tomorrow. Then it hit me. What flight? What was the point in New York when there was no painting any more? Still I couldn't afford to let the full horror of what Patrick had done to my painting – my future – hit me. I shut off the sense of grief that threatened to well up, and focused on my situation here and now.

I moved over to the window. I could see nobody out there. The wharf was empty and silent. There was nothing, only the distant rattle of a train, the low purr of a single launch out on the river. I would make one more supreme effort to get to my car. I hugged Pepper to me and crept back down the stairs, to a half landing where there was another window, and moved across to it.

The lights around the wharf lit up a tall figure moving towards the containers where my studio was.

Patrick.

I was weak with terror. He hadn't gone after all! He must have known I would get out somehow, or feared that someone would come for me. And he'd waited, especially.

He was barely limping, no crutches, his bad leg hardly perceptible. I thought back to all the times he'd seemed so capable on his prosthetic. What a fool I had been. He had only been in hospital a week, why hadn't I clocked that he would never have recovered so quickly if he had really lost a leg on the road that night? For some reason the evening Ben and Caroline had come to the pub came back to me. No wonder Patrick had left, afraid Caroline would recognise the little boy with a leg missing, and give his game away. And the way he'd grown cold when I'd wanted to look at his childhood photos – he was afraid I'd see he'd always had his disability. That if I knew I hadn't caused it I would walk away from him. Yet at that time I had been in thrall to him, so convinced I loved him I would have stayed anyway.

As I crouched at the window, watching him, I thought how Patrick's true disability wasn't physical, it was emotional. It was the way he had been abandoned, by his mother, by my aunt, by Stef and perhaps countless others, and now, as he saw it, by me. In spite of everything, watching him moving back across the wharf to find me, I experienced a surge of the feelings I'd had for him before I knew how very damaged he was. I had believed I might change him, heal him in some way. I had failed.

And in the process look what other damage I had done! I had neglected Timothy. I had lost my friends. And Patrick had nearly killed Pepper. He had vandalised my painting! Destroyed my future.

I watched him walk towards the containers. He *was* coming back for me. But to free me?

Or to kill me?

He was at the containers now. Walking round the front, the riverside. I saw him take a step back as he found the door unlocked. Then turn round and start to jog back. I shrank away into the darkness, but then saw he was heading towards the entrance to the wharf, assuming no doubt, I had left, was on the road. He had his mobile to his ear, probably calling a cab to follow me.

I would make a run for my car now, while he was heading the other way, out of the wharf. I ran down the stairs and out into the yard again. But as I arrived in the open air, a deafening revving sound startled me. Pepper began to yap.

'Sshhh, Pepper!'

I could see Patrick across the wharf, he had stopped too. He turned, staring around confused.

The car – my car – came so fast around the back of the containers, there wasn't time for anyone to move. The blazing headlights caught Patrick full on, lit him up, dazzling him. I saw his hands go to his eyes. He stepped out, waving his arms, trying to stop the car – trying to stop the driver who he must have assumed was me.

And I could see it all.

I began to run, out onto and across the yard.

'NO!'

My throat was parched, I couldn't make a sound. 'Watch out, stop!'

A faint ridiculous croaking sound. I had to stop the car before the cycle was completed. The cycle I realised with a horrible inevitability I had begun the night I became obsessed with the hit-and-run.

The thump was louder than anything I might have imagined that night on my journey to the cottage.

Patrick's body flew up, up, arms spread like a seagull in flight, flipping in the air, his prosthetic detaching from his body, just like a branch broken in a gale from a tree.

I still couldn't scream, the sound in my throat was nothing more than a hoarse whimper.

My vocal cords silenced by the hands of the man who now fell to the ground, and by the shock of recognition.

I ran to Patrick. His head was buckled beneath him. One arm splayed out to the side.

Without thinking, I placed Pepper on the ground, sat beside this man who had caused me so much terror and cradled his head as he faded away. It wasn't the man I was comforting, I thought, but the abandoned boy.

I knew he saw me.

I bowed my head over Patrick's and wept.

The car, my car, had disappeared up the street away from the wharf. I watched the tail lights fade and sat for a while longer.

The cable cars continued to move on their thread-like wires above the river. I watched them, thinking how everything happens without us being able to see it, unless we are far enough away and can look back upon ourselves and see where all the joins are. A small boy on a beach yearning for a family, a little girl blamed for a drowning that had made her think she had to check on things all her life. A fear of causing damage, and in an attempt to stop it, to atone for it, making it happen anyway. It had, after all, as Finn had joked, been like a soothsayer's prophecy from the ancient Greeks, Patrick would die in a hit-and-run. Whatever I did to avoid it, it would happen anyway.

I sat there, Pepper under one arm, Patrick's head in my lap as the lights over the river flickered, and the beacon on Canary Wharf flashed on and off and the tide began to turn.

366

EPILOGUE

My New York buyers were informed that my painting had been vandalised, and agreed to commission another for the autumn.

I returned Pepper to Frank and the two were so happy to be reunited it made tearing myself from the little dog easier to bear.

Finn had turned back after the accident, helped me call an ambulance, though we both knew it was too late.

He had come down to find me that night, he told me later.

'I saw the words you hid in the painting,' he said. 'The day I came down with the beer and crisps and you were so determined to keep me at bay.'

'Really?'

'Yes. You'd put "I'm afraid".'

'I know.'

'You were too frightened to tell me out loud though, so you used our old messaging system.'

'Yes.'

'And earlier, after you came and found me with Louise, I knew something was up. I sensed it. I tried and tried your mobile and when you didn't answer all evening I knew to come and see what had happened. You'd left your keys in the ignition of your car.'

'Because I had no idea I wouldn't be coming straight back to it when I returned to the studio to put the lights off.'

Finn was charged with reckless driving, and in court, where I was a witness, I tried to argue that I'd seen Patrick step in front of the car – and that if I'd never got involved with him in the first place Finn would never have driven into him, but it didn't hold up and Finn was given a six month sentence.

Louise gave up on him, but I wrote to him regularly, reminding him that I was the real culprit, not him.

But in the end we can trace everyone's actions back to another source, Patrick's, Aunty May's, my own, Finn's.

In the end we only have ourselves.

I decided to sell the blue clapboard house, when I returned from a two-year sabbatical painting in New York. Just as my mother always thought I should.

It was summer again when I went down to see the house for one last time.

Having my daughter Rebecca here brought my own child-hood slap-bang up in my face. Aunty May's back, only slightly stooped, moving down the rickety jetty in sun hat and bare feet, jeans and a checkered blouse, my certainty that she would return with treats – chocolate-covered raisins or ice-cream cones. The sting of the salt wind as it must have felt on my newer, tender skin. Images: a child, only a little older than Rebecca, a green nylon fishing net lying beside her on the boards of the jetty, hauling out crabs on a string. A little boy, in the corner of my eye, looking on.

I came out of the house for the last time, ready to set off, with the last bits and pieces packed in the car,

I shut and locked the door with the big brass key and Rebecca ran out onto the sand. I dropped everything and ran after her, resisting the urge to tap the gatepost three times, because if she kept on running she would come to the sea, where riptides could grab a human body – especially one so small – and carry it away in seconds and then there was no knowing how things would twist about and take us back around again on some perpetual loop. I knew now that the obsessive compulsions I had always performed to keep myself and others safe were the opposite. They tricked you and veiled you from the truth and sometimes they caused the very accidents you were trying to prevent.

I caught up with Rebecca and scooped her compact weight up in my arms and put my nose into her impossibly soft hair, and the wind lifted a lock and it brushed my cheek and then blew for a moment in front of my eyes, blurring with the bleached sea grass beyond.

The beach was empty but for the tiny squirming figures – rather like the sperm-like marks on a Miro – of a dog and its owner at the sea's edge. We stood and listened. To the waves slamming on the shore, to the plaintive mewl of the gulls, and the beginnings of the church bell pealing up in the town. Beyond that – beyond that was the massive, unsettling silence of East Anglia, miles of woodland and field and hedgerow between us and our new home in London.

I rubbed my nose on Rebecca's cheek, and turned back to the car.

'She your daughter?'

It was Larry on his bike, pointing at my child.

'She got that man's face,' he said. 'Same face as the man with one leg.' And then he turned and wobbled away on his bike towards the town.

I fastened Rebecca into her car seat and got in. Glanced round to check she was comfortable. She was engrossed with the pop-up toy I'd rescued from May's, her head down, her feet crossed over, humming gently to herself. I set off over the shingle, towards the road. I glanced in my rear-view mirror, and saw my Aunty May's house.

A blue clapboard house, stark against the grey evening sky, diminishing in size as I drove away, a beacon of my past, my childhood, growing smaller by the minute until it was just a dot on the horizon. I imagined all the children who had come and gone inside its walls.

And I vowed that I would give Rebecca, Patrick's little daughter, with his cheeky blue eyes and his long child's lashes, the childhood he should have had.

And then I looked ahead and drove into the magic hour.

ACKNOWLEDGEMENTS

Many thanks to John Burton for the residency at Trinity Buoy Wharf in my own steel container!

Thank you to Steve Wright, captain of one of the Thames Clippers, who took me on a trip up the Thames and gave me a personal commentary on its geography, its history and its secrets.

Thank you to crime writer Sara Cox for your information about police procedures in hit-and-run incidents.

Thank you to Stephanie Glencross and Emma Lowth for all your work on the early drafts, Carla Josephson and Jo Dickinson for your work on later ones and Angles writing group for feedback on the first chapters.

As usual, thanks to Jane Gregory, and to the team at Simon & Schuster for their continued belief in me!

Thank you to Emma for reading, and for giving me your young person's perspective, and thank you so much Polly,

Jem, and Andy for your continued support, contributions, and tolerance. And massive thanks to Susan Elliot Wright.

Enormous gratitude also goes to my mother and late father for providing us with a place to stay in Southwold when my children were little and for some very special memories.

Last but not least, Tilly, upon whom Pepper was based.